Superior firepower

The Stryker trying to crash into them had been effectively neutralized…tires were being blown out, main gun empty and the armor was being torn away. It was no longer a major threat even though it was chasing after them.

The bunkers too had been neutralized. The men in them couldn't stick their heads up without being shot at by first one, then the other HUMVEE's heavy machine gun.

Their hunger for battle, something to kill, had been whetted by the zombies at the truck stop earlier that morning. Now they saw an opportunity to satiate their hunger by defeating the entrenched farmers and taking down a Stryker. This morning the reward had been beer and canned food. This evening their reward would be women.

Their confidence was as high as it had been since entering the farm.

True, they had lost two of their HUMVEEs and some of the soldiers in those were dead, but the two others were still mounting a good offense. They knew they had the upper hand and were going to end the battle with discipline, superior firepower and a better battle plan.

Published by White Feather Press, LLC
www.whitefeatherpress.com

ISBN 978-1-61808-066-0

Printed in the United States of America

Cover art courtesy of Rubber Chicken, LLC

Reaffirming Faith in God, Family, and Country!

Hell Revisited

BY

Terry & Jordan Stenzelbarton

Preface

The Rapture, The Great Death, The Second Plague, The Killer Virus, Armageddon, The End of Times.

It was called many things by the few people who remained alive. In some cities around the world, thousands of people lived when tens of millions did not. If there had been a census taken, Shanghai in China was still the world's most populace city after the Great Death with more than 2,600 survivors.

In other cities and towns around the world, no one survived. Every last person, from the richest to the poorest, healthiest to the sickest, leaders of the community and criminals locked up in the local pokey, all died with equal rapidity. It was a quick end to civilization, as ends of civilizations go. It started everywhere with thousands of deaths the first day and several thousands by the third day.

Major news networks started reporting the deaths at the end of the first week. It was difficult for them to cover because the speed at which it started and then how it spread through the populations around the world.

In an effort to slow the progress of the virus, governments shut down mass transportation, every airport and train station, all subways and shipping stopped. Highways were blocked off by National Guard and Active Duty units until they either left their posts to return home and die with their family, or died while on duty.

By then, however, there were few people left to drive the highways.

The world's people stopped gathering at malls and theaters, churches and restaurants. If someone had a home, they went to it and died there with family. If they were homeless, they died alone on the street. People living in crowded environments and those living far from anyone, isolated in mountains or on islands met the same fate.

No edict by a country's leader did anything to stem the flow of the virus. Everyone around the world, from the northern-most city of Longyearbyen, Norway to the scientists working at the South Pole scientific station were infected and most died. First, second and third-world countries all had their populations dying at a rate unseen in the history of man.

Scientists tried to find a cure, but most died before making any headway and the ones who didn't die, found no cure. The virus ran its course and when done, the world had less than 1/100th of one percent of its pre-virus population.

The deaths weren't like on television or in the movies. There was no dramatic death scene. It was suspected, some people might not have even known they'd caught the virus. The person infected coughed a little, ran a low fever and within three days their brain shut off. Those who survived found people dead crumpled against their cars while fueling up at a gas station, sitting in chairs by their pools, some still at their desks, others in wrecked cars or trucks on the highway.

It was surreal for the ones left alive. Some of those who witnessed the deaths of everyone they knew and loved, lost their minds and stepped off the edge and into the chasm of insanity, eventually ending their own lives.

Others found some way to make it from one day into the next. They were survivors who didn't have the answers to why so many had died, but after the tears had stopped falling, they continued to make the best of the life they still had.

Some of those who lived did not survive as human. For them, life went from bad to worse. They coughed, ran a fever but instead of dying, their body mutated into something not Homo Sapien. They lost the ability to reason as a human. They became what some people called the not-deads, mutants, monsters or zombies. Their strength and speed increased 10-fold over that of a normal human. Their night sight became as keen as any night fighter and sense of smell that'd rival the greatest bloodhound ever bred.

The zombies, for unknown reasons, hid inside dark areas, and lusted for human flesh. No one knew why their only desire was human flesh, but it was the horrific truth many found out. The zombies hunted singularly or in packs, like wolves, and attacked with ferocity and no concern for one of their own. Entire survivor camps were wiped out by the packs. No one knew how long the zombies could live without food, but rumors were that buildings abandoned for nine or ten months still had zombies waiting inside for some hapless survivor to enter.

Zombies were also almost impossible to kill. Clean head-shots that separated the brain stem from the body and shots that destroyed the spine worked well if the shooter used a heavy caliber weapon. Machine guns worked for shredding them apart, but the problem was getting enough lead flying to take down an entire pack before one of them jumped you and began his meal. It was better to avoid the zombies altogether.

The survivors of the Great Death had to learn to live their lives in a much different world than before. It was harder for those who had grown up with a dependency on technology and the corner store for food. People who couldn't grow their own food had to rely on non-perishable foods they scavenged from stores or other homes. At best, it was just enough until they could start growing their own food, raising animals or learning the art of fishing. At worst they encountered zombies and became something else's meal.

Many people living in areas that didn't have an agricultural environment, deserts and snow-bound areas of the planet, didn't live past the end of food stores. With the end of petroleum distillates, gas stations no longer provided fuel for cars. There were no longer any public services and electricity producing industries shut down.

Dams and coal fired producers also shut down and electric grids no longer provided power. Without power, water towers weren't re-filled and sewer processing plants stopped, frozen foods thawed and air circulation systems stopped. Everything taken for granted was now yesterday's memories.

Nuclear power plants were put on emergency shut down before the fall and worldwide only three ejected radioactive gas into the atmosphere after people no longer operated the units. The radiation made areas in Germany, Japan and the

South Africa unlivable for thousands of years. In the middle east, oil refineries and drilling stations shut down, but fires happened and burned until the fuel was exhausted.

All the documentaries written about what would happen to the earth when people disappeared were remarkably accurate. Animals moved into homes of the dead. Lack of maintenance caused man-made structures to collapse. Vegetation re-took roads and tracts of land that had been managed by humans.

The only major difference was that not every man had died. Some still lived.

The sun that now rose every morning was on civilization much different than one from the previous year.

Chapter 1

Jerry Saunders stretched as he lay down on the fold-out bed in the back of the Prevost tour bus that he and his friends had acquired a few hours earlier. They'd located it at a destroyed truck stop south of Montgomery, Alabama.

Jerry's tee shirt and blue jeans were sticky with sweat from the work he'd done today and he still smelled of salt water. His three-day brown and white beard itched.

He was tired from constant activity through the 22-hour long day, but his mind was still filled with how much his life had changed in the past few months and was sluggish in letting him drift into a dreamless sleep.

The bus they found had been saved from the recent hurricane by what was left of a cinder block building and several semi trucks that had piled up forming a protective barrier. It was one of the very few vehicles that hadn't been thrown around by the winds and debris from the hurricane that had recently ravaged the south with a ferocity Jerry had never seen in his 50-plus years.

The fold-out bed was also surprisingly comfortable compared to the bed he'd been sleeping in for the past four months back in the shelter.

Since the fall of civilization, Jerry and his friends had been literally living in a hole in the ground.

The "hole" began as a way to work off anger from his divorce years earlier and evolved into a shelter with three sleeping rooms, a kitchen and living area and a cellar for storing food. He'd had a lot of anger to work off after the divorce.

He hadn't meant it to become a survival shelter, but it did help him and the others survive the recent hurricane that had passed though the area, destroying brick and mortar and steel buildings, toppling sky scrapers, bridges and wiping entire cities off the face of the earth.

The shelter he built had electricity from windmill-driven generators and a paddle wheel that recharged the batteries in the cellar. It had food that was grown on the farm or salvaged from abandoned stores, heat from an outdoor wood burner and a state-of-the-art air filtration system.

What the shelter provided most for the people was protection from the elements and the dangers that lurked in the night. It wasn't roomy and no one called it comfortable or pretty, but it was better than the alternative.

Before the fall, Jerry had been a farmer, living on the same tract of land he'd inherited with the passing of his parents. He worked the small farm with his own son and some seasonal help, raising a few crops and some cattle. He lived a life without much excitement but without boredom. He worried about his crops and milk prices, weather fronts and taxes.

In the evening, he and his son Randy, a part-time community college student, would eat dinner while watching the local and national news most nights. One of them would do dishes and both would go do their own thing until the next morning. Jerry often went to his garage or barn to work on repairing his farm equipment or whatever project he had, Randy would go to his room and play video games or work on his homework.

It was a simple life.

At least once a week Jerry would email his daughter, Amanda, who was serving with the US Army when the fall came. He loved his daughter but she was never one to stay down on the farm. As soon as she graduated high school she'd joined the Army to fix helicopters. He and his ex-wife had disagreed with Amanda's decision, with Jerry supporting his daughter. It was the last brick to come down in their marriage and soon his wife had filed for divorce and moved out. He had to sell 40 acres of his farm to a developer and cash in all his savings to pay the woman off. They'd been together for more than 20 years and the judge said she'd earned her fair share.

Jerry didn't agree with the judge, but he had no choice.

When the President of the United States ordered martial law, stopping all air traffic and interstate travel, before the internet ceased operating and phone service no longer worked,

Jerry received an email from Amanda telling him that she was afraid and people on her base had started dying. She told him how much she loved him and wished she could be there when her end came.

Jerry missed his daughter and wished there was something he could do, but she'd been stationed at Fort Wainwright in Alaska, 4,000 miles away. Jerry replied to the email, but didn't know if she received it before the internet did stop working. He tried calling her, but the calls never went through. He didn't know if she survived but prayed everyday that she had.

There was no reason for him to believe Amanda survived just because he and his son had, but there was no harm, he told himself, in asking God for the favor.

The world collapsed around them and Jerry and his son Randy continued to work hard to survive. Gone were all the conveniences they'd grown used to. There were no more public works, no government, no law enforcement, no regular television or radio broadcasts, no internet and no phone service. Fuel for their tractors and equipment was salvaged from other vehicles or fuel tanks they could find. The stores they could safely raid provided them with canned food and dry goods, but even that had to be a carefully planned out project.

Hundreds of millions of decaying bodies were now occupying millions of homes and churches, hospitals and clinics, in cars and trucks on the highways, in the streets and scattered about the countryside. The bodies were drawing in wild animals, but the bodies had grown too old for the zombies that inhabited some building. Zombies, for some reason, only fed on live or recently dead bodies. It was something they both talked about, but knew there was nothing they could do.

Before the hurricane that had blown through, Jerry and his son had grown anesthetized to the bodies they'd seen when they went on scavenging hunts. The hurricane had washed most of the bodies from casual view, but for several days he had to clean the paddle wheel in the river of bodies.

Jerry pulled the pillow over his eyes and laid his arm across it. He felt the driver, an elderly Mexican-American, Juan deJesus, put the luxury bus smoothly into gear and pull back onto the interstate. They'd be second of the three-vehicle convoy.

Leading the convoy, driving his used and abused dark blue Ford F-350, was Rusty, a recent arrival to the farm. Rusty was a former tattoo artist from Florida. He was a heavy smoker and surly, but was a hard-working man and good with a gun.

Eddie gave over the driving duties of his SWAT truck to Monica while he got comfortable in the passenger seat with his feet on the dashboard. They brought up the rear of the convoy. Eddie was his son Randy's best friend from high school. He had untamed orange hair and was rail-thin. His thick eyebrows gave his face a slight Neanderthal look, but he had a quick, albeit sarcastic, wit.

Eddie had found the SWAT truck while on a supply run with Jerry and a few others and took it as his own vehicle.

Monica was a heavy-set woman in her early 20s and was the team's first aid expert. She'd been found shortly after the fall of civilization by Jerry and his son, sitting outside a Gas & Go eating Little Debbie snack cakes. She had been overweight and confused, manufactured drama and craved attention.

That had been months earlier. Monica was still overweight, but she was becoming more fit because of the work that had to be done on Jerry's farm to keep it functioning. Eddie, Randy and Tony, the shelter's electronic specialist, were all within a few years of age and the three men hadn't put up with the drama Monica's personality exuded. They had found a balance to their friendship which wouldn't have been probable before more than 99 percent of the people in the world had died.

Tony was curled up with a blanket on a cot in the back of the SWAT truck now. He wanted to be near the electronic equipment he'd installed in the truck.

Tony was still nursing the injuries sustained when he had been captured by vigilantes a few weeks back. He and Jeff had told Jerry they were going to look for weapons and ammunition, but in reality they were looking for drugs. The two had been captured and tortured then used as bait for zombies.

During their rescue by Jerry, Eddie and a former soldier named Terrill, the soldier had been killed by a booby-trapped grenade. Jeff hadn't survived either. His neck had been broken by the heavy foot of a vigilante.

Tony suffered a broken ankle, bruises on his face and chest

and missing teeth, but he survived.

Also on the bus with Jerry were the three astronauts from the International Space Station. The convoy had left their shelter and farm near Moody Alabama very early the previous morning to drive to Gulf Shores, Alabama to rescue the two men and woman.

The four astronauts on the station had spent months trying to reach someone left alive on earth after contact had been lost from ground stations. Tony had been the first to hear their call and arrangements had been made for three to return to earth. The Russian commander of the station had remained behind.

Chances had been slim that a rescue could be effected, but Jerry and the rest of the people on the farm had decided to give it their best effort. They drove to the gulf, found a catamaran that had been washed two miles in shore that hadn't been totally destroyed.

The group re-launched the cat and Juan, an experienced weekend sailor, piloted it five miles out into the calm waters of the gulf. The rescue spaceship had landed more than a mile from the catamaran, but Juan's piloting got them to the craft before it sank and the crew was rescued.

They were now resting in the Prevost as well. It would take weeks for their bodies to re-adjust to earth's gravity, but at least they were home on earth and not dying a slow death in space. That was what they'd asked for and what Jerry and his team had provided.

The rhythmic hum of the tour bus lulled Jerry close to sleep. He was on the cusp between awake and asleep. His mind was drifting though everything that had transpired since people around the globe started dying.

The plague, or virus or Act of God and what caused it was still a mystery. There was speculation it was started by terrorists, or renegade microbiologists or even the strange meteor storm that had crossed paths with earth.

On some days it had been reported millions were dying, even tens of millions. There was panic from some, but it was quelled with the swift deaths of more than six billion worldwide.

No inoculation had time to be developed. No social standing, no amount of money or devout belief in a Creator helped. No one knew what started the virus and the scientists who could have determined what caused it were all dead now. It might be years or never before the real cause was ever found.

Earth's population was dead…most of them.

Jerry was the leader of a small band of people who survived the end of the world, along with his son Randy. Eddie, Monica, Rusty and Tony survived. Juan and his wife Margarita, Kellie, Josh and his daughter Marissa, Tia and her two children John and Hannah, twin 12-year-olds Tara and Sara, Danny, Nick and his friend Sade, Katie and Jamal all survived and found their way to Jerry's shelter and farm.

They lived there now in the ad-hoc self-sustaining shelter Jerry had begun building years before the fall of civilization and finished as the world died around him.

Jerry was glad there were other compounds or camps like his. Tony had made contact with the Smith Compound in Kentucky, run by a former military officer. Jerry was sure there were others and when he got the astronauts back to the farm, Tony could take the time to find them.

Jerry thought about the people who didn't die, the ones who had become some sort of monster. Randy had called them zombies even though they weren't dead. They were not-deads who lived off the flesh of people who were still alive or recently killed. No one knew why they survived, how they were turned into monsters or what motivated them.

Jerry and his son had fought off a pair of the zombies and survived only because of luck and the shotguns they had with them. On another occasion, it was a brick wall and two hand guns wielded by Randy and Eddie that had saved Monica when they were caught unaware in a pharmacy.

Fortunately the zombies lived, if that was what it could be called, in darkened buildings and avoided the light of day.

The zombies were what they were -- another part of this post-apocalyptic world.

Jerry thought about the vigilantes too. The laws from before no longer applied. There were some roving bands of vigilantes or brigands who raided settlements like Jerry's looking for food or women or weapons. They were ruthless and lawless and dangerous.

Jerry's farm had survived one terrible attack, but it had cost the life of Mike, a dear man who had been a bank executive before the fall of civilization. Mike had been helping Tia's son with a project when the farm was attacked. Mike had been shot in the head and died in the driveway of the farm.

Kellie, the middle-aged woman who had taken over the supplies and maintenance of the shelter itself, had killed one of the vigilantes when she shot through the door of the shelter. Monica killed another with her .22 rifle and Eddie had killed two when he ran over their escape vehicle with his SWAT truck.

The one vigilante captured was now being held in confinement until they could find some place they could release her without fear of her retaliating against the farm, or turning her over to the soldiers at the military installation with whom they'd made contact. She'd been wounded and there were questions about her guilt and complicity, but Jerry had already decided she had to go. She was bad for the farm. He didn't believe her story about being a victim.

For everything that was different with the world of yesterday, Jerry was happy that he had the safe haven of his shelter and farm. He was happy his son had survived and was right now probably sleeping peacefully in the room of the shelter he shared with his friend Eddie.

Everything wasn't right with the world, but it was right enough considering how bad it could be.

~ ~ ~

CHERYL'S ESCAPE FROM THE FARM AND CAPTIVITY LEFT AN UGLY scene in the shelter. There were no vehicles left on the farm except tractors, quads, Josh's truck with the camper on the back, and Tia's motorhome. None of them could catch Cheryl in the minivan. If there had been something to drive, someone would have chased her and caught her and probably killed her on the spot.

The woman had been captured when she and her younger brother had attacked the farm with three others, hoping to take over the place and set it up as a base of operations. Their plan had gone awry when Kellie had killed her brother by shooting through the oak doors of the shelter.

The other man with her had been wounded while reaching for a grenade. Monica had shot him dead. Cheryl had been hit in her left leg and shoulder by parts of the door and was trying to make it back to their truck when the two others who had killed Mike drove off, abandoning her.

Cheryl later learned Eddie had driven his SWAT into them on the highway, killing them both. Cheryl was cheered to hear that story from Randy, but not for the reason he thought. She was glad they were dead so they couldn't tell anyone she was the leader of their group. Randy was led to believe she was happy because they had taken part in her capture and torture.

Cheryl had escaped from custody, a collar with a padlock chained to a wall in the barn, and leg irons. She'd cultivated a friendship built on lies with Jerry's son. She flirted with him and teased him with her body, a knack she'd honed while in college and serving in the Army. She knew she was pretty and she used it on the hormonally-charged Randy. With Jerry gone to the gulf and another team away from the farm searching for motorhomes for the astronauts, she realized it was her best chance to escape.

Randy had just delivered to her "cell" in the barn a TV and DVD for a "date" with her when she bashed him on the head with a piece of steel pipe she'd stashed. He dropped face first onto the floor and blood started flowing from his mouth. She hated Randy, knowing he was only being nice to her in hopes of getting sex, so she kicked him in the groin just for the pleasure of it. When he didn't grunt, she guessed he was dead. He'd been "courting" her, allowing her out of her cell, not putting the leg irons or collar on her so she was free to leave her cell.

What she needed was weapons and she knew the layout of the farm and shelter because Randy had laid it all out for her in an effort to impress her. Now was the time to use what she'd learned.

In the time she had, she attacked the people in the shelter, shooting Kellie and Danny, before escaping in the deJesus' minivan. She left believing Randy, Kellie and Danny were probably dead and was rather pleased with the look of horror on the old women and children. She laughed at the memory of her kicking Kellie's little dog out of her way. The dog flew across the floor yelping loudly.

~ ~ ~

AMANDA SAUNDERS PULLED ONTO THE AIRPORT RUNWAY AND turned her HUMVEE off. She wanted to make sure there was a lot of space between where she was and where anyone else might be. She was still struggling with this morning's shock. She would never forget the look of fear on her young friend's face after being shot. She would never forget the fear she felt while running away.

What she wanted to do more than ever right now was to break down and cry.

Everything was wrong. Nothing was normal. Amanda was sure she'd make it through the night, but it wouldn't be a night at the Holiday Inn. It wouldn't even be as comfortable her bed back at Fort Wainwright, but it was better than being dead or on a base with her dead friends and co-workers.

She'd watched the news like everyone else. She'd seen the newsmen talking about the end of the world. She, along with three others in the day room saw the president order martial law. The order came a day after the post commander and most of the command staff had died. Her first sergeant, company commander and boyfriend died that day.

The pressure of going crazy was nearly overwhelming. The only thing that kept her on the right side of the canyon of insanity was a desire to return home to Alabama.

She always found the Army's wisdom at sending a soldier, born and raised in the south, to the middle of Alaska, a bit questionable. She'd requested Ft. Rucker, a helicopter post in Alabama, so she could be close to her dad and brother, or Ft. Lewis in Washington so she could be close to her mom and her new husband.

Somehow the Army didn't seem to care too much about these requests because she was assigned to Ft. Wainwright in the middle of the cold freaking state of Alaska. It didn't seem fair, but then that was the Army. She had been assigned to Headquarters & Headquarters Company, 1st Battalion, 52nd Aviation Regiment, known as the "Flying Dragons." She learned a lot from her platoon sergeant and leader in the two and a half years she'd been stationed there. She'd received orders sending her back to the continental United States for more advanced training when the end came.

As she got comfortable in the HUMVEE, preparing for another long night she started singing the song sung to her when she was a little girl by the man she had called daddy. "Amazing grace, how sweet the sound, that saved a wretch like me...."

The song got her crying, something she did not do very often, but now had done twice today. She missed her dad, and if someone were to pull the braid in her dark blond hair and force her, she'd even admit to missing her older brother Randy. She also missed her mom who had divorced her dad after Amanda had joined the Army. And she missed the days when they all lived together on the farm and her worst worry was if she would pass calculus.

She hadn't heard from any of them since the end of the world came. She didn't know why she survived, or the other three from the fort, but they did. It had been horrible. It had been worse than horrible and Amanda didn't know if staying alive had been worth it.

All the friends she'd made, her boyfriend, co-workers, had all died, from the lowest private on base to the commanding general of the post. No one but herself, Capt. Jim Poitra from accounting, Spec. 4 Roy Johnson the cook and Pvt. 2 Shep Sheppard a soldier straight out of Military Police training, had survived.

The end came swiftly on post. It took less than a week from the first death until half the soldiers on post were dead. By the end of the second week, no one was even trying to bury the dead because there were so many. Civilians from Fairbanks had tried to get on post, thinking maybe the military had some secret way to save them, but there was none.

Amanda and her roommate, Sgt. Shauna Lawrence, had no real belief they would survive. Both sent emails to their parents, telling them how afraid they were and how much they missed them. They tried calling, but no calls were going through.

Shauna died that night, quietly in her sleep, just a few feet away from where Amanda dreamed of Alabama. Amanda didn't know if her mom and dad had gotten her emails, but she hoped they had.

Nine days later, everyone who was going to die of the virus on post was dead. It had taken 25 days from start to finish.

Amanda didn't want to be around the dead. As machinery stopped working, the cold temperatures would delay the decomposition of the bodies that were outside, but not the ones inside of buildings. Soon the animals of Alaska would come and there were too many bodies for Amanda to bury by herself. She decided to leave.

Trained as a helicopter mechanic, Amanda thought about taking one of the many UH-60s that were on base. The helicopter had a range of more than 800 miles without spare fuel tanks which was well within the distance to Anchorage.

She was not a pilot, but was she was a crackerjack mechanic on Blackhawks and she might have risked it if had been just herself. She'd learned to fly a little from her boyfriend and knew how the collective and cyclic worked to move the helicopter in flight. He'd allowed her to do it several times under his close direction and supervision. She felt she could fly to Anchorage and land and was willing to do it just to get away from all these dead people. She knew it would be a risk because there were mountains to fly around, but if she flew a few hundred feet above the highway, she thought she could navigate there in two or three hours. From that altitude, she'd also avoid the higher winds the pilots were always complaining about.

Ft. Wainwright was a large military base and she'd spent half a day driving around trying to find someone else but had failed. She stopped trying. She even stopped believing someone else had survived. She was living in a dream from which she couldn't wake. She was afraid and on the verge of doing something just to wake up from the nightmare.

There was no reason she could see that she was alive and

no one else. The only thing that kept her from checking to see if she was in some relentless dream by killing herself, was her dad's collection of books she'd read growing up. There were too many science fiction stories where the good guy was the one to live, only to go crazy.

Amanda vowed not to go crazy.

Once she had made up her mind to fly a helicopter to Anchorage in hopes of finding someone else alive, she started filling her company commander's HUMVEE with her cold weather gear. The man had died at his desk, in the middle of the day.

She wanted to make sure she was ready in case her flying wasn't as good as she pictured it in her mind. She'd already survived one auto-rotation when the bird she was in lost power. Chief Warrant 2 John Jackson had auto-rotated them to a survivable landing. It was a minute in hell as she heard the helicopter engine stutter and stop. The pilot used language usually reserved for drunken bar fights. She felt her stomach protest as the bird went into freefall and the pilot frantically nosed the Blackhawk forward to keep air moving over the blades. He flared at the last moment to a jarring landing, but at least they were alive.

She was relieved to be in one piece after the landing, but she was more relieved she wasn't Jackson's mechanic. Jackson was one of the senior pilots and ripped into his maintenance crew like a drill sergeant with three ex-wives. A fuel line that had been checked by a private and inspected by a specialist and signed off by a sergeant had become fouled.

Amanda had been in the bird at the invitation of the co-pilot who was also her most recent boyfriend. While officially, they were on a check-flight for the Blackhawk, Amanda knew it was the pilots' way of looking around for new camping grounds. She would be going with them on a hunting trip in two weeks and they were looking for movement of the elk herds. They never made the trip after the auto-rotation landing. The regiment commander had found out and he was not pleased.

Amanda had watched and listened as Jackson landed the bird and thought, if she flew to Anchorage and ran into trouble, she could do what he'd done.

She never got that far. She was loading the HUMVEE when she saw another soldier walking between the barracks. At first she wasn't sure she was just imagining him. He was walking in no particular direction, stumbling once in a while. She hollered at him to make sure she wasn't hallucinating. "Hey!" she hollered. "Hey you!"

Pvt. 2 Sheppard took four more steps before stopping. He looked around, not sure if he were imagining her voice. When he saw her, he wasn't even sure she was real despite her standing 30 feet from him.

"Hey soldier. Are you real?" she called to him, stuffing her sleeping bag into the back seat of the HUMVEE and walking slowly over to him. Something told her his mind had already cracked. His boot laces were untied and dragging in the mud, his uniform was wrinkled and field jacket unzipped and he wore no headgear.

"Are you real?" he asked her in return. He had the same southern accent she had. She placed him from someplace other than Alabama, but she didn't know why. His very dark skin was smooth, causing the whites of his eyes to stand out in stark contrast. By the number of veins she could see in his eyes, it looked like the kid hadn't slept in too many hours.

Even though she was just shy of 21, the young man looked too young to be in the Army and too afraid to be left by himself.

~ ~ ~

WHEN 12-YEAR-OLD MARISSA CAME IN TO THE SHELTER OF JERry's farm, she told them the minivan and Cheryl was gone. Boomer, the large Bull Mastiff who was Tia's pet, had taken chase. Marissa said she heard a gunshot but the big brown dog was still chasing the van when it was leaving the drive. He'd be back eventually.

As it was, once Cheryl left the shelter, Katie and Mrs. deJesus ran for Danny and Kellie. Both had first aid training and ordered 13-year-old John to find towels and the other girls who were eating supper with them when Cheryl broke in, to get the first aid kit Kellie kept by the cellar door.

Jamal, the tall, dark, lanky 16-year-old Cajun raced up the stairwell to latch and lock the hatch door. The hatch was the second exit from the shelter and was at the top of a spiral staircase that led to the bedrooms. It was how Cheryl had gotten away without having to go through the shelter's doors and having to face the very protective dog.

Katie gently pulled Danny off Kellie's body as he was finally regaining consciousness.

Mrs. deJesus took care of Kellie who seemed to be going into shock.

"Both injuries are superficial on him. Nothing broke. He's lucky," Katie said to Mrs. deJesus as she bandaged Danny's wounds. His head, two inches above his left ear, had been grazed by the 9mm bullet. The hair and skin were ripped off and she could see the bone, but it wasn't cracked. It was bleeding like all head wounds do. She put gauze over the wound and wrapped his head with a towel.

"Hand me that superglue there," Katie, who had learned first aid as a girl scout and worked for a summer at a veteran's home where she listened to stories from Viet Nam, ordered one of the twins. Their names were Tara and Sara and they were identical. She was in no mood to try and guess which was which now. She finished cleaning the arm just below the elbow. She saw muscle, but the wound was not too bad. The bullet had taken a lot of skin and very little muscle, but hadn't severed any major blood vessel. It had already started clotting. She used the superglue to hold the skin together, added a large band-aid and wrapped the arm in a clean towel, using a safety pin to keep it in place.

Kellie was in worse shape as Mrs. deJesus discovered. She was face down on the floor and struggling weakly to turn over. Her face was blood covered and a pool of blood was forming under her. She had been held down by Danny until Katie was able to move him.

Mrs. deJesus, who had advanced medical training as a school administrator, had rushed to her side. John was bringing more towels and another first aid kit that Josh had in his camper as Mrs. deJesus was examining Kellie's injuries.

Just as Katie had done, Mrs. deJesus went to work on the

head first. There was a lot of blood and it was flowing freely. She instructed Tara, who was kneeling opposite her over Kellie's body, to hold the towel John had brought on the wound in Kellie's side until she could finish on Kellie's head.

The young girl, crying but doing as instructed, held it where she was told.

Wiping Kellie's head wound clean as best she could, she saw a flap of skin had been lifted. She folded it back into place and put a four-inch band-aid over it. She'd clean the blood later. The point where the knife had punctured her neck wasn't as bad, but was still dripping blood. A smaller bandage was used to close that wound as well.

She then turned to the holes in Kellie's side. The pool of blood under her friend was still getting bigger. She had Tara pull her hands back so she could see the hole and immediately told the girl to put the towel back.

"Johnny," she said looking at the boy who looked like he was in the first stages of shock. "In the cellar, by the bed there is a bottle of Tequila. Get it. Hurry." The boy was shaken out of his thoughts and dashed down the stairs.

Kellie tried to talk. "Randy," she croaked out. "Where's Randy?"

"We'll find him," Mrs. deJesus told her. He's probably still working and didn't hear the noise in the barn. She was just making that up. She didn't know, but she wanted Kellie to calm down. "I'll send Johnny after him when he gets back up here."

Mrs. deJesus asked Jamal for a knife. The young man who had been helping Katie tend to his friend Danny looked at the other twin girl who wasn't helping those on the floor and told her, "Back of my belt, on the left." The girl, who had been standing out of the way, reached under the young man's shirt and pulled a razor-sharp knife with an eight-inch blade out of its sheath.

"Perfect," Mrs. deJesus said taking the knife from the little girl. John returned with the half-full bottle of Tequila. She took it from the boy and unscrewed the top. "Drink this. A lot of it." Kellie shook her head and Mrs. deJesus insisted. "This is going to hurt, and you are going to try to move, but I want you to stay as still as you can.

"Believe me, this will help."

Kellie took a swig with Mrs. deJesus' help. "Johnny, find me a stapler." Kellie didn't hesitate and took two more big swallows and started crying.

When Kellie handed her back the bottle, Mrs. deJesus poured the rest of the liquid over the blade of the knife, causing Kellie to almost pass out.

Mrs. deJesus found both the entrance and exit holes of the bullet that had traveled through Kellie by using Josh's knife to cut away the clothes, then scraping the blood off. She cleaned the one in front first and saw it was clotting nicely. The hole was the size of her little finger and had stopped bleeding so she just covered it with a bandage.

The back hole was larger. It was leaking blood, but not heavily. She thought she might have to staple the hole shut, but if it was clotting already, maybe she should wait for Monica. She'd had only so much first aid training during her time with the Dallas school system.

What was happening here was way over her skill level and she hoped what she was doing wasn't more damage to her friend Kellie.

"Johnny. Randy is probably in the barn. Go find him," Mrs. deJesus told Tia's 12-year-old son. The gangly boy took off with Boomer who had just returned from chasing the minivan.

Mrs. deJesus looked at Katie, then to Marissa and the others. Danny was coming to, but he would have a concussion at least, and a headache to beat all hangovers.

The bleeding that had been flowing from Kellie's side had been staunched and bandaged.

"We are very lucky no one is dead," Mrs. deJesus told them. "Very lucky indeed."

Katie and the others had to agree. She then heard Kellie's walkie-talkie. It was John. He sounded near hysterical. "I found Randy. I think he's dead!"

Chapter 2

KELLIE'S EYES SHOT OPEN AND SHE STRUGGLED TO GET UP but Mrs. deJesus held her down. "You," the older woman said, pointing to Jamal, "stay with her and do not let her get up. Tara, grab the kits and come with me, hurry." She grabbed the walkie-talkie from beside Kellie and got up off the floor. "Where are you, son?" she asked levelly into the unit as she was racing out the door. "And Sara, find another walkie-talkie and turn it to channel three so I can talk to you up here."

"I'm in the criminal lady's room in the barn. Please hurry. I think he's dead." Mrs. deJesus could tell the 12-year-old was near panic. "I'm on my way Johnny. Don't move him." She was running as fast as she could down the path. Her heart was pumping and memories of a school shooting in one of her middle schools flooded back to her.

"There's been enough death, God. Please don't let young Randy be dead," she prayed as she ran. Tara caught up with her and ran beside her with the two first aid kits.

Mrs. Marguerite deJesus and her husband Juan had survived when nearly everyone else in the world had died. They found themselves alone in their town and had decided to drive to the gulf coast and bring their lives to a close. They were on their way when they came across Josh and his daughter and later Nick, Jamal, Sade, the Craven twins and a couple of others. When they all got sick, they went in search of medicine. They came across Jerry and his friends. Monica, their medic was able to help them.

They all moved back to Jerry's farm and there they stayed.

Mrs. deJesus found 12-year-old Johnny, Tia's son, at the door of the room where Cheryl had been held prisoner in the farm's barn. There was a box with a TV half out of it on the floor and a new DVD player still in the box.

Randy was lying on the floor where Johnny found him. Blood pooled under the young man's face and there was a tooth on the floor.

Randy was Jerry's son. He was a very kind and soft-hearted young man who Mrs. deJesus liked very much. He was always helpful, never said an unkind word and had a smile that reminded her of Jerry.

Mrs. deJesus knelt down and placed two fingers on Randy's neck. With her heart pounding from her run she couldn't tell if he was still alive. She moved her fingers to check again and felt a faint pulse. She thanked the God she'd just prayed to. "He's alive. Tell them he's alive." Johnny, who was crying and holding on to Tara let go of the girl and fumbled with the walkie-talkie.

"He's alive! Mrs. deJesus says he's alive!" he shouted into the radio.

Mrs. deJesus saw Randy had a massive bump on the back of his head and his short brown hair was matted with drying blood. She leaned down and listened to his breathing. There was gurgling but it was steady. She took two fingers and pulled the clotted blood out of his mouth. There was a lot of it, including another broken tooth.

Randy breathed easier but he was still unconscious.

"Johnny, tell Jamal I need him down here," Mrs. deJesus told the boy. When Jamal said he'd be down shortly, she looked at the two kids standing by the door, both looking too young to have to experience this type of horror. "Johnny, can you drive a quad?" He shook his head silently. "I can," volunteered Tara. "My dad and I used to ride them." Tara and her identical twin sister Sara had been found by Danny and Jamal.

"Excellent. Go get the big one from the garage and bring it over here. Johnny, go find a wooden ladder if you can." The kids ran off to do what Mrs. deJesus had asked. They might be scared, but they were doing as she asked without complaining and she couldn't ask for more.

She gently probed the bump on the back of Randy's head.

She wasn't sure the skull was cracked or not, but it wasn't staved in. She gently rolled his head to the side and saw his nose was nearly flat. He was unconscious now and if she waited until he came to, the pain might be too much. Using two fingers, one on each side of his nose, she set it. A blood clot broke free and she wiped his face and waited until it started clotting before laying his head back down on one of the towels Tara had brought with her. She didn't want him choking on his own blood.

The quad arrived at the same time as Jamal. Young Tara turned it off and waited for further instructions. John came out of the barn with an aluminum extension ladder. Mrs. deJesus told him to pull it apart so there was just one piece.

"Jamal, take the blankets off the bed. John put the ladder beside young Randy," Mrs. deJesus directed them. They finally understood what she had planned. Jamal ripped the blankets from the bed and heard the iron bar hit the floor. Everyone stopped what they were doing and looked at it.

Jamal looked at Mrs. deJesus. She nodded. "Good thing it was not longer or heavier," he said. She nodded again. He folded the blanket in thirds and laid it on the ladder John had put next to Randy.

The three of them then rolled Jerry's son onto the ladder. He weighed at least 250 pounds and for the kids and the elderly woman, it was a weight well over their ability to move easily. Mrs. deJesus held Randy's head as best she could as they moved him and Tara jumped off the quad to help.

Once Randy was on the ladder, Mrs. deJesus made sure the bump on his head was not against the rungs. When she was satisfied, they each took an end and lifted Randy out the door and onto the rear luggage rack of the quad.

Jamal started to get on the quad to drive it back to the shelter. "Tara, you drive," Mrs. deJesus said stopping him. "Jamal, turn around and sit backward behind Tara. You're strong enough to hold on to the ladder, the little girl is not," she instructed. "Tara, go slow. We're right behind you."

Tara nodded, got on the machine, started it and waited for Jamal to say he was ready. When he nodded, she put the big Polaris in first gear and slowly released the clutch. They started moving at walking pace, which was good for Mrs. deJesus. Her heart was still pounding like a jackhammer. John walked beside her, tear stains on his face.

The sound of the quad kept them from hearing the four motorhomes until they were halfway up the driveway. In all the excitement, Mrs. deJesus had forgotten Tia and her crew of three men was due and here she came with a convoy of four motorhomes. She told the others to continue to the shelter.

Tia, an Army wife with two kids whose Army husband died in the plague, had left later than Jerry that morning. She'd gone with Josh, Marissa's dad, Nick, a man in his early 30s, and Sade, a Nigerian-born refugee who had come to the United States years before and had formed a friendship with Nick, to search for a motorhome for the astronauts.

While Jerry and his team were driving to the gulf, Tia and her team were fighting zombies and recovering the new motorhomes at a place south of Anniston they'd found.

Mrs. deJesus waved at the driver of the first motorhome towing the damaged Escalade on the back. She ran to the door and opened in, climbing the two steps.

"Cheryl escaped and shot Kellie and Danny. Randy's hurt bad. Drive out back and park right in front of the shelter," she said rushing up to the driver's seat. Tia didn't stop to ask questions. She maneuvered the big motorhome up the overgrown path. Mrs. deJesus filled her in on everything as she drove. The other motorhomes followed.

Tia parked right in front of the parapet that Jerry had built when he was first building the shelter. Tara had parked the quad as close as she could to the door of the shelter and was just shutting it off.

Both women rushed out of the motorhome. The drivers of the other motorhomes must have seen the makeshift stretcher and came running too.

Tia, Nick, Josh and Sade carefully lifted the ladder off the quad and took it inside the shelter.

Everyone else followed.

~ ~ ~

It took a lot of talking and holding of his hand before Amanda could convince the young private she was real and alive. He was 18 years old and had just arrived on post three days before people started dying. He was fresh out of AIT (advanced individual training) at Ft. McClellan. He'd started in-processing and was assigned a billet, but that was all. He had no idea what had happened or would happen. When he couldn't find anyone else alive, he thought he was one of the living dead from the stories his grandma used to tell.

Amanda assured him he wasn't and told him of her plan to fly to Anchorage. Sheppard, looking young and scared said he'd do whatever it took to get away from here. The dead bodies frightened him while he was awake and tortured his dreams.

They found some gear for Sheppard and loaded it into the truck.

Sheppard, who said everyone called him Shep, slowly began showing more life as he realized he was not inside some living-dead nightmare from the tales of his grandmother's voodoo.

Amanda drove them back to the maintenance buildings where she usually worked. She knew of a helicopter, a Blackhawk, that had just finished its flight check after an overhaul, which was fueled and ready.

They were driving down Neely Road on the base when Amanda saw another soldier, her second that day. He was running out of a building off to her right. He was waving a white table cloth. Amanda brought the truck to quick stop. Shep looked at her, fear as real as the shaking in his hands.

"Stay here," she told him before climbing out of the truck. She knew right then she was going to get a weapon. With no one else alive, she hadn't even thought about it, but if this soldier was crazy, she had nothing with which to defend herself.

The soldier turned out to be Capt. Poitra. He was an accountant with finance and, like Amanda and Shep was working on leaving the post. The captain had been gathering food to take with him. Amanda, who had planned on flying the 370 miles hadn't thought about food. She didn't think she'd need to eat if she was going to be flying for just a couple of hours.

Poitra didn't pull rank, but did get her to reconsider flying to Anchorage. If she failed, she'd probably die and kill Shep as well. If they took trucks, if something mechanical broke, chances were they wouldn't end up dead in fiery wreckage on the side of a mountain.

Also, with two trucks, if one broke down, the other would be there as a back up.

The captain was a short, husky man, with close-cropped dark hair. He looked like a man familiar with the north and the cold.

As they talked about plans, she learned this was his second tour of Wainwright and was headed the same direction as she was. She found out his wife had not survived the plague. She had been pregnant with their first child and a lot of who Capt. Poitra was died when his wife did. He thought about taking his own life, but chose instead to drive to Anchorage, then on to Sterling Alaska where he'd grown up.

"Safety in numbers, Saunders," he'd said to her and she was forced to agree. It'd take them a full day to drive to Anchorage, but it was probably safer than flying and saving a few hours.

They spent the rest of the day preparing for the trip. They decided on Army trucks because they could mount machine guns on them. They didn't expect trouble, but Alaska had wild animals that were already encroaching onto the base. Mounting an M60 machine gun on top of the HUMVEE might mean the difference if they needed food or were attacked by a wild bear or moose.

After an hour of hearing her say "Yes, sir," to him, the captain said the world had ended and so had the United States Army and she should call him Jim. The captain had already left the Army. Amanda saw no reason to think she was still in the Army, but part of her couldn't stop believing it.

They slept in the Post Exchange that night, snacking on the food and looking for anything they might need for survival. The HUMVEEs had radios, but they went ahead and got walkie-talkies with extra batteries as well. Jim said it wouldn't hurt to be too prepared. They slept on inflatable mattresses in the sports department with extra blankets from linens. The heat and lights were still working here, unlike many of the other buildings on post, but the thermostat must have been on a timer because it cooled off after 9 p.m.

It was a brisk 15 degrees above zero when they began their drive the next morning. They had their headlights on because of the short days. They'd only see the sun, if it wasn't obscured by clouds, for about five hours this early in the year. They'd jump on the George Parks Highway which would take them all the way into Anchorage. They had already seen a number of vehicles on the road, wrecked after the driver had died.

Their HUMVEEs were fueled and each truck had four five-gallon fuel cans strapped to the rear deck. The trucks had a range of about 300 miles on a tank of fuel and they were going at least 370 miles. Amanda had packed the same manual pump they used to fill the fuel cans in case they had to forage for fuel along the way.

Jim drove by himself, leading the two-truck convoy. Amanda took the wheel first and followed the captain at a respectable distance so her headlights didn't bother him. He'd told her already they would stop every two hours for a 15-minute break and every six hours for a rest break. He said there was no reason to hurry. The trucks were winterized, but Alaskan roads could be tricky, more so now that there were no road crews.

~ ~ ~

THE INJURED WERE TREATED AND FUSSED OVER AT THE FARM IN Alabama. Beds were moved from the upstairs rooms and furniture from the living room moved temporarily outside.

All three patients were resting comfortably. Randy hadn't come to yet, but Kellie was lucid, although a little drunk. She cried a lot and everyone re-assured her that everyone was going to be okay, even though no one knew if it were true.

Danny came to, but Tia made him lay down in the bed they'd made for him.

Danny was pissed and used a lot of words the young kids shouldn't have been hearing. Mrs. deJesus laid her hand on his arm, the good arm, and told him he needed to settle down because he was scaring the children and if he didn't, she would change his dressing and pull off the superglue.

Tia, Tara and John took care of Kellie; Josh, Sara and Katie hovered over Randy and Mrs. deJesus, Marissa and Jamal were at Danny's side. Nick and Sade moved the motorhomes from in front of the shelter and parked them where they'd be out of the way for now.

Most of the talk between everyone was how to break the news to Jerry. Some thought they should tell him as soon as he came within range, but Kellie voted everyone down. Her head hurt and her side hurt, but she was still nominally in charge of the house.

"Starting now, I want someone on the CB. Every 15 minutes call for Jerry. If he answers, I will talk to him. Even if I am asleep, wake me. I will tell him. No one else." She looked at everyone, the tears in her eyes as plain as the pain in her face. They understood why she must be the one to tell him, so they didn't argue. She and Jerry had become close.

She started making up a schedule for everyone, but Katie, the farm's horticulturist, shushed her. "You just lay there, sweetie." Katie was one of the people who had come to the farm with the deJesuses too. She had been wandering a highway when Josh and his daughter came across her. Josh, a butcher who spoke softly, allowed the former nursery manager to ride with them.

"We'll take care of the radio. You have a big cut on your head and lost some blood. You need to sleep and drink your water. We'll take care of everything else."

Kellie laid back and closed her eyes. It had been a horrifying evening, the worst part hearing John say Randy was dead. She thanked God John was wrong.

Randy was hurt bad, but he was alive. She would have to find a way to tell Jerry that he'd been hurt, and the first thing she'd tell him would be that his son is alive.

She cried knowing Jerry had left her in charge of the farm and trusted her. Kellie knew she should have been more careful of that manipulating vigilante Cheryl.

Kellie saw how Cheryl had paraded her pretty young body in front of kind-hearted Randy. She'd seen women like Cheryl treat men that way before. She'd seen it in the schools where she'd taught and seen young men do stupid things for pretty girls. She kept asking herself how she was going to tell Jerry how her fear of pissing off his son kept her from telling him how dangerous Cheryl could be. She looked over at Randy. His eyes were turning black and blue and his upper lip swelled and there was still some dried blood in his hair. His head was on a pillow, slightly turned so the bump on his head could be iced.

She finally fell asleep wondering what words she'd use to tell Jerry of the injuries she'd allowed happen to his son.

Jamal, after being given the okay from Mrs. deJesus, went to his tent and got Danny his bottle of Jack Daniels. He poured his friend two shots, which was all Mrs. deJesus would allow. Danny said it helped his headache and the pain in his arm. He fell asleep thinking of how many ways he was going shoot the lady who shot him.

~ ~ ~

CHERYL LEFT THE SHELTER IN THE MINIVAN AND WAS DETERmined to put as many miles as possible between her and her prison in the shortest amount of time. It had been a difficult month for her after being wounded during the ill-planned attack and her subsequent capture by the farm's defenders. She hadn't been hurt bad, but bad enough, and held prisoner in the barn, a dog collar around her neck at night and in leg irons during the day were added insults.

Her problem this time, she decided, was her choice of compatriots. Her brother had picked her up at the St. Clair Correctional Facility where she'd finished a 30-day stint for assault. They were living in a trailer park when the end of the world came. She was working at a small store chain as a cashier to make a little money while her brother worked odd jobs in construction. With death all around them, including everyone they knew, they thought they hit the jackpot.

All their mistakes, brushes with the law and lies were behind them and they could build their lives over.

The one thing both wanted, after they stopped questioning why they'd been so fortunate to survive when most of the population hadn't, was to be in charge, especially Cheryl. She wanted to control her life like she'd never been able to before. All her life she had been controlled by someone else.

Growing up, her mom and dad controlled her. They told her what to do, what classes to take in school, what sports to play and whom to date. Her younger brother was an afterthought to her parents and was freer to get in trouble, which he did.

After high school, Cheryl was told which college to go to, which degree to get and to whom she should get engaged.

The man her parents wanted her engaged to, Mark Kennedy, was wealthy, well-educated, well-connected and a thorough and complete prick. She dated him through college and put up with his attitude, but she never loved him. He was always making sure she felt indebted to him and seldom listened to her opinion. He controlled where they went, what they did and with whom they made friends.

Cheryl allowed him to do it because it was expected of her.

After two years of college, she was expected to marry Mark and have beautiful children and Cheryl might have done just that if she hadn't met Devon.

Devon was a contractor who was remodeling the dream house Mark had picked out for them. Devon was tattooed and vulgar and everything Mark wasn't. He was also in the house nearly every day for three months.

Where Mark was cultured and intelligent and chose every word he spoke carefully, Devon was brash and outspoken and cared more about having a good time than making more money.

Cheryl loved the looks of Devon's hard sweaty body when he was working and hated Mark's long, lean tennis body. It wasn't an affair, because she was still just engaged to Mark, but she felt liberated when she flirted with the carpenter and later when they ripped each other's clothes off in the dream house.

Mark slapped her when he found out. He then used his connections to ruin Devon's business. His anger led him to make sure Cheryl got fired from any job in any position at any company anywhere in the area.

Everywhere she went, or any job she got lasted only long enough for Mark's influence to get her fired.

Even her parents shunned her. They'd worked so hard to raise her right, put her through college and plan her future and she threw it all away to screw a broke carpenter. They cut her off from family money and seldom talked to her. She hadn't lived up to their standards and they never let her forget it.

After being fired from her fourth job in as many months, she was walking back to her one-room apartment when she passed an Army recruiter's office. She walked in, knowing Mark couldn't mess with the Army.

Her parents were furious that she joined the Army, thinking it was below their social status. Cheryl didn't care. She liked thought of her parents being pissed at her and she felt like a rogue for choosing to become a soldier.

Six months later she was a second lieutenant. She found the organization of the military, the level playing field where everyone was equally nothing, a good fit for her. Cheryl knew she was attractive compared with most of the other women and she used her looks to get the men to help her get by.

For the first time in her life, she felt like she had some control of her life. The male drill sergeants seemed to go easy on her because she was pretty, although the female drill sergeants treated her as equal cannon fodder. After basic training, she was transferred to Ft. Benning for officer candidate school. It wasn't easy, but she graduated and was given 2nd Lieutenant bars.

She was made an officer.

She was assigned to a post in Germany as a supply officer. She'd stayed mostly out of trouble; at least enough so nothing was put in her official record. There were some problems but batting her eyes at the right man, or a flirtatious glance in the right direction, covered up her mistakes or errors in judgment. She finished her first tour and rotated stateside with a promotion.

~ ~ ~

SHEP, STILL LIVING IN HIS OWN NIGHTMARE, DIDN'T TALK MUCH on the drive from Fairbanks to Anchorage. He rode in the passenger seat and looked out the window. Amanda was okay with it. Her dad had once told her that too many people spoke without thinking about what they were saying. That comment had stuck with her. She was always careful about what she said and didn't push Shep to talk.

The drive was boring. There was no music in the HUMVEE and with the winter tires, it wasn't a quiet vehicle. After two hours, she was happy to see the captain pull off the side of the road. It was still dark, but they could see the first rays of dawn.

After a good brisk walk and tending to personal business, they got back on the road. Shep had offered to drive, but Amanda said she was good for the next leg and pulled out to lead.

She wasn't ready to trust Shep behind the wheel. If he was like she'd been when she first arrived, the snow-covered roads might be too much for him to handle right now.

The captain had suggested keeping her speed to about 50 miles per hour, which was good because every few miles they'd come across a vehicle on the highway. Twice they'd had to leave the road because a semi had wrecked, blocking the entire two-lane road.

Amanda kept the same speed and the captain fell in behind her. The sunrise was beautiful, nothing like the sunrises in Alabama, but still amazing and she might have appreciated the grandeur if the rest of the world hadn't died.

As it was, she thought about her boyfriend and how he died in his bunk. She wondered if her dad and brother had gone the same way. She knew the two had planned on moving into that damned hole her dad had been digging for years in the hill behind the barn. Her last email from him had been telling her that she was always in his thoughts and prayers.

He was like that. He wasn't a bible thumper, but he was a devout believer in God. It sometimes bothered her, but he never forced his faith on her or her brother, so it never became an issue. For her, the best thing about his faith was the Sundays with no work.

She thought a lot about her dad's faith during the second leg of her drive. She had never really been a believer or given God much thought. She had other things to think about. She hoped if her dad had passed from this life into the next, that whatever God he believed in had taken him peacefully.

The convoy was just about to their second break when Amanda saw a little bit of civilization. A Chevron station was off to her left, but it had been set afire and was nothing but rubble and a burned out building.

Further along the highway a Tosoro Alaska gas station and eatery could be seen. They should be able to re-fuel their trucks and stretch.

She pulled in and turned off the truck. Amanda looked through the front windows of the building while Shep went to the back of the store. It was typical of many of these stations that were far from the cities -- pumps out front of the station and an attached restaurant, probably run by the same family as the gas station. This one also had a bait shop to one side.

There were six 4-by-4 trucks parked in the lot, a front loader off to one side and a bulldozer on the other. When the captain pulled into the parking lot and turned off his truck, the silence was so absolute she could hear the echoes of his truck for several seconds afterward.

They stretched and looked around the area. Jim showed them bear tracks in the dirt and suggested they not spend much time here. Amanda tried the diesel pump, but it didn't work. Jim jumped up on the loader and found it had a full tank of fuel.

It took them 20 minutes to re-fill their HUMVEES. There was not much else to talk about. They weren't even half way to Anchorage after four hours of tedious driving. Amanda said she was still good to drive but Jim said he could use a few hours of sleep if Shep could drive for him so the young black man took his turn behind the wheel.

Amanda pulled out first and took the lead again. For everything that was wrong in the world, the steady sound of her HUMVEE gave her comfort. With the sun now above the horizon she could see why so many people were in awe of the Alaskan countryside. She was a born and bred Daughter of Dixie, but Alabama had nothing like this for wilderness beauty. She saw two herds of elk and several other smaller species of wildlife, but no more people.

Amanda concentrated on the road in front and picked up speed on the two-lane highway. They hadn't seen as many car or truck wrecks in the last few hours so she drove down the middle of the road. She picked up her speed to 60 miles per hour and kept it there. Shep fell back a couple hundred yards but he reported on the radio that he was fine with the speed. There was snow covering the highway, but the tires on the HUMVEEs handled it easily.

Two more hours came and went. Jim called her on the radio, asking if she needed to pull over. She told him she didn't but would if they needed to. Jim said they were fine and to stop when she was ready.

She was ready when they came up to Willow Way, about 90 minutes out of Anchorage and near the intersection of Alaskan Highway 8. She hadn't planned on stopping, but there was a truck parked in front of the little strip mall and a man in Army uniform was running from the store waving his arms.

That was how they picked up Spec. 4 Roy Johnson.

Johnson had come to the same conclusion as Amanda and the captain, but he'd left a day before them. He had lived off post in Fairbanks and when his friends had died and no one answered the phones on base, he figured he'd head to Anchorage where his fiancée was attending college. The large black specialist hadn't heard from her and knew she was probably dead, but he had to know. He'd just finished a two-week leave with her to become engaged, and gotten back to Fairbanks the same day the president implemented martial law.

He hadn't returned to the military base, just got back in his car and drove.

Roy's car had broken down the previous day and he had to walk back several miles to find the truck he'd seen off the road. He'd pulled the dead body out and got this far before it too broke down. He'd pulled into this strip mall to get some sleep and the truck stalled and refused to restart. It was already dark so he broke into the thrift store for some blankets, the liquor store for something to drink and the food mart for something to eat.

He drank more than he should have, admittedly getting so drunk he passed out, and didn't wake up until late in the morning. He decided to get something to eat and search for another vehicle before getting back on the road. Five minutes earlier or later and Roy would have missed them completely. He hadn't found a vehicle, but he wasn't feeling tired anymore so was glad to ride with them.

Jim suggested he take over driving from Amanda and Shep continue driving the second with Roy as his co-driver. Amanda was fine with it. She'd been behind the wheel for more than seven hours. Roy packed up what he had in the second truck and the four started on the last 80 miles to Anchorage.

Jim left Amanda to her own thoughts once they'd been on the road for 20 minutes. Amanda closed her eyes and listened to the sound of the truck. She'd slept the night before, but after the last stop, she'd had something to eat and a good rest break so she covered herself with her field jacket and a blanket, put a pillow against the window and closed her eyes to be alone with her thoughts. She felt the sun's warmth on her eyelids.

By the time the sun had reached the horizon, they'd be in Anchorage. Each of them had a different reason for heading there and she hoped to find more people. She'd hate to think they were the last four on earth.

Amanda had drifted in and out of sleep and sat up when Jim stopped the truck. She looked around and it was getting dark. There were no lights except for a few fires in buildings far off the highway.

Anchorage was without power.

Jim had chosen to pull off the interstate near Midtown. He pulled into a gas station that had diesel tanks on pedestals. It would make it easier to refuel the trucks in the morning.

The four disembarked from the trucks. Bones cracked as they stretched in the cold weather. It was snowing and the wind was picking up.

"What do you guys think? Stay with the trucks tonight or do we try to find others by driving around and looking for lights?" the captain asked.

"I remember reading that Anchorage has almost 300,000 people living here. Fairbanks had 30,000. We should find some people tomorrow," Amanda said.

Roy didn't like her figures and pointed out that just because they didn't find more people in Fairbanks, it didn't mean all of them had died. When his friends and neighbors had died, he'd left the city. He hadn't looked for other survivors.

There might be more people alive than any of them knew, but in all honesty, Roy told them he didn't care about anyone else. Tomorrow he was going to go to the University of Alaska Anchorage and look for his fiancée.

He wasn't asking. He was telling.

Jim said he wanted to continue on to Sterling in hopes of finding family in the morning.

Shep, the young private who hadn't said much looked at them with the same look Amanda had seen on her dad's dog when it had been caught digging in the garden. Her dad had hollered at the dog, something he seldom did, and the dog hung its head, put its tail between its legs and slunk up to the back porch of the farm house. The poor thing looked so sad and lost, just as Shep did now.

"I don't know," the young man said, his soft southern voice bringing a smile to Amanda's face. "I guess I just want to find some more people."

Amanda told the others she wanted to go home as well. Her mom lived east of Spokane and Amanda would start there. If her mom and her step dad couldn't be found, she would continue on to Alabama to find out if her brother and dad were still alive.

Shep lifted his head enough to look at her. Alabama was close enough to Mississippi, so he said it. "I'll hang with the sergeant for a while I guess."

Chapter 3

A year before Armageddon, 1st Lt. Cheryl Paxton became the new assistant command information officer assigned to the public affairs office for a combat division home based at Ft. Stewart, GA. She'd arrived there with a clean record after attending an eight-week course of study at Ft. Meade, Maryland. She was excited about being in charge of the community relations side of the Public Affairs Office.

Cheryl was less excited about it four months later. She found her job boring. She wrote articles for the community newspaper, spoke at lunches with local companies, attended formal evening parties for local politicians.

None of it she found fun. There was no spice in her life and when she wasn't working, she was attending officer enrichment classes and fulfilling other military responsibilities.

It was not the fun life for which she'd been longing; instead it was the same monotonous drudgery week after week.

The Public Affairs Officer, Maj. Bob D. MacKenzie, was a gregarious and jovial leader. Everyone in the office liked him because he led with flair and energy. The command group of the division liked him because he was smart, had a sharp wit and writing talent, while the PAO staff respected him because he knew how to train them to be better public affairs specialists.

Cheryl liked him too, at first, before she found out he was also a man who was serious about training his junior officers.

He was there to train her and teach her, not let her run rough shod over his office. She forgot that and she paid for her mistake.

She recalled with perfect clarity her fall. He'd called her in his office just before the end of the work day. She knocked and looked in to his office. “You wanted to see me, sir?”

“Yes, come in,” he said, not looking up from the laptop on which he was typing furiously with two fingers. Cheryl felt comfortable around the major. He wasn’t a hard-ass like the instructors at OCS, but more laid back and fatherly to all in the office, from his assistant PAO to the lowest private.

“Please close the door,” he said quietly. He didn’t look up from what he was typing. She closed the door, thinking maybe he had a special assignment for her. His was watching his fingers, then looking up to make sure he’d correctly spelled what he thought he typed.

Cheryl closed the door a little too loudly and giggled when the major looked up. “Sorry,” she apologized and smiled the smile that would make some men willingly walk into hell’s fire.

He looked back to his typing so Cheryl walked over to the major’s “brag wall” where he had awards for his writing, leadership and service. She’d been called into his office before and he’d counseled her how she could better serve the office. He was always friendly and helpful and always informal.

In a voice that was both quiet and stern, he said without looking up from his work, “Lieutenant, when you to report to me, you will report at the position of attention in front of my desk and you will stand there until I tell you differently.”

There was a brief pause as it sunk in and an icy chill worked its way through the office. She moved smartly to stand in front of his desk at the position of attention. “Lieutenant Paxton, reporting as ordered, sir,” she said, wondering what she’d been caught doing wrong.

The major finished his writing a long minute later and closed the laptop’s cover and looked straight at her. “Lieutenant, I am displeased with your performance. You are here as the community relations officer and in the past 12 days I have received reports from two of our local vendors that you have neglected your duties, instead ordering one of the enlisted personnel to do jobs for which I made you personally responsible.”

Cheryl had made plans to spend a weekend at the ocean with a lieutenant colonel from G-2, but one of the local suppliers wanted a representative from the division for their annual party. Cheryl sent frumpy SSgt. Hines. A week later, another supplier had an employee accepted to West Point and wanted to have someone from the division on hand for the presentation. Cheryl thought it sounded boring so, again, ordered Hines to do it.

"Sir, Hines wasn't doing any…," was all she got out before Maj. MacKenzie stood up with authority, his chair rolling to the wall behind him.

Without raising his voice from conversational level, he leaned across his desk, both hands flat on the glass.

"I did not give you permission to speak, lieutenant, so shut your face hole." The temperature in the room dropped again for Cheryl. There was a bearing in the major's voice she had never heard from anyone. It was a conviction that he was right, and Cheryl was wrong and he had all the power.

"Staff Sergeant Hines is one of the finest NCOs I have *ever* had the privilege with whom to serve. You have done nothing but drop shit jobs on her that were *your* responsibility.

"I've also heard your comments about her looking like 'Mrs. Potatohead' to the other officers here, and you've treated her like she's your personal labor force. These actions are unacceptable.

"She is ten times the asset you are and if you could see past your own self-aggrandizing, you'd see how valuable a soldier she is to everyone in this office.

"No one takes advantage of my soldiers and my staff, especially some lazy-assed lieutenant who thinks she's got more important things to do than her job." The major kept a steady stare into Cheryl's left eye. He wasn't flinching, nor giving her a chance to find a way to talk herself out of the mess she'd gotten in to. "From this day, no, from this minute forward, lieutenant, you will carry out the orders I gave you the first day you arrived.

"You will carry those duties out correctly and effectively or you will find out how much of a hard-ass I can be. The Army owns you 24 hours a day, seven days a week, and that means I own you 24 hours a day, seven days a week."

He straightened up from leaning across the desk. He wasn't

a tall man, but his confidence and authority filled the room. He wasn't sure he was getting through to her. "I've seen officers like you ruin good soldiers, but I will not let you ruin the soldiers under my command." He reached for the sheet of paper that had been spit from his printer. It was a record of Cheryl's actions and the major's corrective action. He let her read it.

"I am forwarding a copy of this conversation to your company commander and requesting a letter of reprimand be placed in your personnel jacket...."

Cheryl tuned out with his last sentence. A letter of reprimand in her personnel jacket would probably keep her from any command positions. He had just ruined her career and he was doing it because of frumpy old SSgt. Hines.

She heard the major dismissed her and she went back to her office. There were no tears, no recriminations and no self-motivational speeches on improving herself.

Instead she was plotting ways to get even with SSgt. Hines and Maj. MacKenzie. They couldn't get away with treating her like this and she wouldn't stand for it.

In the following weeks, Cheryl did the work she was assigned, without enthusiasm, but with just enough effort to keep MacKenzie off her ass.

To destroy Hines' life, she had an affair with Hines's husband, not because he was handsome, but because it would drive Leena to tears. Which it did. Cheryl laughed in her face, then in the face of Hines' husband. She didn't care about them except to ruin their lives.

When Maj. MacKenzie called her in his office about the alleged affair, Cheryl was prepared and told him of sexual harassment complaint she was going to file against him, something the Army took very seriously.

She told him the stories she had made up, with times of when the two of them were alone in the office which would be borne out by the sign-in logs or witnesses, along with some other evidence she'd manufactured, and how the major had offered to "help" her career in exchange for sexual favors.

She'd set him up to ruin his military career, and even if she couldn't prove them, the allegations would be on his record.

MacKenzie smiled at her and picked up the phone to dial

the MPs. Cheryl leaned over his desk just as he'd done to her and told him not to try and bluff her. He turned his laptop around and she saw that he was recording every word she had said.

Her military career ended after a brief court martial and three months incarceration. At 25 years old, her military career was over with a dishonorable discharge, reduction in rank to E-1, forfeiture of two-thirds pay and allowances and a criminal record. Cheryl knew what she'd done wrong -- she hadn't given friendly old Maj. MacKenzie credit for being smarter than her.

She vowed that mistake wouldn't happen again.

From there, it was a series of failed relationships over the next six months before she knocked a man's teeth out at a bar and was sent to the county lock up for 30 days.

Then the world ended and everyone in her past, except her brother, was probably dead. She could start clean on her terms and her brother, two years her junior, did everything his big sister told him. They found a few others still alive and formed a gang, with Cheryl in charge.

Anyone who wasn't with them was against them.

If they didn't like following Cheryl's rules, they became bait for the zombies.

~ ~ ~

RANDY CAME OUT OF HIS UNCONSCIOUS STATE SHORTLY BEFORE three in the morning. He groaned slightly and Katie, who was sitting watch, reached over to wipe his mouth.

"Easy there, Randy, you've got a nasty bump on your skull," she told him. She reached over and woke Sara who was sleeping on the floor, acting as Katie's aid. "Go wake up Kellie," she told the twin. The little girl did and gently helped Kellie sit up in bed. She got water for both of the patients and helped Kellie drink while Katie helped Randy.

"Wha' 'appen'?" Randy asked, feeling his missing teeth.

"Don't you remember?" asked Kellie softly.

Randy thought for a minute, concentrating as best he could. He then shook his head. "Las' I rem'm'er," he said slowly, "I wa' hel'ing 'anny, I 'ink. I ha' a 'ad 'eadache." He reached up and touched the bump on the back of his head, then bandages on his nose and finally his teeth. "Oh 'od, wha' 'appen' 'o me?" he asked again then started crying. He also felt a bruise in his crotch, but he wasn't going to feel it with two women and a young girl right there.

Katie touched his arm softly. "You were hurt, but you're going to be okay," she comforted him. "Try to sleep now, sweetie. You need your rest and we'll talk more in the morning."

Randy didn't notice that Danny and Kellie were lying next to him, he just closed his eyes. Katie saw the young man run his tongue over his missing teeth for a moment then slip off into a deep sleep. Katie looked at Kellie. "That's a good sign," she mouthed and for the first time that evening, Kellie felt the load of the world lift slightly from her chest.

Kellie couldn't sleep any more and had Sara bring her the tablet she used when she couldn't be at her computer. She did a lot of typing. She typed an entire page before she realized her headache had receded to a dull ache.

~ ~ ~

JERRY UNKNOWINGLY WOKE UP AT ABOUT THE SAME TIME AS HIS son back on the farm. The bus drove off interstate bypass 459 onto I-20, having to leave the road because of the interchange being totally collapsed. He'd gotten two good hours of sleep. He sat up just as the bus was accelerating. Juan was still driving and looking extremely happy to be doing so. The two American astronauts were in the front talking quietly with him.

The female Canadian astronaut was writing her thoughts down on a note pad.

Things seemed to be going well. He looked at his watch, then out the front window. He recognized their location and figured at least another 20 minutes before they could make radio contact. He was excited to get back to the shelter. He missed his son and Kellie and the others who had become special to him. Despite the hell they'd experienced with all the death, the zombies, the vigilantes and the weather, he was happy on his farm. He looked forward to expanding the living space over the winter when there was less farm work to do and more time for building.

He mentally made plans to build another windmill and water wheel generator for the shelter. He was sure he would find more batteries for his power grid so he could expand power distribution. He also needed to dig another septic system, and a place to bury garbage. Those would be big projects to keep people busy. They'd need more fuel, mostly diesel, for the tractors. More seeds for plants and a bigger garden. With all the people they had, they could use more of everything.

Lost in his own thoughts, he was caught unprepared when Juan hit the brakes of the big bus. Jerry fell off the bed, but quickly scrambled to his feet. Juan had unbuckled from his seat and was headed for the door. "Hurry," he encouraged Jerry.

From the vehicle behind them, Eddie was already getting out of the SWAT truck even as Monica was bringing it to a halt.

Juan was out the door without his gun, but Jerry took the time to grab one of the AR-15s before leaving the bus. The Ford had stopped in the highway in front of them. Rusty had been driving on point for the convoy.

He was now leaning into a car that had cashed on its side against the median barrier, its motor still smoking from the recent crash. He was reaching inside the Volvo, trying to pull someone out of the driver's door. Jerry handed the AR to Monica and pulled Eddie along with him as they ran up to help Rusty.

"Move the bus so we have more lights over here," Rusty yelled to Juan. The bus had three times as many lights on the front as the old Ford and Juan understood immediately. He ran back to the bus and a moment later, everyone at the car could see like it was daytime.

Rusty gripped a woman's hand and arm, holding her from flopping onto the passenger side of the car and onto the dead man who still had blood flowing from his ears and nose. She'd obviously been the driver and he the passenger. Jerry jumped on the car and got the back door open after Eddie got it to unlock. Eddie jumped inside and used his knife to cut the woman's seat belt and helped Jerry and Rusty get the woman out.

She was unconscious and very pregnant. They carefully carried her to the bus where Astronaut Kayla Schaeffer of the Canadian Space Agency took over.

"Let's go, Juan," Jerry told the driver of the bus. "I'll be in the Ford. Saddle up everyone and let's get home!" He ran from the bus to his truck and got the convoy moving again. He didn't know why a pregnant woman was driving at this hour on this highway, but if she was as far along as he suspected, he knew why she crashed. He didn't give anymore thought to the man they left in the car. His time on earth had come to an end.

Ten minutes later, after getting back on the road, they were pulling off I-20 and getting on local roads, he heard a voice on the CB. "Come in Mr. Saunders. Can you hear me?" It was the voice of a young girl, but he didn't know which one.

"This is Jerry, come in. Who is this?"

"This is Sara. Lemme get Kellie. She wants to talk to you."

Jerry waited, wondering why the little girl was up so late. He looked at the clock on the dash which said 5:34 a.m. He wondered why the little girl was up so early. He'd been on the road for more than 25 hours with a little over five hours of sleep, three on the way down and two from which he just woke.

"Jerry this is Kellie, come in."

"This is Jerry. What's up Kellie? We're seven miles away and I got that souvenir you wanted."

"We've had a problem here, Jerry, but everyone is alive and doing a lot better. Randy, Danny and I were all injured," she didn't want to say wounded. "I'll tell you all about it when you get here."

"Was it zombies," he asked her, "or vigilantes?"

"It was one vigilante and it's my fault. But we'll tell you everything that happened when you get here. I just wanted you to know everyone here is alive and doing better." He voice sounded weak and different. It didn't have the sultry, husky timber it usually had. She didn't want him to ask her for any more details so she ended the conversation. "Kellie out."

He called back twice, but she didn't answer.

Jerry was left to worry about what had happened for the final 20 minutes of the drive. The worrying was interrupted when Monica, who had stayed with the crash victim, along with the Canadian astronaut, called him on the walkie-talkie from the bus. "We got the baby, Mr. Saunders," Monica told him, "but the woman just died. There was nothing we could do."

~ ~ ~

CHERYL'S CREW HAD DONE WELL WITH STOCKING THEIR HIDE-out, but three were killed on a raid of a food store. They'd captured two strangers who were used as bait, but someone came looking for them and rescued them right under the noses of her team. Five people were killed that day, one at the light post, blown to hell by a grenade, the drug addict whose neck got broken by being stepped on, and three from bullets from the rifle of one of the rescuers. Her crew had been wrecked by locals with no military training and she wasn't going to have that.

Cheryl had made a tactical error attacking Jerry's shelter by sending Cooley and Martha to the farm first after the owner and others had left. She should have known that stupid bastard Cooley would shoot first, which he did. When she, her brother and another guy who was also former Army, went to the shelter's door, she thought they'd frighten whoever was left into giving up. She hadn't expected the door to explode, killing her brother and injuring the other former Army soldier and herself.

It went from bad to worse when the guy who was still struggling with getting a grenade through the hole in the door was shot in the head. The man fell and the grenade rolled away from him with its pin still in.

Cheryl struggled away from the door, glad she had given her gun to her brother. She was hurt, but was treated by a heavyset lady, younger than herself. She knew she had made a mistake and didn't know how she was going to get out of it.

She was locked up in a cattle barn and remained that way for days. She had no way she could see of getting free until the boy-man Randy started fawning on her. That's when she started building her story that she used on his dad and his girlfriend. If it hadn't been for the girlfriend, Cheryl might have convinced both men she was a victim. Cheryl saw that Kellie didn't believe her so she began really working on getting Randy to do as she wanted him.

It wasn't supposed to end with her killing Randy, but if she did, it was his own fault. She did however hope she'd killed Kellie and the Danny Rambo who came running in. They got what they deserved.

She decided she would exact revenge on all of them, starting with the guy who locked her up, Jerry, when she got back on her feet. But first she had to get to the Smith Compound. They had tanks at Ft. Knox and damned if tanks wouldn't blow that shelter out of the ground once and for all.

~ ~ ~

Amanda and Shep shared a HUMVEE for the night. They moved the trucks to a large parking lot and parked them side by side, facing opposite directions, letting them idle.

They thought about turning the trucks off to save fuel and so they wouldn't attract attention from the wild animals, but the temperature was already below zero so staying warm was a higher priority.

By the time they finished eating and sharing one of the 12-pack of beer Roy had smuggled along, they settled in for the night, closing up the windows, leaving just a crack for fresh air.

It was more than eight hours before there would be enough light to see anything beyond their headlights. Amanda put the pillow between the window and her head and she worked to get comfortable. She thought about her dad a lot and how she had told him she didn't want to stay on the farm but to get away and see the world.

"Dad, I'll never get into a good college with my grades," she told him. "But in the Army I can learn to do something more than farm. I can earn some money and see more of the world than our part of it."

Jerry had reluctantly agreed with her choice. He'd always thought she wasn't like her brother or like so many of the girls with whom she went to school. She wasn't one to become a mother at 19, a wife at 20, ex-wife by 23 with two kids and living at home with her parents. She was too headstrong and smarter than her grades showed. There was too much she'd read about and seen on television.

Her dad had supported her decision, but her mother had not. It caused a lot of arguments in the house during her last year of high school. She knew it wasn't the cause of her mom moving out and divorcing her dad, but it was part of the cause and it hurt her.

Jerry showed up for her graduation from basic training from Ft. Jackson, but Randy hadn't. He had been left to work the farm. Her dad was proud of her. He showed up again when she finished 14 weeks and three days of school at Fort Eustis, VA. He only spent a few hours with her, but he made the drive and it meant a lot to her.

Amanda loved working on the helicopters. She didn't like the winter weather at Fort Wainwright, and wasn't gung ho for the military lifestyle, but she passed all the physical tests and fit in with her teammates.

She was promoted to specialist E-4 after only 15 months of service and was recently made acting sergeant while waiting for the Army to catch up with orders. She had the points to be promoted and was just waiting for the rank to be made official.

By the time her orders came in for more advanced schools in leadership training, she was contemplating applying for helicopter flight school at Ft. Rucker Alabama. She worked on the birds every day and the pilots often told her how much fun it was to fly the UH-60s. Her boyfriend was 21-years old and used to be a 15T UH-60 repairer like her before going to flight school. He had been a UH-60 pilot for six months before he died.

Amanda hadn't talked to him about her orders to report to Ft. Lewis for a month at the NCO Academy there for PLDC before her re-assignment to a permanent duty station there. It would have been a month before she had to begin out processing and she didn't want to upset the apple cart with his training. A lot of military relationships were like that, temporary. Some got used to it, others didn't.

~ ~ ~

AMANDA WOKE EARLY IN THE MORNING, LIKE SHE HAD DONE ON the farm and in the Army. Shep was snoring softly with his head against the passenger window.

She was glad he was sleeping but in the reflected light, saw tear stains on his face. She didn't want to wake him, but she had to go to the bathroom. She reached quietly behind her and pulled out her over night bag with the tampons she'd gotten from the PX, a roll of toilet paper, the wet-naps she picked up, a pair of clean underwear and the large flashlight.

She got out of the truck as quietly as she could and gently closed the door. Both men in the other truck were still asleep, which she was glad to see. There was no reason for her to be embarrassed for being a woman, but sometimes this time of the month came at the worst time of the month.

The fresh snow, four or five inches she figured, showed no tracks from any animals either. She found a spot of bushes between the Lowes and Office Depot buildings where she could relieve herself and clean up.

The temperature had fallen to below zero over night, but in the three minutes it took her to change, she'd suffer through it.

When she finished, she was shivering, but she felt clean and that was important to her. She walked back to the trucks and climbed in. Shep was already awake. "Sorry," she apologized.

"No problem," he said to her. "Can I use your light? I'll be back in a minute." Amanda turned the heat up as soon as he got out. Her feet and fingers were really cold and her nose had started to drip. When Shep got back a few minutes later he too put his hands by the heater vent.

"I miss Mississippi," he said to her. "I want to go back and find out if my mama or brothers or sisters made it."

"How many do you have?" she asked him, trying to keep him talking a little.

"I have four brothers, but Leo was in prison. I don't know if'n they'd let him out before everyone died. I got three sister and they all live around Meridian. You probably never heard of it."

"You're wrong there, Shep," she said, a smile growing. "I live on the other side of Birmingham. My dad has…or had…a farm about 150 miles east of Meridian."

"Well, I don't know what caused everyone to die, but if I lived, maybe some of my brothers and sisters are still alive. Maybe even my mama. I'd like that. She says I'm her pride and joy because I got out of Mississippi."

"My dad wasn't happy about me leaving Alabama, but he knew I had to get out of there," Amanda told him. "Right now, I'd give anything to be back there.

"So, are you going back?" he asked, voice full of hope.

"If I can find a way, I want to," she admitted to him. "But it's a long way away. I think I'll first try to get to Spokane, that's where my mom lives."

"Can I go with you? I can help drive."

"Shep, as long as you carry your own weight and mind your manners around me, we can be partners."

"You don't have to worry about that Sergeant," he said, a smile reaching his face for the first time since she'd met him. "My girlfriend lives with my momma."

Chapter 4

There'd been a few days with snow recently, but the weather had turned remarkably mild over the past few weeks. Those at the shelter of Jerry's farm needed it. A spring storm moved through the night before and Jerry had walked down to the river to check on the paddle wheel generators. Both were running smoothly and the deeper water caused by the storm didn't appreciably raise the river level.

The three months since coming back from the gulf coast with the astronauts had been busy for him and everyone else at the shelter. Keeping the wheels that powered the generator that charged the batteries for the house was one of the more important things he did every week.

Every day had been busy with surviving and making preparations for the future.

This morning the sun was just rising over the trees and reflecting off the underside of the clouds. It was a beautiful sunrise by anyone's standards and something the people living on the farm needed with so little beauty left. The slapping of the water wheels was calming, but it sounded like a bearing might be going in the generator. He'd have to make a note to change it as soon as possible.

Jerry stood silently, watching the water and reflecting on the past five and a half months.

Randy's head injury had healed under the tender ministrations of Monica and Dr. Kayla, but he was a different young man than he'd been. He was quiet more, less ready with the smart remark. He blamed himself for what Cheryl had done to his friends Kellie and Danny, blamed himself that she used him to get away with the minivan. He blamed himself for being naïve and nearly getting people killed. He'd thought she was a good person and was a woman who could be trusted.

Randy had been fooled by Cheryl. He realized upon reflection how she had used him and manipulated him. While he tried to believe her story of woe, everything she told him that night more than three months earlier had been a lie. She lied as easily as he breathed and she did it with the expertise of a professional poker player.

On the morning Jerry and his team returned from picking up the astronauts, the Ford slid to a halt in front of the shelter. He ran into the shelter and saw Randy on the bed they'd made for him in the living room. The older Saunders stroked his son's hair until his son awoke. Jerry smiled down at his boy and spoke softly. "How are you son?"

"Hi dad. I fee' like I got ki't by a horth," his son said softly, then started crying, something his dad hadn't seen him do since he was six years old and his dog had died.

"Oh dad, it's my faul'. I believe' she wasn' a ba' perso'. I let her get loose and 'he hurt Kellie and 'anny."

"Oh no, son, she had me believing her too. It's not your fault for being a good boy with a kind heart. This is on her and on me, not you. We were both used by her."

Jerry now had a very rare tear on his face as well. It was a partial lie to his son because Jerry hadn't believed the story Cheryl had spun. He just didn't want his son feeling like he was totally at fault. It was a lie Jerry told to his son without hesitation.

That was when Monica came up to Randy's side. "How you feeling, jerk?" Randy smiled, showing the missing bicuspid and canine teeth, one upper and one lower. "Damn, she really did a number on you guys," she said unnecessarily, and hugged her friend gently. "It looks like Katie and Margarita have taken good care of you, but let me take a look."

Monica spent 10 minutes with Randy and certified the care he had received was good enough until Kayla could do a thorough examination. The real doctor would check him over more when she finished with Kellie, who had the most severe injuries.

Jerry let Randy sleep some more and moved over to Kellie's side. Kellie was asleep and Jerry held her hand for several minutes. She started to wake up to talk but Jerry shushed her and told her there would be time for that later. She closed her eyes and drifted back off to sleep.

Capt. Kayla Schaeffer, who aside from being a pilot and scientist, was also an MD. She fussed over all three of the patients that morning. The Canadian looked over the medical supplies the shelter had in stock. After checking the two more severely wounded patients she declared the equipment was insufficient for the surgery she needed to do.

Kayla and the others had moved to the kitchen area to give Jerry what little privacy they could while he sat with Kellie. He heard their low whispers and after kissing her gently on the forehead went to join them. They were trying to decide what to do about getting Kayla some better equipment.

~ ~ ~

CAPT. KAYLA SCHAEFFER WAS THE OVER-ACHIEVER OF THE farm. She was born and raised in North Bay, Ontario, Canada. She moved to the United States with her parents when she was 16 to attend college at Dartmouth in Hanover, New Hampshire. Her parents were both blue collar workers, but her exceptional intelligence and perfect scores on the ACT and SAT and 4.0+ in her three years of high school got her accepted with a scholarship.

She studied microbiology and after three years decided to get her MD at Geisel School of Medicine. After finishing residency, she realized she didn't want to start a practice and work in a hospital so took a year and worked with the Peace Corps in Africa.

While there, she learned to fly fixed wing, single engine airplanes from a man with whom she almost fell in love. They became engaged and came back to the United States where the man had an affair with one of Kayla's friends. With him out of her life, and no direction, she got a job doing research with NASA and one of her co-workers got her hooked on helicopters. She already had a pilot's license and learning to fly helicopters was easy for her.

Within two years she was flying helicopters for emergency organ transplants along the east coast when called.

Her research supervisor got her a placement with NASA as a mission specialist aboard the International Space Station where a long list of experiments would keep her busy for months.

The training for the mission was just another challenge for her and she put everything she had into it. She launched aboard the Soviet Soyuz space ship with Col. Polkóvnik Rustov, who would be taking over command of the ISS from Marine Lt. Colonel William "Buff" O'Reilly.

O'Reilly had been on the station for four months as an emergency replacement commander when the previous commander got appendicitis and had to return home.

Also going up to the station with her was Commander Cleve van der Graff who would be working with the electronics aboard the station. He was a handsome Air Force test pilot who'd recently completed his Masters Degree from MIT.

The speed at which people began dying on earth left NASA and the Russian space agency scrambling to launch a ship, but in four tries, there were four failures because astronauts and cosmonauts were dying even as they were waiting on the pad.

It was the family man, Buff, who had a wife and two children, who suggested using the rescue capsule to return to earth. Cleve and Kayla wanted to return as well. Col. Rustov, who was starting his third tour as station commander wanted to stay behind.

The three were cautioned of the dangers and the risks. The rescue capsule might fail to orient correctly and burn up on re-entry, might sink into the gulf, or might land in the wrong place so they couldn't be rescued in time or any number of other problems of landing the capsule without the help of ground control.

They took the risk and Kayla, last to enter the capsule, kissed Col. Rustov and wished him well, even though she knew once the capsule landed safely or burned up on re-entry, he was going to move the station into its highest possible orbit, then open it to space to preserve it for some future astronaut.

~ ~ ~

Kayla was trying to describe to Eddie and Tia some of the equipment she would need for a proper surgery and the two were speculating on places to find the equipment. Jerry asked how much time they had.

Kayla, looking gravely up at Jerry, suggested the sooner they got the equipment, the better.

There was a health center in Moody before the fall of the world and after getting a list of supplies from "Dr. Kayla," Jerry, Juan, Josh and Nick went to look for supplies, but the place had been wiped off the face of the earth from the hurricane.

Jerry was glad he'd slept on the bus the night before, but even so he slept on the return from Moody back to the shelter. He woke with a start when Nick turned off the truck in the driveway.

Jerry checked with Kayla and Kellie wasn't getting any better. He recalled a hospital off the interstate near Huffman and another foraging party was sent, this time with Eddie and his SWAT truck, Dr. Kayla, Tia, Nick and the American astronaut Commander Cleve van der Graff, the former test pilot. Cleve was still weak from four months in space, but he wanted to help and he was well rested.

Buff, who they'd discovered to be a fanatical chess player and dog lover, was also an electrical engineer. He would spend a lot of time helping Jerry re-design his power grid in the shelter and had volunteered to go along, but Jerry suggested his skills would better used improving the shelter and communication systems with Tony.

Jerry decided to stay at the shelter with Kellie. Not only was he exhausted, he wanted to be with her in case her condition changed for the worse.

The five took two trucks to go look for the hospital. Kayla alluded that it would save time if she was with them and time was of the essence now.

Dr. Kayla knew she'd find what she needed in the rubble as soon as they found the building, but it took the party most of the afternoon to get at it. The building, six stories high, had collapsed on itself and the two wings at either end of the building had caught fire. Eddie, pulling into the parking lot, said it looked like the quest might be a wash.

Still, there were some areas that looked promising and Dr. Kayla urged them to check out the parts of the building still standing. Eddie was armed with his favorite rifle, the Bushmaster 308, Tia and Nick with AR-15s and Cleve with a BAR 30-06 he'd found in the stash the boys had picked up months earlier.

They began searching for a safe way into the building.

Staying in the truck as backup, Kayla kept in communication with the four searchers. The sound of gunfire startled her and it lasted for nearly half a minute. Kayla called Eddie as soon as the shooting stopped.

"Cleve got three zombies, Nick got two. Me and Tia got one each," Eddie told Kayla, breathing heavily. "Here's an interesting question we gots to ask you doc. How the hell are these things still alive? There ain't no food in this place, but they're still big, ornery cusses who just don't like dying."

Dr. Kayla didn't have an answer, so urged them to hurry clearing the building.

Twenty minutes later, Eddie gave the okay for the doctor to come in. The corridors of the hospital were dark and the doctor followed Eddie and his high-intensity flashlight beamed up the hallway. There were cracks in the walls and ceiling tiles on the floor, broken equipment and dead diagnostic device with clear tubes plugged into long-dead-patients.

Every patient still in the hospital was dead. There were also decomposed and half-eaten bodies on the floors in the rooms and in the corridores. Beds still had bodies in them, but, to her disgust, some had been devoured to the bones. She didn't know if the person had been alive when eaten or the feasting had taken place post mortem. She could think of no greater terror than to be incapacitated in a hospital and have one of the zombies start eating her flesh.

Just the thought of it made the hairs on her neck stand and a chill work its way down her back.

Eddie, Nick and Tia had become accustomed to seeing such horror, but the two astronauts hadn't. She heard Cleve at the end of the corridor throwing up what food he had in his stomach and Tia giving him words of solace. Kayla, being a doctor, wasn't immune to what she was seeing, but she wasn't sickened by it.

Kayla looked through a dozen darkened suites before finding the supplies she knew she would need. Most of the supplies she came across were useless and she wasn't prepared to risk her patients' life on something she wasn't sure was safe.

The doctor was careful in what she chose, but she took everything she could and put it in the bag she'd brought in with her. She sent Nick and Cleve back to the truck for more totes when the bag was full. She found the pharmacy and the safes and secure cabinets were open. She and Eddie worked on moving some of the ceiling tiles and fluorescent lights that had fallen.

Everything she wanted wasn't available because of the damage, but she was able to get the basic necessities.

With everything she believed she would need, she told everyone they needed to get back to the shelter. Eddie suggested they look around more while they were there, in case they could find some more supplies they might need, but Kayla looked at him with her ice blue eyes and told him there wasn't time, adding "I don't even know if I can do what I'm going to have to do," she told Eddie. The young man read her intensity and between the lines, but they did pick up a laptop and two computers with monitors on the way out. Kayla said they might have medical texts that she could use on the hard drives.

They all hurried to the trucks and broke speed limits, not that there any cops left to catch them on radar, getting back to the shelter.

It was a good haul of medical supplies and Kayla, who spent the ride from the hospital sorting through the haul, had two totes filled with what she needed first.

When they arrived back at the shelter, she had the totes unloaded into the shelter while she and Monica cleaned up. She then threw everyone out of the shelter while the two women worked.

The doctor, with Monica assisting as nurse, was able to

stitch the wounds in Kellie's head and Danny's arm with confidence and a local anesthetic in a sterile environment.

The bullet holes in Kellie's side were trickier and Kayla wanted more time to examine the woman and get her more stabilized and hydrated before deciding what to do.

With Kellie and Danny now resting more comfortably, she'd turned to Randy. Dr. Kayla, after more than an hour of examining Randy and giving him both visual and oral tests, concluded he'd gotten a sever concussion. She was able to determine that Cheryl's kick to his groin had missed its intended target which was fortunate.

The two teeth that had been broken had to be removed, but it was nearly painless for Randy with the amount of Novocain she pumped into his gums. He would heal and, except for the teeth, be okay.

Kayla said she needed rest, telling Monica to get some as well. Before retiring, she asked Buff to set up the laptop and two computers they'd retrieved and to wake her in four hours. Jerry let the doctor sleep in his bed, while Monica slept in her own in the shelter. Everyone else was kept out. Four hours later, Buff had the computers up and running and the passwords had been hacked. They had medical texts she'd hoped for and Kayla read through them. She then told Jerry what she was going to do.

Kellie hadn't progressed as well as the other two people attacked by Cheryl, and by the time Jerry had arrived with the astronauts, she was just barely holding on to consciousness. Kayla did everything she could to stabilize her, but her condition wasn't improving as the doctor hoped, which had spurred her to get more equipment and supplies just in case.

Kayla, once she'd returned with the medical supplies, put Kellie on a saline drip with antibiotics, and took slides of her blood to look at under a microscope. She and Monica made regular checks of her blood pressure, heart rate and breathing but Kellie wasn't getting better and after a four-hour nap and two hours of reading, Kayla made the decision to look deeper into Kellie's wound.

Kellie was moved to one of the motorhomes, even as Jerry and Buff were supplying it with power, and the operating area made as sterile as possible. Tony and Nick used 25 feet of plastic surgical tubing for a rudimentary suction that they ran through the sink's drain and outside the motorhome to a small shop-vac.

Kayla operated with Monica assisting. Two hours later she came out. "The bullet hit her ascending colon and some blood vessels. She has lost a lot of blood which was pooling in her guy. I would like to see if we got a blood type testing kit in all those supplies."

They found one and an hour later, everyone had been tested. Katie had the same O+ blood type and willingly donated a pint straight into Kellie.

During the entire procedure, Jerry sat next to Randy, who was now setting upright and holding onto Kellie's dog Molly, who whimpered continually.

Neither man talked much. Jerry was playing out every bad decision he'd made in the past two days and Randy continued to beat himself up over the way he'd allowed Cheryl to play him.

Danny, head bandaged and with the stitches Kayla had put in his arm left the shelter to sleep in his tent. He came by after a few hours to check on Kellie. He felt a lot of guilt for what he failed to prevent and he wanted to make sure Kellie and Jerry knew how sorry he was. Jerry told Danny he'd done nothing wrong and asked if he'd sit with he and Randy while they waited for the doctor.

Five hours after moving Kellie to the motorhome, Kayla came to talk with Jerry. She's weak, but her stats are finally coming up. I've done all I can. I haven't practiced medicine in 12 years, but I was able to close the hole I discovered in her colon and stop the bleeding. There was an infection I cleaned out. Now she is going to have to heal on her own.

"Can we see her?" Jerry asked.

"Not now. She's resting and I want to keep where she's at, as sterile as possible for as long as possible. Why don't you wait a day or two? She's still sedated, so she won't even know you're there."

Jerry spent the days alternating between sitting with Randy and helping the astronauts move into their new homes. Tia had brought four mint-condition motorhomes she'd located near Anniston.

Danny, Nick and Cleve cleared and leveled areas for the new motorhomes and the tour bus they'd found when picking up the astronauts. To keep his mind busy Jerry helped Tony and Buff run wiring and cables for electricity and networking of all the computers at the farm, and plumbing for the septic systems.

Randy was moved into his and Eddie's room and given lots of time to sleep and recover. His eyes were black and blue but the swelling on the back of his head had gone down considerably, making it easier to lay on his pillow.

On the third morning after their arrival, the spacemen started an exercise regimen for themselves. The kids loved it. They did jumping jacks and push ups with them and the astronauts helped the kids learn the right way to do the exercises, and how to stretch before running.

The American astronauts moved into the home Tia had driven, Kayla and Monica took the tour bus as their home. Eddie had called dibs on the bus, but Jerry told him no.

Nick and Rusty were still in tents so they were allowed to move in to the second motorhome. The deJesus' took the third home and Danny, Sade and Jamal took the fourth, so no one was sleeping outside unless they wanted to and no one wanted to.

Josh, Katie and Marissa were still living in the cramped camper on his truck and hadn't complained once. Katie took the baby from the mother who had died, because Josh insisted.

Between Katie and Marissa, the baby was pampered. The little guy got his fill of fresh cow's milk six times a day through an ingenious IV bag feeding bottle Kayla cobbled together. The newborn was certified healthy by Kayla and Josh told Jerry how Katie had never had children of her own and when Katie had first seen the child the night he was brought in, he knew she was in love with the little guy.

Eddie and Tony thought the four in the camper, as well as themselves, needed to get out of the shelter and into something with a little more space to live.

Eddie convinced Jerry to allow him to take Tia, Nick, Sade

and Rusty back to Anniston to pick up the other three new motorhomes they had located four days earlier and Jerry agreed.

There were no troubles this time, something for which Tia was grateful. The last time she had gone to Anniston, she had a building collapse on her truck and she and her team had to fend off several zombie attacks. She'd driven over two that had attacked her, and the men who had gone with her killed another six before they were able to safely retrieve four new motorhomes.

In less than a day every one had a comfortable home. The motorhome in which Kayla had operated was converted to the farm's "hospital" and had two patients, Kellie and Randy. All that could be done, by Kayla, by Jerry and all the others on the farm had been done. Now only time would tell if Kellie would survive.

~ ~ ~

JUST AS HE SAID HE WOULD, WHEN SPEC. 4 ROY JOHNSON WOKE up, he insisted on locating his fiancée at Anchorage University. He told them he'd get another vehicle and head off by himself, but Jim and Amanda agreed there was safety in numbers. They'd stay with him while he went to the campus. If he didn't find her, they'd decide what to do next from there.

The sun was just coming up when they got to her dorm. Roy went in by himself, knowing without being positive, that when no one came running out of the building, she was probably dead. "Maybe she isn't here and went home to Juneau," he told them. "But this is where I last saw her and I have to check."

He went in the building himself while the others waited outside in the trucks.

A few minutes later, a window opened on the third floor. The young specialist looked down at them and said she was there. It was the way he said it that they knew his fiancée was not alive. Roy stepped away from the window, back into the room.

They'd give him time to mourn.

A gunshot report and a splatter on the window told them all

they wanted to know about how Spec. 4 Roy Johnson, Army cook and native of Milaca Minnesota, mourned the loss of his fiancée.

The captain lowered his head and Shep said some kind of prayer that echoed his Cajun heritage. Amanda teared up and looked to the captain for help. He shook his head.

"Let's go," he told them after a few moments and got in his HUMVEE. Amanda and Shep got in their truck and followed him. He drove for about 15 minutes until they were on the south side of Anchorage. He pulled over and got out.

"I'm going on to Sterling, which is about three hours drive from here," Jim told them. You're welcome to come along. We haven't seen anyone here and we should have seen someone by now. Anchorage is a big city. You might drive around some more and find someone. It's up to you."

"If it's all right with you, sir, Pvt. Sheppard and I are going to try to get back to the lower 48. We know it'll be a long drive, but like you, we're going to try to get back to family," Amanda told him. There might not be an Army anymore, but still Amanda felt it the proper thing to say.

"Well, good luck to you. Take 1 to 2," the captain told them, referring to the Alaskan highways. "Then 2 to White Horse, and then the Alaska Highway all the way south. You'll end up in North Dakota. It's about 3,500 miles and should take a week or two.

"I'd like us to stay together, but I know how you guys feel. I grew up in Alaska, so let me give you some advice. Remember your cold weather training, Sgt. Saunders. Your HUMVEE should make it as long as your perform maintenance on it and keep her fueled. Fuel up every chance you get. You do the same. Eat a lot. Drink a lot. Don't take any chances and you might make it."

Amanda nodded to the officer and looked at Shep who was looking at the captain like he was being abandoned. The captain saluted the two, got in his truck without looking back. Roy killing himself after the two had ridden together yesterday must have bothered the captain as much as the deaths back on base.

Amanda knew how to get back onto the highway. She was

afraid of what was to come, but she couldn't fault the captain. Her HUMVEE was fully fueled. She had four five-gallon cans filled, enough food and water for herself and Shep to last at least a week. There was nothing to do now but drive.

~ ~ ~

JERRY SLEPT ALONE IN HIS SHELTER FOR THE FIRST TIME SINCE the fall of the world. It was almost too quiet and he missed seeing Kellie in the bed across from him.

With everyone else sleeping in relative comfort of quarter-million dollar motorhomes, he felt the shelter was like the low rent district, with cots for beds and almost no room to move without tripping over something.

Before falling asleep, he thought of a gift he could give Kellie.

He was awake earlier than usual after a restless night and was working on the plans for her gift even as he made his morning coffee. He scribbled notes on a sheet of paper and looked around the empty shelter.

He poured a second cup of coffee and walked down to the barn to begin morning chores. He saw the astronauts putting all the kids through morning "PT." Both dogs were playing along and everyone looked like they were having a good time. Tia, Monica, Josh and a couple of the other adults were also working out with them. He hurried through the chores because he was looking forward to seeing Kellie that morning. He finished milking the herd which had grown to 33 head and threw some feed out for the chickens that had found their way to the farm.

By then he couldn't wait any longer.

Walking back up to the shelter, he saw Tony at the graveyard where Mike was buried beneath the slate markers Jerry had carved for him and Terrill, two men who had given their lives in defense of the shelter and the people living here.

Tony was finishing a project on which he had been working. The marker he placed read "Polkóvnik Александр Rustov – a man of the stars." It had taken Tony two days to carve. He'd refused any help.

Col. Rustov, after making sure his fellow astronauts from the International Space Station were safely rescued, wished them all Godspeed, said goodbye to his friend Tony.

Alone in the International Space Station, the Russian officer turned off all the equipment, purged the air and fluids from every system he could and opened the station to space.

No words needed to be said. Jerry left Tony to his thoughts and privacy. Tony and the cosmonaut had shared hours of friendship in the final days of the ISS and the young man on earth felt a kinship to the man who orbited above them.

Jerry showered and put on clean clothes and wondered how Kellie had always been able to find something clean for him. It wasn't that he wasn't organized; he just didn't seem to find the time to fold and put away his clean clothes.

~ ~ ~

JERRY HAD MET KELLIE FOR THE FIRST TIME IN A FIELD BEHIND the farm. She was in her early 40s looking disheveled and lost. She'd been a teacher of special education students and the punching bag for an abusive husband.

When her sister and her family had died, Kellie's mind came apart and she tried to kill herself by driving her Lexus into a tree. She cried when she failed. After that, she and her dog Molly, a small mutt of undetermined breed, started walking. They'd avoided a band of vigilantes and was fortunate enough not to encounter any zombies in the manufacturing plant in which she'd spent a night.

Jerry, his son Randy and Mike, before he was murdered, found her walking…stumbling more often than not…in the back field. She'd been afraid at first, but eventually found she fit in with the farmer and his friends.

All her life she'd had it easy. She'd married a wealthy man and lived an easy life. She never wanted for anything except someone to love and respect her. Her ex-husband had said he loved her, but the violence and abuse he'd inflicted upon her belied his words.

In Jerry she found an honest man with weathered but gentle hands. She didn't plan it, and was hesitant about admitting it to herself, but she was sure she was falling in love with Jerry. They slept in the same room, a necessity brought on after Jeff had been killed and Tia and her kids came to the shelter, but in separate beds. They became friends and Jerry trusted her with responsibilities of the farm, but Jerry had kept his feelings close to his vest and she was unsure where their relationship was headed.

When Cheryl had threatened Hannah, the nine-year-old daughter of Tia who loved spending time with Kellie, Kellie was more afraid than anytime in her life. When Cheryl shot her and Danny, she felt like she'd failed Jerry.

When John reported over the walkie-talkie that he'd found Randy and that he was dead, Kellie wanted to die herself.

She heard later as she drifted in and out of consciousness that Randy was still alive and the doom she felt clouding down on her life lifted. She made sure, since Jerry had left her and Randy in charge of the farm, that she would tell him what had happened. Her failures had almost cost his son his life, and might still cost her hers, but she would tell him.

~ ~ ~

DR. KAYLA MET JERRY AT THE DOOR OF THE MEDICAL MOtorhome and told him Kellie was still unconscious, but doing better that day. She allowed him 15 minutes to sit with her which he did.

He walked up the three metal stairs and saw Kellie lying on a comfortable bed, on the other side of where Randy was sleeping. There was a makeshift barrier of linen between them. Randy was sleeping, but Jerry had been able to speak with him while he was recovering in the "hospital."

Kayla or Monica must have brushed Kellie's dark brown hair because it had been neatened up since the last time he'd seen her on the stretcher being taken into surgery. There was a clean bandage covering the wound on her forehead and another on her neck, but her color was less pasty than he'd seen. She also didn't have a waxy look to her fine features anymore.

When he'd first seen her in the field, he wondered how a woman, slender and obviously someone who had lived an easy life, could have survived as she had in the wild that was now the norm.

But over the days and weeks, he found she had a hardiness of the soul and no fear of working and getting her hands dirty. She was a highly-educated woman, but simple in her words and her likes. He wasn't sure she'd stay at the farm, but not only did she stay, she began to fit in and help. She was excellent at reasoning and problem solving and without trying, she fit in with the people on the farm already, and helped the new people feel welcome.

Jerry sat in the chair Kayla must have placed there for him and he took Kellie's hand. He didn't know what he should say or was supposed to say, but he was happy to feel the warmth in her once delicate hands that during her time at the farm begun showing her first calluses.

He told her everything he'd done since he arrived back at the shelter with the astronauts. He did it all while holding her hand. When he was finished, he thought he felt her squeeze his hand, but wasn't sure. When Kayla came in to tell him his time was up, Jerry told her about the squeeze. Kayla nodded and didn't tell him it was probably just muscle reflex.

The best news the doctor gave him that day was Randy was being released. Jerry waited for his son as Monica helped him dress. He then helped his son down the steps of the motorhome, telling himself it might be a good idea to build a ramp for it.

Jerry and Randy walked around the shelter for just a few minutes because Dr. Kayla said the young man needed some exercise, but not too much yet. He discussed his gift for Kellie and Randy agreed it might be a very good idea. Randy respected Kellie, even though they had disagreed on Cheryl. He now saw how right the older woman was and wanted to find some way to apologize.

Jerry called Eddie on his walkie-talkie and the three met in the shelter. Eddie thought Jerry's plan for Kellie's recovery was "boss" and agreed to help. Danny, who was recovering nicely overheard the conversation and also wanted to do something for the woman he was unable to save from being knifed and shot.

With Danny came Jamal and from there, everyone who heard about Jerry's plan wanted to contribute what they could.

It took three days for Jerry, Eddie and Danny and the others to find everything they needed. Then the real work began.

On the fifth day after Kellie's injuries had been tended, when Jerry was sitting with her, her eyes fluttered awake. She had a new bandage around her head that hid the stitches Kayla had to put in her forehead. She opened her eyes and looked around. She realized she was in a rather well appointed-room in the medical motorhome.

Jerry called softly for Monica because Kayla was off checking on a child who had gotten hurt climbing a tree.

Monica hurried into the room and checked Kellie's pulse and temperature. She relaxed and told Jerry that everything was fine.

"Jerry?" she asked through dry lips.

"Right here, Kell."

"Oh Jerry. I'm so sorry," she said and started crying.

He didn't know what she was sorry about, but he was glad she was still alive and nothing she'd done wrong made any matter to him. He kissed her gently on the forehead, stroked her hair and told her nothing was wrong now. "As soon as you get out of here, I have a present for you."

It was not a speedy recovery, but four days later, Dr. Kayla allowed Kellie, who had lost a lot of weight and was still weak from the ordeal, to leave the medical motorhome for the first time since the surgery to sew up the bullet holes Cheryl had inflicted on her.

Everyone was there, outside the motorhome as Jerry held her hand, helping her down the long ramp. No one had found a wheelchair, but Kayla said if Kellie leaned on Jerry, the exercise would be beneficial.

There was applause and cheers from everyone who lived on the farm. Even Boomer barked.

Kellie started crying again. She hadn't realized how loved she was. No one had forgotten the story Katie and Mrs. deJesus had told them of how Kellie had sacrificed herself for Hannah.

Jerry escorted her into the shelter.

It wasn't the shelter she had left. All signs of the blood had been cleaned up. Jerry and the others spent 18 hours a day, with everyone who could, helping to fulfill Jerry's plan of a gift for Kellie. It showed Jerry how much everyone loved Kellie and re-affirmed how important she was to this shelter.

The shelter, which had been a hodgepodge of make-shift accessories, plywood walls, well-used furniture and small rooms, had been remodeled to every extent Jerry could imagine.

Still holding on to Jerry's arm, Kellie was escorted slowly through the doors of the shelter. The kitchen, had all new appliances on a brand new, real hardwood floor over the concrete which she'd grown used to.

There were real counters with marble tops and all new matching dinnerware, pots and pan and a dishwasher. The living room had been gutted and rebuilt. All of Tony's electronic equipment had been moved to his motorhome. In its place were comfortable furniture and a real desk for her computer and tablet.

There was a large flat screen TV for watching DVDs in one corner and music playing softly from speakers hidden in the ceiling. There was another large screen which had the feed of the 16 surveillance cameras around the farm.

Tony had installed a base station CB within easy reach for her, right next to the player for her music.

Jerry let her take it all in; everyone else had stayed outside, watching through the doors, not wanting to intrude on this special moment for Jerry.

He helped her up the 10 new and wider spiral steps to what used to be Eddie and Randy's room. She wondered if Jerry had re-modeled the room for her personal use, but when he opened the door, she started crying again.

All three bedrooms had been converted into one split-level room. There were real walls and real pictures of scenery. He'd built in a real closet and real dressers and a real bathroom with a tub. The inside and outside walls were curved and lighted along the ceiling and baseboards and each of the three levels were separated by five wide steps to the next higher level.

There was just one bed in the room, a king-sized bed with

real linens between night stands with individual lamps.

The bed and everything else in the shelter had been scavenged from the wrecked motorhomes in Anniston, and a home improvement store that hadn't been totally destroyed in Harrisburg, transported here and installed.

Molly jumped off the bed when she saw Kellie enter the room. Molly, who had been punted by Cheryl had recovered and was thrilled to see her owner. The little dog was yipping and running in circles. Jerry had made the dog stay in the bedroom because it had a way of climbing on Kellie's lap given half a chance.

"Welcome home, Kellie. You like it?" Jerry asked, picking up Molly so Kellie could pet her little mutt.

"Oh you dear man, I love it," she said through tears. "And I love you, too," she told him as she kissed him. She finally had to admit to him and to herself that Jerry was the man she was destined to be with.

"Can I stay here now? Do you think Kayla will let me?"

"I don't think Kayla could stop you, even if she wanted to," Jerry told her, as he helped her sit down on the bed. It was the most comfortable bed Jerry could find within the specifications Kayla had given him.

She would have suffer many visits from Kayla every day for a while, but she was permitted to stay in the shelter as long as she took it very easy, didn't lift anything and was careful in her movements around the grounds.

"I think she's had enough excitement for the day," Kayla told them, coming up to the bedroom and checking on Kellie's condition. "Now I think she needs to rest for a while then see if she can eat some solid food."

Jerry agreed and told Kellie he had some work he needed to finish, but he'd bring her something to eat in about two hours. He helped her get comfortable on the bed and pulled the blankets over her. Molly curled up beside her.

As Jerry leaned over to kiss her forehead, Kellie reached up and pulled on his tee shirt. "No sir. Now you kiss me like this." She pulled his lips to hers and kissed him with a fiery passion that was only tempered by her state of recovery.

Chapter 5

Once they were back on the road Amanda told Shep they could probably drive 200 miles at a time and stop for a break and fuel. At 60-65 miles per hour, they'd go about three and a half hours at a time and that would eat up the miles. "If you sleep when I'm driving and I sleep when you're driving, we could make it to the states inside of a week, allowing for breaks and fueling and both of us being too tired to drive."

Shep agreed with her and the two former soldiers from Ft. Wainwright got on the road. They had a long day ahead of them.

Their first stop was in Palmer Alaska, less than an hour after leaving Anchorage. They were passing a sportsman's club and Amanda wanted a hand gun and rifle to go with the M-60 that was mounted on the roof of her truck. They broke into the building and found more than she could have hoped for. She found a Baretta 92 and enough ammunition to fill five clips. She also picked up a 12 gauge shot gun and two boxes of slugs and 00 buck shot.

Shep said he wasn't much of a gun enthusiast and let Amanda find one he could easily use. She chose the Marlin 336 30-30. She showed him how to load it with five rounds. When and if he needed to shoot, all he'd have to do cock the lever and it would load. Then it was aim and shoot. She told him it would kick more than an M-16, but if he pulled it tight into his shoulder, he'd never notice.

They also stopped to fuel the HUMVEE and take a rest break. Amanda wanted to drive as many miles as she could the first day so she suggested Shep try to get some sleep. She'd wake him if anything exciting happened.

He adjusted his pillow and closed his eyes before saying.

"If what has happened over the past few weeks and this morning hasn't been exciting, there's something seriously wrong with you sergeant."

Amanda drove for almost five hours before stopping at the intersection of Highways 1 and 2. Shep had slept most of the time and was ready to get out and stretch. She saw that everything to the west had been destroyed by fire. The visitor center had also been burned to the ground, but the Chevron gas station and restaurant were still standing.

Best of all, was the semi at the Chevron station. It was a tree-hauler nearly full of diesel fuel and it took Amanda and Shep less than 20 minutes to top off the HUMVEE. Amanda was still wearing her combat boots, but took a short run a couple hundred yards down the highway and back. Five hours was along time for her to sit and she was feeling a few of the cramps she got every month. Amanda drove three and a half more hours before giving over the truck to Shep. He'd slept on and off and was wide awake when Amanda pulled over beside a wrecked semi. The truck had slammed into some construction equipment and the two found enough diesel to fill their truck back up.

It was dark now, but the snow had stopped and the moon was bright in the sky. It would be easy for Shep to drive through the next few hours. Amanda was finally feeling tired and with her blanket and pillow, by the time they were five minutes back on the road, she was asleep.

They continued the process until arriving in White Horse.

In White Horse they found a restaurant with a big sink. They noticed they were beginning to smell. They filled it with water and heated some over a fire so they had reasonably good water to wash their bodies. There was a clothing store so both found clean underwear and socks. Amanda kept her Army jacket because it was well-made and very warm, but she found some jeans and flannel shirts she could change into.

During their entire stay in White Horse they saw nothing move except a bear in the distance and many smaller animals already reclaiming the town.

Before getting back on the road, they pulled out of the truck everything they packed at Ft. Wainwright. They aired it out so the truck wouldn't smell so bad. They also found some stuff, like empty MRE bags, they wouldn't need and left it there in White Horse.

The sun was just setting as they finished and they decided to spend the night if they could find a house with a wood burning stove. They did and Amanda fired up the potbelly stove after making sure there were no bodies in the house.

An hour after dark, the house was reasonably warm. The HUMVEE was parked outside, fueled and ready for the next day. They had plenty of food and water and for the night, two queen-size beds with heavy comforters.

Both slept surprisingly well after talking for a little while about their respective families.

Amanda was up first and stoked the stove. She heated water and washed again and put on all clean clothes. She looked out the window as saw no new snow had fallen over night.

They would be driving with clear skies at least to start out.

Shep woke up and except for stoking the stove, did the same thing Amanda had done. They had a light breakfast and got back on the road. Both had slept well so they were ready to continue their crossing of Canada. By the end of the day they would have crossed the half way point and from there, Amanda had convinced Shep, things were all down hill.

It was their third full day and two nights of driving when they entered the city of Edmonton. From there they would drive straight south to Calgary then to Spokane.

Amanda was beginning to feel like they might make it to the United States without any problems. The HUMVEE was running smoothly. She checked the fluids every three breaks, the tires every break and kept fuel in the tank above a quarter filled. They'd seen no other signs of people.

They stopped before taking the 216 bypass around Edmonton to refuel. They found a diesel tanker parked under the Century Road overpass. It had parked there and wasn't wrecked so they assumed the driver's body was still in the cab. While they were fueling, there was something about getting on the bypass and heading straight south that lifted their spirits more than the break. The highway was clear of snow with the temperatures rising above freezing during the day time. They felt safer driving 60 – 65 miles per hour now.

The 180-mile drive to Calgary was as pleasant as any part of the trip. The sun was out, but not blinding with the high clouds. They both knew that from Calgary to Spokane was about a 10-hour drive so they were going to fill up after driving through Calgary and drive until sunset. Then they'd find a place to stay that had beds and a wood stove and get a good night's sleep before driving the last four hours through Southern Canada, Northern Idaho and into Washington State.

They stopped for the day in a town in the mountains called Coleman. They got fuel and found a house near the interstate that had a nice fire place and no dead bodies they could find. They didn't search the house, just the main floor, believing ignorance was bliss in this case. Amanda started a fire in the fireplace to warm the house. There was no running water, but they had seen 5-gallon water bottles at a nearby gas station. Amanda drove to get a few so they could bathe while Shep cooked. She had to pick up some iron cookware to heat the water in the fireplace, so they were able to have a hot meal and a hot bath that night.

While they were talking, Amanda told Shep that any number of young men would have given five years of their life to have an evening like this with her. Shep told her of the troubles he'd had getting together with his girlfriend, who was white. Mississippi had come a long way in the past dozen years, but being a mixed couple in the south was not quite as acceptable as in places like California and New York.

There were two bedrooms on the main floor and Amanda took the master for the night. She looked at the pictures of the family who had lived here. They had left family photos on the dresser and walls. They must have been elderly because they had adult kids with children. She hoped they were all together when the end came for them.

As she lay in bed, she thought about how tomorrow they'd be back in the United States she was familiar with. Maybe she'd find out about her mom or maybe they'd find other people. She hoped for both but expected neither.

Sleep came easy to her with nothing but the sound of the fire in the fireplace and Shep's snoring in the next room.

Morning came cold and clear. All the driving had left Amanda feeling out of sorts, so she went for a run while Shep made them some breakfast and stoked the fire. The temperature was in the teens, but her mittens and hat kept her from freezing while she worked up to speed. She ran about 20 minutes from the house and turned around to return on the same street. She did not want to get lost.

She was reflecting on the miles she and Shep had put behind them in the last eight days and hoped the next two days went just as well. She looked forward to getting back into the United States.

Two blocks from the house she and Shep had been staying in, she slowed to a fast walk to cool down. She almost felt like singing a cadence while walking. It would have echoed in this dead town where there was no one left alive. That was what she was thinking when she heard the gun shot.

~ ~ ~

THE FIRST NEW EXTERNAL BUILDING WENT UP FOR STORAGE ON Jerry's farm. It was built into the side of the same hill where Jerry had planned to put his second windmill back up. Both windmills had been destroyed in the hurricane, but they were still finding parts to re-build and re-erect the second one.

No one staying on his farm had ever been a contractor, but Jerry and Rusty had both done some construction work. Months earlier, Jerry and Mike had raided a lumber yard and they still had a lot of the wood stored in the garage near the front of the farm. The garage and barn had been severely damaged during the hurricane, but both had been salvageable.

Eddie and Cleve took the SWAT truck with trailer to a lumber yard they'd found to scavenge more of anything they could use to help build a storage shelter. Most of the lumberyard was gone but they were able to garner a pallet of cement, a dozen railroad ties, a man door and some insulation from what was left.

Cleve wanted to drive through the town of Trussville, looking for more electronics. The strip mall where Monica, Eddie and Randy had been attacked months before was gone except for foundations. The building where they'd gotten guns and the shortwave radio Tony still used was gone as well. Fire had ripped through the town of Trussville and it was being overgrown quickly, to be reclaimed by Mother Nature.

The Home Depot and Best Buy on the west end of town were scattered over several dozen acres now. They drove the main road down to the 459 bypass and saw nothing but devastation being reclaimed by nature.

Eddie decided he didn't want to drive back through what was left of the little town, so he took 459 south to I-20 to take that way back to the farm. He was glad he did when off to the east he saw some heavy equipment. Eddie elbowed Cleve.

The two men looked at each other and grinned like only men seeing heavy equipment will. "Toys," said Eddie.

"Damn straight. Let's go look," Cleve told him. Nothing could have stopped Eddie short of another hurricane.

It took an hour of picking through debris for the two men to find something worth their time. It took four more hours for them to get it to the farm.

Cleve felt like a 12-year-old who had just conquered the middle school bully when he drove a Cat 420E backhoe loader through the back gate of the farm. He was pulling a trailer with DK32 bulldozer strapped to it.

He was followed by Eddie, who had two 1,000 gallon diesel fuel tanks on his trailer. They weren't full, but they had enough fuel in them that the trailer was at its weight limit and maybe a little over. Eddie didn't care. He'd seen other trailers if they broke this one and there were other implements they could scavenge at a later date.

Everyone knew, eventually, their ability to find fuel would run out. It might be years before they couldn't find anymore or work on a way to manufacture their own, but for now, they'd find all they could and use it as best they could.

Rusty, Sade and Jamal spent a week on fuel duty. The spare 500-gallon tank was strapped to a trailer and pulled behind Jerry's Ford and the three found every semi, bus, piece of heavy equipment within 20 miles that had fuel in it and filled the two 1,000 gallon tanks. When they were full, they filled the 500-gallon, unloaded it, loaded the other 500-gallon tank used for storing gasoline and filled it by emptying cars and trucks. They were careful of gas stations because they found the underground tanks were often contaminated. They were marked on a map and kept track of by Kellie, who was still recovering, but wanted to help in any way she could.

The first storage outbuilding was finished and a small celebration was held.

To Jerry, it felt like real progress was being made. The storage building was filled over the course of the next week with canned food and non-perishables, as well as an office for Tony and Cleve and their surveillance and radio equipment and a server Cleve set up.

The shelter also took in two more groups looking for a safe haven. The first was encountered walking along 59 south out of Gadsden. There was a man and three women who told their story of misery to a stunned Randy, Nick, Danny and Jamal.

The four had escaped a small compound in Georgia that had become militant, with the capturing and ritualized killings of zombies, execution of members for minor infractions and women being forced into group marriages.

The man, who said he was a man of the cloth, and three women of varying ages ran away one night, not knowing where they were going, but knowing they needed to head somewhere safer.

It was a tense meeting. The four had been caught by surprise on a long stretch of highway. They hadn't been able to hide fast enough. They were tired of running and hiding and gotten careless when Randy spotted them.

From 100 yards away and with Nick and Danny covering the four, Randy called to them. They were starving and exhausted. Randy thought it might be a ruse and made them lay flat on the pavement. Nick and Danny stayed behind him and kept the four covered while Jamal manned the BAR 30-06 pointing out the front of the SWAT truck.

All four were searched carefully. Randy still felt suspicious of strangers and made sure to search them thoroughly even though one was a young girl of 17, the other two women in their mid 30s and the man claiming to be a minister in his 40s.

He found no weapons and the minister was carrying a bible. They begged not to be hurt and two of the women started crying, including the young waif of a girl. They asked for water and food. Randy and Danny had seen this play before and were hesitant to trust the four refugees, ready to send them on their way with no help at all.

It was Nick who helped the situation most. "For by grace are ye saved through faith; and that not of yourselves: it is the gift of God," he quoted, looking at the preacherman. The man of the cloth knew this passage as well as he knew the opening of Genesis. "Ephesians 2:8 from the King James," the minister said readily.

"Story checks out" Nick said confidently.

Randy still wasn't ready to trust them implicitly, but the threat was lessened and they were taken back to the farm for the others to meet. Randy took the precaution of blindfolding the four, but he did give them water and reassured them they were not being held captive. He just wanted everyone to be as safe as possible until they got back to the farm.

The second group they found was coming north from Orlando. Their camp had been mostly destroyed by the hurricane and the flooding that followed. Of the 60 who had started the compound, they were the three who survived. They were headed to Texas, where one of the men used to live. They were intercepted by one of Jerry's foraging parties. Two of the men decided not to stay at the shelter and wanted to continue on to Texas.

The Escalade might have seemed an extravagant gift before the fall of civilization, but it was just one of five SUVs that were at the farm now. It was dented and dirty and the back window was broken, but the two men were grateful for the generosity and full bellies and tank of gas. Jerry gave them enough food for a week, some ammunition for their guns and wished them the best of luck in their search.

With five more people living at the farm, two more motorhomes had to be located. It took more than a week and the search parties had to go to the far side of Birmingham to find them. The minister, who everyone started calling "Padre" and the man from Florida, Tim, moved into one of the new homes, and the two women, Natalie and Karen, and the teenage girl,

Cindy, moved into the other motorhome.

Other improvements came with another water wheel and generator, further upstream from the first and the second windmill was completed. The people on the farm also dug a better septic system, installed a much larger water storage tank, better water filters, and completed repairs to the barn and garage.

Tony and Cleve improved the power grid, installed larger transmitters and antenna for Tony. Tia found bicycles when she was on the crew looking for new motorhomes and brought them back and Buff built a small soccer field among other projects.

Tony had contact with Keith from the Smith Compound at least once a week. Keith was the first outside contact Tony had made months earlier. He was the communication specialist for a military compound in Kentucky.

He also made contact with two encampments in the western U.S. There was a Mormon group with 76 people that was suffering a food shortage near Wendover, Utah, just past the Salt Flats. The second little bit of civilization was the Perry Cooperative near Sacramento that had more than 175 survivors. They were struggling, having lost a third of their number in an earthquake months before, but C.J. Perry had radioed they were still strong enough to keep the cooperative viable.

Since it was Sunday morning, Jerry knew everyone would be taking it easy. Jerry had never been a religious man, but he was a believer in God and his dictate of a day of rest and, truth be told, he liked the day of rest idea.

For those who wanted to attend, the Padre would provide a non-denominational service on Sunday morning after breakfast.

Of the survivors, four or five would show up for the 15 minutes of prayer and reading from the bible. Sometimes Jerry would go with Kellie, but most times they would just relax in bed. No judgment was made for those who attended and no recriminations to those who didn't.

The night before was the weekly get together of everyone on the farm. It was an informal gathering where everyone was free to speak their thoughts, as long as they kept their language proper and didn't make any false accusations.

Jerry had originally suggested that to be fair, they should decide on a leader who would be the final authority on the farm. He understood that before the Armageddon as it was now being called, he had owned this place. Now, he didn't think that claim held much weight without a government to back his claim.

Also, he didn't think he had made the best decisions for the people living here and brought it up at the informal gathering. "If you all agree to appoint someone else as leader of this group," he told them, "I'll understand."

Cleve, the senior American military person, even though there was no real military left, put the kibosh on Jerry's idea. "Jerry, I don't think anyone here believes they could have done even half the job you've done with your generosity, compassion, thoughtfulness, foresight, leadership and work ethic, especially with the stresses you've been under.

"Unless someone feels differently, I think you should remain the top dog for a few more years," the former astronaut said, "then we'll worry about creating a republic."

Everyone started applauding Jerry until they could see how embarrassed he was becoming. "Okay, if you say so," he said in his usual self-effacing manner that any politician in the past would have given his first born to be able to fake.

~ ~ ~

AMANDA WAS IMMEDIATELY AFRAID FOR HERSELF AND SHEP. There was no reason for Shep to have gone to the truck and gotten their guns out so she assumed it must have been someone else.

She worked her way between buildings until she could see the house she and Shep had holed up in the previous night.

Now that she wasn't running, she was getting cold.

The house they'd stayed in had smoke coming from the chimney, but the front door was open. She knew she'd closed it and knew Shep wouldn't have left it open. They hadn't seen anyone in their 3,200-mile drive so far and didn't expect to find anyone in this little town.

Just as she was about to move closer to the house, she saw a strange man in the door. He was looking outside as if looking for her. He was talking to someone over one shoulder and had a rifle leaning over the other.

She was getting colder where she was hiding, but wasn't going to get nearer to the house without knowing more.

The man in the door was huge and he was dressed like a man who knew how to survive in the cold. He came out of the house and opened the door of the HUMVEE to look inside. Amanda was hoping he didn't notice the keys in the ignition or rifle in the back. He did notice the M-60 covered on the roof.

The man heard something from inside the house and he walked back toward the door. There was something inside that was more important to him than the HUMVEE right now. She heard another voice from inside the house. It wasn't Shep's.

Amanda moved from her hiding position, keeping the HUMVEE between her and the door to the house. She was going after Shep's gun which was in the back seat of the HUMVEE. She'd just reached the door behind the driver's door, when she heard another gun shot.

She opened the door, threw off a mitten and grabbed the 30-30 which had been lying on the floor of the truck. She could have reached for her pistol, but she'd put it in the front seat pocket and the shotgun wasn't loaded. She chambered a round and leaned across the hood of the HUMVEE. She surprised the two men who were pushing the young black soldier out of the house. He was alive, but had been shot at least once.

"Hold it!" she hollered at them, causing them to pull their guns up. She fired two rounds at them before they could aim. The first shot hit the man in back in the leg and the second shot went through the arm of the big man in front.

Both men dropped their guns and put hands over their wounds.

"Hey lady, this is our town and this guy was in our house. We had the right to throw him out," the big man said, his accent decidedly French-Canadian.

"I don't care. Just shut your face or I swear to God you won't breathe another breath."

Then, not moving her eyes off the two men and their guns on the ground, she spoke to Shep. "How you doing, partner?" she asked the man on the ground.

"Bastards kicked in the door and shot me in the leg," he told her raggedly through the pain. "When I wouldn't tell them where you were, they threatened to shoot my dick off. The little guy even shot between my legs to let me know he was serious."

"Can you get in the truck and start it?" she asked him.

"I think so, sergeant," he told her. He was still wearing just his regular clothes, but they could find winter clothes once they were away from here. Because she had backed the truck up to the house to unload the 5-gallon water bottles, the passenger side of the truck was closer to Shep. He climbed in and turned the key, giving the truck time to heat the glow plugs. Amanda didn't take her eyes off the two men, one who was on the floor inside the house, the other still in the doorway.

"Kick the guns out where I can see them," she ordered the two men. The big man standing in the doorway, looking pure hate at her, kicked both rifles out of the house and onto the walk. He then spit chewing tobacco in her direction. Amanda didn't care.

The HUMVEE started up and Amanda knew she would have to stop aiming at the two long enough to get into the truck. She could kill both of them right now, but she wasn't prepared to take a life. Instead she shot the two guns on the sidewalk. She hit both of them and throwing bits of concrete at the man still in the door. It was a bit of payback for his spitting. "Go inside and close the door. If I see your face again, I'll put one or two rounds in it just to watch it splatter."

The big man spat again, but still closed the door. As soon as it was closed she fired a round high into the door frame which should make the men hesitate long enough for her and Shep to get away.

She was throwing the 30-30 to Shep even as she was jumping into the driver's seat. She had the truck in drive and pulling out of the driveway even before her door was closed all the way. She knew the men might come after the two, but maybe they wouldn't after being shot. She hoped the damage she'd done to their weapons had disabled them as well. Thinking back, once they'd closed the door to the house, she probably should have grabbed them.

Amanda was as scared as she'd ever been in her life. They were on the highway to the United States again when she heard at least one bullet impact on the back of the HUMVEE. Someone had shot at them, but checking her rear view mirror, she didn't see anyone following. She drove as fast as she dared and Shep didn't utter a sound as she swerved around other cars on the road. She was a mile from the house when she finally slowed to a safer speed. Her heart was still beating hard but there was at least a half mile behind her without anyone following her.

She looked over at Shep and the man was pale. She looked down at where he'd been shot. There was a puddle of blood. Amanda looked in her rear view mirror one more time then looked for a place to pull over. There was an industrial complex and she pulled in, being as careful to not raise dust or leave easy to follow tracks. She pulled the HUMVEE behind some buildings and turned it off so she could hear if anyone was approaching. She then jumped out and ran to his side of the HUMVEE. She opened his door and blood ran down onto the tennis shoes she was still wearing. Shep fell over on her and she caught him as he fell out of the truck.

She helped him to the ground and reached for anything in the truck she could that would stop the bleeding from Shep's leg. She tried to remember everything she'd learned about first aid and she got the tourniquet on and tightened in less than 30 seconds. Shep's eyes fluttered and he opened his eyes for the last time. He was whispering something and Amanda had to lean down to hear him. "Thanks for helping me, sergeant. Sorry I couldn't help you more," he whispered.

He closed his eyes and breathed two breaths. When he opened them again he whispered "Momma."

Then there was a stuttering breath from him and he expired.

Amanda held him and cried.

Chapter 6

Jerry had been up for hours to milk the cows and feed the chickens and hogs, regular chores that needed to be finished no matter what day it was.

This morning, if it were like the past few Sunday mornings, would begin slowly as some slept later than usual.

Eddie was scheduled to help him, but Jerry had told him the previous night that he could sleep in. Eddie had liberated some Jim Beam and would probably be nursing a hangover this morning.

It was just himself doing the chores and he had finished an hour ago so he was walking the farm, just reveling in the peace this morning was bringing him.

About 9 a.m. the younger children would come out of their motorhomes and begin playing on the soccer field, or riding bikes or playing kickball or some other sport they'd make up. Some adults would come out for the church service; others might do laundry or watch a movie, read, play video games or whatever they did to relax.

Jerry loved Sunday mornings.

Walking back to the living area, Kellie was sitting at the picnic table with Monica, Dr. Kayla, the deJesuses, Tia and Buff, the former Army wife who had become close friends with the Marine astronaut. They were drinking coffee and watching the twins, Tara and Sara, with John and Hannah, and Marissa, Josh's daughter, face off in a soccer game against Jamal, Cindy, the 17-year-old refugee, and Rusty.

They played without a lot of noise because there were still many people sleeping.

Josh and Katie had baby Adam bundled up for the cool morning and were heading for the picnic table as well. Everyone else was either still sleeping or busy in their homes.

It was a quiet morning even with the kids kicking the ball and Boomer running around and getting in everyone's way.

It was a peace Jerry loved.

It was a peace shattered by gunshots, a lot of them.

Everyone at the picnic table ran for their homes without saying a word. They didn't have their weapons with them; the peace they'd experienced over the past few months had relaxed them into thinking they were safe.

The people on the farm had become complacent.

The younger kids were herded by Cindy as she took the sleeping baby Adam from Katie, to the cellar of the shelter as they had been previously told to do in times of danger. Cindy had never fired a weapon so was chosen to watch over the younger children. Her life before the fall had been high school cheerleading and fending off the advances of the football quarterback and what to wear that day at school.

Jerry noticed the workouts the astronauts had been holding four days a week hadn't been wasted on Monica who outran Josh, but she stopped to pound on Eddie and Randy's motorhome.

Jerry, who was furthest from the shelter, had the longest run. He watched as no one panicked, just ran like holy hell.

While he was running he heard more shots, but from the echo, they sounded like they were coming from the other side of the hill from the shelter, probably from near the barn or garage. It was hard to tell from the way the echoes bounced off the hills.

Kellie had his Desert Eagle ready for him when he got to the shelter, even as she was pulling her AR-15 from the gun safe.

Jerry buckled the holster on and picked up a Model 70, bandolier and walkie-talkie she had ready for him. He put the earpiece for the walkie-talkie in his ear so if someone were talking, no one could overhear.

She'd also looked at the surveillance monitors and as he was running up the spiral staircase that led to the hatch above the shelter, was telling him what she saw. "A dozen men by the farm house and eight or nine more in the driveway," she told him. She then repeated the information to others who would be armed by now and have taken up their positions.

Eddie and Lt. Col. William "Buff" O'Reilly, who would be the reserve force in the SWAT truck, would be monitoring everything from where they were parked between the motorhomes and the shelter entrance.

Commander Cleve van der Graff was their best tactical officer and would be coming up the back of the hill to take up a position under the antenna. He would be hearing the same information as Jerry.

Over the walkie-talkie, Jerry could hear everyone telling him they were in the positions they'd predetermined would be good spots to hide and fight back in an emergency. They'd gone over their placements more than a month ago, building rudimentary bunkers, not really thinking they'd ever need to use them.

However, Jerry and Cleve had insisted they all know where to go in an emergency like this.

Jerry slowly opened the hatch at the top of the staircase. It was well hidden by bushes, but he didn't want to take any chances. He crawled out of the hatch and closed it quietly. He heard more gunshots, louder now, and men laughing. They were shooting the cows that were free ranging around the old farmhouse, barn and driveway.

In his ear he heard Cleve say he was in position. Cleve had found parts and designed the communications equipment they were now using. It was 50 years more advanced than the walkie-talkies they'd been using before.

Jerry peered through the bushes and saw the men. The main group was shooting the cows in the legs and laughing at them as they stumbled and fell. The group of about nine men in the driveway, which had become overgrown because the rear entrance had made it easier to reach the storage building and the motorhomes, was shooting at the chickens that laid eggs for the shelter.

Another two cows were shot and the men laughed and walked up to them and put rounds in the cow's back legs and watched them struggle and moan in pain. The other cows ran.

Off to the side he saw Boomer running at the men. He'd forgotten about the big Bull Mastiff and Jerry made the situation worse as got to his knees and hollered at the dog. "Boomer! No!" But it was too late. Boomer was in full sprint at one of the closest men heading up the path toward the shelter entrance.

In full stride and before the man could aim his gun Boomer leapt on him, tearing at the man's neck. The dog was shot by several other gunmen, but it was too late for the man attacked. His neck was spurting too much blood for anyone to save him. The man had also been hit by bullets fired by his own people.

Boomer fell to the side of the man he attacked and laid still.

Jerry fell back on his belly when someone started shooting at him. The shooting of the cows was bad enough but killing Boomer pissed him off even more. He loved that big, stupid, loyal, playful dog.

Their aim was not that good and whoever was shooting at Jerry missed by a wide margin. These were brigands, as Jerry came to think of them, living off whatever they came across with no concern for anyone but themselves.

He heard Cleve in his ear. "Stay down, Jerry. There are a couple of men searching with scopes. Let me try something. Maybe we can end this peacefully."

Jerry kept low and tried to see as much as he could through the heavy bushes.

"Stop shooting!" Cleve hollered from his concealment. So far, not a shot had been fired by anyone from the Saunders's Farm. There were three more shots and Cleve hollered again. "Stop shooting or we will shoot back!"

"Cleve, they're some guys moving up around back. At least seven of them," Jerry heard Kellie tell the former astronaut. Jerry wanted to say something, but Cleve interrupted him. "Rusty, Danny, Padre, cover the door of the shelter. If anyone tries to get in, shoot a warning round and warn them back...if they don't fall back, drop 'em and stop 'em."

Rusty, Danny, Monica and the Padre had positions which allowed them wide fields of fire around the back of the farm. The parapet which was outside the main entrance of the shelter protected the doors from friendly fire.

"Katie, Josh, give them crossfire cover. Eddie, start your truck and pull it to the edge of the motorhomes." Cleve gave the orders quickly and calmly and Jerry heard clicks from the walkie-talkies signifying acknowledgement.

The men Jerry could see had taken cover, but at least the shooting had stopped. "Who are you?" someone hollered from below.

"We are the owners of the animals and dog you have just killed. We want you off our property now, or we will make you leave," Cleve yelled back.

"Your dog attacked us and killed Bo," was the response from below, then there was a long pause. "We had the right to defend ourselves. And we need to eat. It's been days since we had fresh food. The cows were here and we did not know anyone lived here so we shot them," the voice from below said.

"They're moving to your left, Cleve. Tia, they'll be coming up on you from your left first. Randy and Juan, move along the back side of the hill and cover her left side. Watch yourselves," Kellie said over the walkie-talkie, usurping Cleve's control, but everyone knew she had a view he didn't. Kellie knew Tia was the person to the furthest left of their defensive line and would be the closest to anyone coming up from the left side.

"Don't move," Cleve hollered back down to the invaders. "If you want to live, you will leave this land. Go back to the road and do not come back." He then moved from the antenna to a secondary position he had prepared which would allow him to better defend Tia's position while still being able to watch to front of the farm.

"But we are hungry and need food. You can't keep food from us, that would be inhuman," the voice said. "We are peaceful travelers and like I said, your dog attacked us." Cleve knew the man was buying time for his men to maneuver. He was going to put an end to it. "Take your men to the road and we will provide you with three days worth of food and then you will leave."

"We need more than three days worth of food…" was all Jerry and Cleve heard before the guns started firing again. First it was a single shot, then a fusillade of a machine gun, then quiet.

"I gave them a warning shot," Cleve heard Danny say.

“They machine gunned the hill right below where we are and were working their way to the shelter’s parapet.”

“Take ‘em out,” they heard Cleve order. “They are moving to attack by the looks of it.

“Eddie, get your truck moving to the high side of the hill to the west side of the shelter and park it.”

The Padre, Danny and Rusty all had scopes on their high-powered rifles, where Monica was still using her .22 rifle. The three men each took down one intruder in the first volley. Danny took out the machine gunner. The five remaining men dove for cover in the tall grass. None got within 25 feet of the shelter door. The five tried to return fire at the men hidden on the hill, but the cover the defenders had chosen hid them pretty well.

Eddie started his SWAT truck and was moving toward the shelter and the spot Cleve had told him. Buff was hanging partially out of the open door with the M-249 squad automatic weapon looking for targets. The machine gun could spit out 700 rounds a minute and was belt fed. He had a 150-round belt and was ready to use it.

Neither of them saw from where the rounds came, but one blew through the engine block, causing the engine to choke, smoke and die. Four more ripped through the windshield’s 1-1/4” laminated bullet-resistant glass. There was still a star in the windshield that had stopped a high-powered rifle round from near point-blank range from the woman who had been partially responsible for his friend Mike’s death.

Eddie was lucky not to have lost his face when the fourth came through the windshield in front of him, three inches left of his head. He was cut and bleeding from fragments but still alive.

He also felt fear and the heat of rage in his face. Even while bleeding he grabbed the microphone to tell Cleve what had happened.

Cleve heard the call on the walkie-talkie from Eddie. “Those pricks have armor-piercing rounds!” Two more rounds came through the front of the truck as Eddie ducked for cover and reached for his Bushmaster. This time Buff, who ducked back into the truck, saw the flash of the rifle shooting them.

He put six three-round bursts into the weeds where he saw the shots come from.

"You got 'im, Buff. Nice shot," the Padre informed him.

Cleve heard the results of the brief firefight, but was concentrating on the man talking to him. He was hollering up at him. "We killed your men in the truck and you're next asshole!"

"Okay everyone, stay calm." Cleve said over the walkie-talkies. "These guys are not organized, but they can't talk to each other just like we can. If you get a shot take it because they are not going to surrender.

"We have good defensive positions and they need to come at us more than we need to go at them. They have already shown they are ready to kill to take what we have.

"Do not let them."

Jerry slowly edged through the bushes that were hiding him from the intruders. He pulled the Model 70 Winchester to his shoulder and looked through the scope. He had always been a peaceful man, but now he was pissed and faced with 18 to 20 men, all with guns intent on killing them and they'd already proven they found killing easy.

Jerry saw two men aiming in the direction of where Cleve was hiding. He touched the trigger twice and both men fell. One of the intruders must have seen him because someone started shooting at him with a machine gun. Jerry ducked back behind the brushes and kept his head down. He heard the rounds hitting near him.

Two more shots were fired from his far left and he heard Cleve tell Tia she'd hit the machine gunner and he wasn't going to be shooting any more. Another couple of shots were fired and he heard Juan on the radio for the first time. "Me cago en la madre que te parió! They shot Tia!" Juan, an older man who had been a corrections officer in Dallas for 30 years, had moved up to support Tia and her position.

Jerry got on the radio. "Kayla, Natalie, work your way around the back of the hill to Tia's position. Make sure you watch your back, but I think they are all in front of us. Randy, Juan, cover them. Kellie, tell us where they're hiding. We can't let them pick us off."

"Five around the house. Four in front of the barn, they might be trying to get inside. One hiding behind the dead cows and two more under that fallen tree. There are four or five still alive and hiding in the weeds along the path south the shelter door," Kellie reported. "I see Kayla and Natalie moving now through the back of the homes." Jerry was proud of the woman for remaining calm. "I also have pictures of the back gate area and it's still clear."

Three more shots fired from behind the hill. Rusty reported that two more intruders had been taken down.

"There are still at least four men on the path that are moving toward the shelter entrance," Kellie reported. Buff told Cleve he was in the parapet at the door and would keep anyone from approaching from that direction. Buff was the last line of defense for the children and Kellie in the shelter.

Eddie, whose face and neck were cut from the shattered glass of his windshied, had stopped bleeding. He was working his way up the back of the hill toward Jerry's position to give his friend's dad some cover. He had his Bushmaster 308 and found a good position near the tree ine but to where he could see where Jerry would be hiding, and the line of sight that Buff had, but further along the bend in the path that led to the barn. He had just knelt down behind a tree when he saw someone moving up the hill to get the drop on Buff. Eddie put a bullet in the man's throat. When the man fell, he rolled and someone on the other hill saw the movement and popped two more rounds into the man.

The three others, who were below Eddie's line of view, but had seen where the other shots came from, fired back at the far hill. The three on the opposite hill shot the brigands shooting at them and killed the three intruders with just six shots.

It wasn't all good news however. Everyone heard Monica on the radio. "Looks like the bastards got Rusty. He's not moving."

Buff low crawled forward and confirmed all eight brigands on the side of the hill were dead. One was still struggling weakly so Buff ended his suffering with a knife. "Cleve, we're secured this side, over" he reported.

"Good job so far everyone, but we're not safe yet," Cleve

told them. “Monica, Padre, move up to support Buff.

“Buff, you and Eddie rotate the hill and see if you can draw their attention from Juan. I don’t think the intruders know where he, Randy and I are yet. Juan’s protecting Tia.

“Jerry, crawl backward and come over to the antenna base so you can use it for cover and concealment. Kellie, give us an update”

“Still five at the house, but they’re moving to get a shot at Juan. The four at the barn are looking at the top of the hill looking for Jerry I think. They didn’t go inside. There’s still one hiding behind the dead cows and two more under that tree,” she said.

Jerry, who had gotten to the antenna, saw the four along side the barn. He asked Juan if he saw them and the old Mexican said he did. “Randy, watch the ones at the house. Juan, you take the front one by the barn, I’ll take second one. On three. One, two, three.” Jerry shot the second man in line by the barn. They had been kneeling by the door where young John had found his son bleeding on the floor months ago.

The front two men dropped. Juan had hit his target too.

The two behind them ran back to the back side of the barn away from the gunfire. They came into the sights of Eddie and Buff who dispatched them, Eddie with two rounds from the Bushmaster and Buff with a three-round burst from his machine gun.

“Juan! The men behind the tree see you!” Kellie hollered over the radio.

The intruders fired at least two rounds before a Browning Automatic Weapon spoke its peace. The automatic weapon, on which Randy had unfolded the bipod for steadier aim, ripped the tree apart as well as the upper torsos of the men hiding behind it.

Randy didn’t have the trigger control as Buff and sent five rounds toward the invaders with each pull, but his accuracy with the machine gun was good enough.

The five men around the house and the one who was hiding behind the dead cow started retreating.

With their friends no longer supporting them, the rest of the invaders started running as fast as they could away from the barn and garage and back toward the dirt road that ran in front of the property. They ran through the treeline between the burned out farm house and the road away from the shelter. Eddie took one more long shot and had the pleasure of seeing the man who was in back stumble and fall after being winged in the leg. The brigand got back up without his weapon and was limping away as fast as he could.

"Randy, Buff, Juan, monitor the perimeter," Jerry said across the radio. "Monica, check on Rusty and tell us how we can help. Kayla, who can help you with Tia?"

"She was hit in the shoulder, but she's going to be fine. She's bandaged and Natalie is helping her back to the medical bay. Monica, I'm on my way to you and Rusty." Monica didn't answer. She was crying over Rusty's body. He'd been hit three times. The Padre prayed for the dead man's soul.

The time between the first shot that Sunday morning and the last was less than 20 minutes, but the tears would fall for days. They buried Rusty and Boomer next to Mike. Jerry spent the afternoon carving the name of "Francis 'Rusty' Rutz" and "Boomer - A Beloved Dog" on two pieces of slate. There were now five memorials in their little cemetery.

Everyone except the perimeter guards, Jerry decided one person by the antenna and one in the living room at the video monitor would suffice for now, was at the burial of their two friends.

The minister said a few comforting words and read a verse from the bible. "From the book of Romans, Chapter eight; 'For I am sure that neither death, nor life, nor angels, nor rulers, nor things present, nor things to come, nor powers, nor height nor depth, nor anything else in all creation, will be able to separate us from the love of God in Christ Jesus our Lord.' May God have mercy on our friend Rusty and our beloved Boomer. Amen"

Everyone took a turn tossing a handful of soil into the graves before returning to their homes.

Jerry was the last to leave and filled in both holes with a shovel. He didn't want any one helping him and everyone else retired to their own homes to commiserate with their closest friends or family.

Eddie and Tia, both whom had received quick medical attention from Kayla following the battle, were ordered back to the hospital motorhome to make sure their wounds didn't need more extensive treatment.

Tia had been shot in the left shoulder. The bullet had entered in the pocket of the clavicle and was a clean exit out above the shoulder blade. It was a through-and-through and no major veins or arteries had been hit so Kayla sewed up both holes after cleaning and cauterizing the small blood vessels.

Eddie had glass fragments removed from his face and neck. Kayla told him how lucky he was that he didn't lose an eye. She used butterfly bandaids to close the wounds and sent him back to his motorhome. She told him he had three days off from any work.

Kellie allowed Jerry to close the graves by himself, but sat on the bank, far enough away to not be a bother, but close enough the let him know she was there for him. When he was finished, he stood over the two graves for a few moments. Kellie then joined him and walked him back to the garage to put the shovel away. She didn't say anything and neither did he. She just held to his arm and offered him support.

The dead brigands were buried by the burned out farmhouse in a common grave. Cleve dug a hole with the back hoe and piled the dead inside and covered them with four feet of dirt.

There was no ceremony for the dead vigilantes. Jerry said their bodies would be fertilizer for the weeds that were growing around the house.

~ ~ ~

ONLY THE COLD GOT AMANDA TO GET BACK IN THE TRUCK AND start it. It was still below freezing out and she had begun to shiver while holding Shep. She'd finally stopped crying over his needless death. She thought, as the truck warmed up, on what she should do. She wouldn't leave Shep where he was. That wouldn't be dignified and the young soldier deserved better.

When she was warm, she reached for what clothes they'd left in the truck. There were no jackets, but there were some blankets and their Army sleeping bags. She used Shep's to wrap him up and she buried him in a pile of what looked like pea-gravel. She didn't have a shovel, so she did the best she could.

There was a lot going through her head after she had him buried, but her priority was getting back on the road and as far away from here as possible.

She smelled diesel fuel and looked around her truck, seeing one of the 5-gallon cans had been punctured and was leaking. She'd been so caught up with Shep, she hadn't even noticed until now. She unbuckled the can and using a marker that was in the front of the HUMVEE, wrote Shep's name and hometown on the can. She sat it on top of the small burial mound and got back in the HUMVEE.

She had so much adrenalin coursing through her body she didn't stop driving until she weaved through the stopped traffic at the border and entered the United States of America. She stopped and took a break and filled the HUMVEE with fuel before continuing on I-95. It was late afternoon and Amanda had spent the day driving fast and watching her rearview mirror. She was starting to get tired again, but she wasn't going to let her guard down. She spent the night in Sandpoint, Idaho, parking her truck on the airport runway so she could see anyone around. Even so, she didn't sleep as well.

When morning dawned, there was a light mist falling. It was cold, maybe the mid-30s, but it wasn't snowing. It was a little less than two hours to Spokane and she wanted to get an early start.

~ ~ ~

THAT EVENING, THERE WAS A DEEP SADNESS AROUND THE PICNIC table that sat beside the parapet of Jerry's shelter, but not defeat. "We've been reacting to everything. Something happens, we react," Jerry told them. "This is the second time we've reacted to someone attacking our farm.

"The problem is good people die because we get comfortable and think the worst has passed. The worst then comes up and kicks us in the head.

"I think we need to start thinking like the worst has not passed. Starting tomorrow we're going to set up some type of real defense and a real warning system. We don't know who will be coming down the road next, so starting tomorrow we're going to find some way of protecting ourselves better."

Ideas were bandied about the rest of the evening and thoughts on the ideas were debated on the ability to implement, tools, maintenance and upkeep of whatever system they would decide on.

The meeting broke up after just a few hours because there was an unspoken consensus that everyone would be more comfortable discussing these plans more the following day.

As Jerry held Kellie that night, he felt her sobbing at the loss of Rusty and Boomer. He wished he knew what words would comfort her, but he had none. She used one hand to pet Molly who lay beside them and held Jerry's with the other.

Jerry recalled something his mother had sung to him the night of his dad's funeral. She had come into his room where the 17-year-old boy was crying alone, away from the guests who had come to the house. Jerry's mom had held him and sung "Amazing Grace, how sweet the sound, that saved a wretch like me. I once was lost but now am found, was blind, but now, I see."

Jerry now sang it for Kellie in a soft tenor. It was the first time he'd ever sang for her. When he finished she had stopped crying.

Within minutes, they were both asleep.

~ ~ ~

IT WAS A WARM MORNING AND BREAKFAST WAS BEING SERVED outside at the picnic tables. While everyone ate they began discussing what they could reasonably make happen. The terror of the previous day was still paramount to their discussions.

They discovered Cleve, Tia and Kayla to be the best tactical planners, while Buff and Tony would be the ones to make the electronics work. Eddie and Danny knew weapons and Randy and Jamal were assigned to procurement.

Jerry and Kellie handled the organization and resources. The other adults on the farm were tasked with food production and maintenance. The meeting was a catharsis for all of them. Jerry made every person feel like they were doing something to protect themselves from another attack like the one the previous day. The planning meeting seemed to give comfort to everyone.

They were still talking when Cindy came up and grabbed Randy by the arm. She needed another player for a soccer game with the kids and Randy was pulled away. He didn't appear to be upset.

There was a lot to be done, but Jerry was more than willing to allow his son an extra half hour of play before the adults needed to get down to serious work. Randy had been more introverted and quiet since the betrayal by Cheryl and if the pretty young Cindy could bring him out of his shell, Jerry was all for it.

The first day was spent making plans, writing down supplies they would need and a thorough survey of the farm. Someone found some cans of yellow spray paint and Jerry and Cleve walked miles marking trees and rocks to indicate where bunkers or berms needed to be built.

Kayla and Tia used red paint to mark areas Tony felt were best for his purposes. Eddie and Danny, with help from Nick, Sade and Josh cleaned all the weapons and inventoried the ammunition for each weapon. Kellie and Randy inventoried the garage and barn supplies with help from three of the four newest members of the farm Tim, Karen and Natalie.

Katie and the deJesuses worked in the garden with the younger kids and Jamal.

Monica was on cook duty for the day and served sandwiches and fudge brownies for lunch and whipped up a fried chicken supper, with baked potatoes, okra and a salad. No one complained.

Everyone seemed pleased having a part to play and despite the previous day's tragedy.

When the dishes were cleaned, leftovers stored and trash

cleaned away, Kellie pulled out her tablet to update her lists. A lot was accomplished and she wanted to make sure the plan that had been decided that morning, was still on track.

There was a lot of discussion of supplies they didn't have and were going to be needed sooner than later, and that meant scavenger parties were going to have to begin searching further from the shelter and farm.

Both Josh and Katie voiced skepticism of allowing the teams to venture too far from the shelter. Where it was now, 30 miles from what was left of Birmingham and 40 miles from Anniston, it was a farm that few would stumble across. They said the brigands or vigilantes, who had attacked the farm, were few and untrained and there might not be another attack. A few of the other adults also speculated about frequency of the attacks being six months apart might indicate that there were few outlaws still "out there."

Jerry disagreed with them, but he didn't want to come out and tell them their opinions didn't matter. Instead he was firm yet conciliatory. "You might be right and we won't ever have a problem with them again. I hope we don't.

"But I believe the worst is yet to come. We don't have a support system for our farm; it's all on us to defend ourselves and our friends. I think once we get a good early warning system in place, and a better way to defend ourselves if we are attacked, we'll all feel safer at night.

"That's why I'm adamant about this. I want everyone to feel safer at night so if we wake up in the middle of the night to some strange noise, we'll be thinking it's a mouse and not some armed outlaw ready to kill us in our sleep."

It had been the first time Jerry had been so forthright with his view. He suspected a few of the people there could guess what his dreams had consisted of. The few who had been leaning toward a less extensive defensive system, even Josh and Katie, saw the point Jerry was trying to make. If they didn't agree with Jerry, they kept it to themselves.

~ ~ ~

THAT NIGHT AS HE AND KELLIE LAY IN BED, MOLLY SNORING

softly in a basket someone had found, Jerry made sure Kellie understood his resolve. "This shelter was built because I was pissed at my ex and I was looking for a place to hide," he told her. "Now we have 20 people here hiding."

She ran her fingers through his hair, which had grown long. "And no one wants to hide forever," she said. "People want to live and enjoy life and not be afraid."

Jerry traced the scar on her forehead that she'd been self-conscious about for months. "Yes. And feel like they are safe in their home." Kellie'd had nightmares for weeks after the attack by Cheryl and each time Jerry had been there to comfort her and make sure she felt safe.

It had taken months before she quit wholly blaming herself for not being more insistent about her feelings on Cheryl. Randy had been doing the same thing and had fights with both Eddie and Monica. Jerry had gotten the three together, away from everyone else and spoke with both of them. There had been enough blame to go around. All three of them made mistakes, all three had failed and all three had to live with the guilt. There was enough blame for everyone and he told them they had a choice of wallowing like fat hogs in mire, or learn from their mistakes. It wasn't an overnight change in attitude, but there was progress toward what was as normal as this new world allowed him.

Kellie snuggled her head into his neck and felt his arm around her shoulder. "I feel safe with you."

"Tomorrow morning, we start making everyone feel safer," he whispered to her as they fell asleep.

Just as everyone had chipped in to re-build the shelter for Kellie, everyone put in 16 to 18 hours a day making the farm safe. The ones who didn't think they needed to put so much time and effort into the system they were building, kept their opinions to themselves. If they disagreed with Jerry, they went to him and didn't spread the poison that was gossip.

Randy took Juan and Cindy in one direction on the map and Jamal took the Padre and Nick the other looking for supplies on the lists given to them by Tony, Cleve, Buff and Tia. Not everything on the lists was available, but by the end of the week, there was a 12-foot chain linked fence around the entire living area, stretching from the driveway entrance, around the outbuildings, the motorhomes and the cleared-out area behind the shelter.

The fence had four gates for entry and egress. They had found enough of the fence so that now the cattle, chickens and four pigs had pens.

Josh butchered the dead farm animals the brigands had killed and built a smoker with the help of Nick and Tim, where he was preserving the meats. It kept the former butcher busy all week. He worked with his daughter, Marissa, teaching her everything about butchering and smoking.

Six bunkers were built, camouflaged and stocked with weapons. One thing the farm didn't have a shortage of was high-powered hunting rifles and ammunition. Cleve had set the bunkers so they each had overlapping fields of fire and could cover 95% of the fenced in area.

Danny seldom got off the backhoe through the entire week and Tia, despite, or maybe because of her injury, operated the bulldozer. Between the two of them, they built berms on which the fence posts would be concreted into the ground.

Tia spent an entire day, even eating while on the dozer, clearing a clear field of fire 12 feet inside the fence and 20 feet beyond it. She knocked down trees, cleared brush and filled in low-lying areas. The little woman was on a mission to protect her four kids. Some of the time she was working, she would have John or Hannah, her original two, or Tara or Sara, her adopted kids, riding with her, learning how to drive the bulldozer.

John and the twins, all now 13 years old, were tasked as apprentices to the adults. There was no such thing as school anymore, so their educations were being taught by on-the-job-training and lessons of the real world. Tara was with Cleve, John with Buff and Sara with Kayla and Monica to give the farm an extra medical orderly.

Tony scavenged wiring and sensors and was able to put together what he called a "sensor web" that he and Buff installed as quickly as the poles were cemented into the ground and fencing attached.

Katie worked closely with Natalie on the garden, not only with what was growing now, but what they would plant later in the year and next year. Natalie wasn't a smart woman, but she was diligent and trustworthy. She'd never graduated high school and all her life had been spent in the service industries, like cleaning houses or cleaning stores. Katie, who was the daughter of a wealthy nursery owner, was fond of Natalie. She took her under her wing and taught her about gardening and plants. Soon the two were almost inseparable and the bleak look on the dark woman's face was replaced more often by a brilliant smile.

The others on the farm found ways to contribute as well, within the limits of their skills. Juan helped Jerry build a third windmill for power generation, Mrs. deJesus took care of baby Adam so Marissa, when she wasn't with her dad, could take care of the animals with Jamal.

Hannah, who turned eight years old, learned about inventory tracking, spreadsheets and administration, coordinating several projects and keeping track of everything, from Kellie.

Wherever Kellie was, Hannah was there too, with her own computer tablet, hooked into the network of all the farm's computers, taking notes. Kellie started calling the little girl "L-T," short for lieutenant, and the nickname stuck.

Nine days after the attack by the brigands, the perimeter fence was completed and Tony turned on his sensor web. There was a LED light board over a map of the farm right over Kellie's desk in the living room of the shelter. He turned on the switch and the lights blinked once and went out.

Everyone looked at the dark board, then at Tony. He smiled.

Everyone but he and Buff were expecting lights to flash. Tony picked three tennis balls and a racket he'd stashed beside Kellie's desk and handed them to John. "Have at it, Johnny." The boy knew what to do and he ran up the spiral stair case and out the hatch at the top. They watched him go because he had a smile that signaled this was something he'd been waiting to do. They'd not seen him all afternoon while he'd been practicing for his special mission.

They heard the boy holler "One!" and moment later a light lit up under the number three on Tony's board and a buzzer sounded for a second. Tony pressed a button and the Number 3 camera showed on the monitor and a tennis ball near the fence.

"Two!" and a moment later a light came on under the number 7, the buzzer sounded and Tony pressed the button under camera Number 7. Everyone saw the second tennis ball.

"Three" and then an "Oops, missed!" and everyone chuckled. "Three!" John said again, and the light came on and buzzer sounded for camera Number 12. Tony pressed the camera button which showed the third tennis ball.

Everyone was cheering and patting Buff and Tony on the back. "This is just one set-up for monitoring the fence. There's another one just like it I set up in the storage shelter in my office. It's the main one."

John came back down the stairs with his tennis racket and everyone gave him a round of applause. The boy soaked up the praise and took a small bow before running over to where his mother was standing.

"There are also speakers for the microphones for the cameras that have them," he told them. "They're plugged in, but turned off now. Turn them on here," he said, turning a knob on the control set.

He then pointed to a different dial. This is for the outside speaker system. It's a public address system Randy found at a sports stadium. From here you can talk and everyone within a mile will be able to hear you. There are six stadium speakers spread around the perimeter and hidden pretty well. He spun the dial and pulled the microphone down. "Luke, I am your father," he said and everyone heard the echo around the farm. Three lights started flashing and he pulled up the cameras. He'd frightened some birds into setting off the alarms.

Jerry liked the set-up a lot. He told Tony and Buff as much.

Hannah spoke up to let everyone know she and Kellie had already set up a schedule for monitoring the perimeter from the storage shelter.

"I," she grinned sheepishly, turning on her tablet and bringing up the schedule. "I mean *we* came up with a schedule which we think will keep who is in the control room from getting bored. Everyone under 18, except Adam, works only the day shift for three hours. The day shift is from 9 a.m. to 6 p.m. The adults will work the night shift in five hour blocks. That way no one has to watch the equipment every day and no one will become com…compl..compla….” She’d forgotten the word Kellie taught her and was discreetly reminded by her mentor, “Complacent. No one becomes complacent.”

The little girl smiled at her mentor Kellie who was smiling back at her. She’d written down the whole thing on her tablet just as Kellie had taught her.

Mrs. deJesus broke up the meeting with the calling of dinner being ready. It was a good ending to a very busy week and the meal Mrs. deJesus had fixed was the best they’d had together in a while.

~ ~ ~

So much had happened in the last two days and the last two months to Amanda, she was surprised that she didn’t wake up to some new nightmare. Looking out at the empty airport, she realized it was just the same nightmare. She got out of the truck in the mist. She could only see a couple of hundred yards in any direction.

“Well, truck,” she said to her HUMVEE. “What’s say we go to Spokane today?” She walked around the truck, checking the tires, cleaning the windows and checking the fluid levels. Her military training held her in good stead in taking care of the HUMVEE.

She got back in the truck, but left the door open while she ate two breakfast bars and drank one of the bottles of water she kept in the truck. It was cold, but once she got back on the road, she’d warm up. She would need to find some more cold-weather gear. The gear she’d brought from Ft. Wainwright was now in a house in Canada.

She looked at her map and decided to take US-95 into Spokane. She’d never been to Spokane before, but it looked to be the quickest route.

Ten minutes later, she was turning around. The bridge that crossed Lake Pend Oreille was gone. Parts of it were there, but the middle section was now in the lake itself. She couldn’t tell what caused the collapse of the bridge. With the heavy mist she couldn't even see the other side.

She turned around and headed back to take US-2 into Newport then into Spokane. Once there, she would begin looking for her mom and step-dad's place. She'd never been there, but her mom talked about it often in emails.

Amanda's mom was not happy with her daughter being a soldier and for the first six months after she enlisted, her mom hardly spoke a word to her. Amanda's dad had told her to not let the communications stop between her and her mom so Amanda emailed her weekly.

The soldier had never been as close to her mom as she had her dad. Her dad was an outdoorsman, enjoyed getting his hands dirty and working the small farm. Her mom was less interested in farming. Her contribution leaned more toward the farm's yard and house work and taking care of the farm's finances.

Growing up in the south had advantages and disadvantages. She was always expected to help out on the farm, which curtailed her playtime, but it also instilled in her a good work ethic. Her mom, who did a lot of volunteer work in the community was a loving and caring woman, always made sure they were well-fed and made it to soccer practice summer camp. The biggest disadvantage was while her friends in high school were partying in town Amanda was on a curfew that she broke only once.

The night she was 48 minutes late, her parents were both waiting for her when she arrived home. A month of reduced privileges and extra chores followed the raised voices and the excuses. Her mom had wanted to go easy on the girl, but her dad had been insistent. He named three of her classmates who were already pregnant in high school and that was the clincher.

The month dragged, but in that time her dad allowed her to operate the tractors and equipment. He spent a lot of time with her, showing her why things on the farm were done a certain way. He talked to her about his thinking process and what he wanted for her future.

Her dad was a different man around her than he was around

Randy. With Randy, there was often gruffness in her dad's voice. With her, her dad was softer and more gentle but no less strict and demanding. He often said he loved his children equally, but different.

By the time the month of punishment ended, Amanda was as capable as Randy at driving the tractors and operating the other equipment on the farm. That might have been the turning point or the crux of the wedge her mother saw between her and Amanda. They had been close, but now Amanda had more experience with the equipment, she wanted to use them, leaving her mom feeling like she'd lost a little bit of her baby girl.

Amanda and her mom talked for hours when Amanda chose to join the Army. Her mom almost persuaded her to go to the community college and get a degree in accounting so she could one day take over the farm's finances. There was a special bond between them that Amanda didn't have with her dad.

Looking back, Amanda thought that might have been a clue that her mom and dad were headed toward a divorce.

Driving down US-2, Amanda saw now that her mom hadn't been happy in the role she was filling. Her mom might have already been thinking of leaving her dad. Her parents had argued, like all parents do, but it never escalated beyond days of silence and over-the-top politeness between them.

Amanda wondered if it was not her joining the Army that had been the impetus for her mom to file for divorce, but rather the threshold of her mom's tolerance. Once Amanda was out of the house and on her own, her mom had no reason to be a parent anymore.

Amanda hoped her mom was still alive somehow and living in Spokane. She wanted to see and talk with her mom.

Amanda, as she drove through the low mountains felt like she needed to talk with her mom and make sure she knew how much she loved her.

She arrived in and drove through Newport Washington. She headed south and as the sun burned off the mist and low-hanging fog, through Colbert. She'd never met her step-dad, a firefighter, but her mom spoke highly of him.

Spokane was as dead as every other town and city she'd driven through. There were dead cars and dead bodies. She parked along an overpass and looked around. The city had smoldering fires in many parts of what she could see. The smell was as bad as any farm. Carrion birds circled and dropped down to feed on something, Amanda refused to look.

The only movement was that of wild animals that were taking back the city. After two minutes, she couldn't look anymore. Her mom's place was east of Spokane, just off I-90 in a suburb call Liberty Lake. It would be a 20 minute drive from where she was. Getting back into the HUMVEE, she already knew her mom was gone, but she had to make sure.

Chapter 7

The security systems wasn't completed and tested 48 hours before it proved its worth.

The Padre was on watch early that Thursday morning when the perimeter light for camera two started blinking and the buzzer sounded. He figured it must be another animal until he pulled it up on the 42-inch monitor. Camera two had a view of the main driveway and burned out farmhouse.

The grainy picture from the low-lux cameras showed seven zombies ripping the gate off its hinges. They were working together and the Padre was shocked at the savagery he was seeing and hesitated in shock a moment before hitting the big red button in the control room.

The alarm sounded on the farm and everyone was jerked from their sleep. "Zombies at the main gate," they heard the preacher man tell them over the PA system. "Zombies at the main gate. This is not a drill."

Listening to his voice echo around the farm, Journey "Padre" Stone still couldn't believe he was here. It was not where he thought his life would end up.

~ ~ ~

In his 40 years on this earth, he'd spent time in juvenile detention three times and six different foster homes. He never learned who his real parents were and he didn't really care.

When he finished high school, more because the school wanted to get rid of him than because of his grades, he bummed around Texas before heading east, taking on jobs until he had some money. With dollars in his pocket, he'd find the drugs he needed to lose reality.

Once he reached the age of majority, he spent some time in jail for drug offenses. Loud music, drugs, women were all his life was about. He moved around the great state of Texas until it was better to leave the state than to stay.

On his 37th birthday, the Padre walked out of the Garden City jail north of Savanna Georgia. He'd been their guest for 271 days for drug offenses. He had been facing a third strike felony conviction and a lengthy prison term, but the prosecutor agreed to a lighter sentence when the Padre gave up the name of his supplier.

He'd been clean for 272 days, paid his debt to society and was thinking it might be a good idea for him to leave Georgia and maybe head back to Texas. He had $97 in his pocket and was walking to the bus station when he was hit by a car that had swerved to get him on the sidewalk. The car then drove off at a high rate of speed.

As he lay on the sidewalk, he knew his legs were broken and he tasted blood. The pain was more than he'd ever felt, including the time he was shot in the neck during a drug deal.

He was looking up, unable to move, thinking he was about to die.

The Georgia sun was bright in his eyes and he heard himself say, "Oh God, if I live through this, I swear I'll be a better man."

Some woman was screaming and time melted around him. He was in and out of consciousness, but he heard the sirens from the ambulance and police cars. He briefly came to in the ambulance. He heard the attendant saying something about having a hard time finding a vein. He passed out again.

He drifted in and out for days, hearing voices that he couldn't understand. On the ninth day, he finally woke up when a portly nurse in a wrinkled nurse's uniform was giving him a sponge bath. "I see you're finally awake, Mr. Stone. Good to see you're going to be part of the living."

The Padre had been taken to St. Josephs Hospital in Savanna. The state was paying his bills because he had no insurance. He found out the man who had hit him had died later that day after crashing the car during the police chase.

His recovery was long and painful. His injuries, according

to the doctor, should have killed him and it was only a miracle that had saved him.

Journey Stone, remembering what he'd said as he lay on the pavement and during his months-long recovery, spoke with the hospital chaplain as often as he could. He knew he could never attend a seminary, or get into a college, and was really afraid to go inside a church, so he went another way.

Journey was a man from the fringes, long hair, beard, dirty clothes and street-wise. The street became his pulpit. His injuries left him with a limp, but he walked the streets and preached from the Good Book to others like himself. He fore-went trying to preach to those with money and homes and jobs, instead he preached to people like himself.

He became known on the streets as "Padre" when he spoke of salvation and surrendering to the grace of God. It was a simple yet powerful message that crossed all denominations and he preached it with his soft Texas accent, without the fire and brimstone used by most street preachers. Some would mock him. Some threw empty liquor bottles when he preached. Some told him to leave or shut up.

When he wasn't welcome he would go elsewhere until someone wanted to listen to what he had to say.

When people started dying around the world, Padre was on the streets, with his brethren. He stayed with, and closed the eyes of hundreds who passed, asking for God to forgive them for any sins they had committed in this life.

With nearly everyone else dead, he wandered the streets alone until he came to a camp near Atlanta. The camp commander was a militant, too militant for the Padre. He escaped with two ladies who were to be "comfort" women for the commander's men and a 17-year-old girl who would be the commander's newest wife. It was a dangerous escape, and once free, Padre knew he wanted out of Georgia. The four trekked westward, surviving three days of hurricane weather by cowering in a brick building.

They continued their walk until found by the men from Jerry's farm. They felt welcome and they stayed.

~ ~ ~

IN THE HEARTBEATS THE PADRE RECALLED THE PATH HIS LIFE HAD taken, he was also checking the other cameras around the farm to make sure there were no other zombies attacking.

Picking up the microphone he called Jerry. "The zombies are only coming in from the front gate, Jerry. I don't see any others."

Walkie-talkies came to life as the defenders of the farm took up their assigned defensive positions. In three minutes, Jerry, Cleve and Danny were in positions to see what the zombies were doing. Cindy had the baby already, and Kellie ushered her and the teenagers who were running through the main door of the shelter, to the cellar then turned on her equipment to back up the Padre.

The zombies had the gates off by the time everyone was in position. The gates were bent and two of the zombies had been cut by the sharp metal, but the others didn't care. The low-light cameras were proving their worth as they picked up the zombies working as a pack, like wolves, to tear the gate down.

No one was sure what drove the zombies, how they'd become stronger than any normal human had ever been, or why they sought out human flesh, but they were here on the farm and looking for food and they'd already broken through a gate that had taken half a day to erect.

From his position on top of the hill above the shelter, Jerry used his binoculars to get a good look at the zombies. The zombie's eyes were all black, blacker than the darkest night, and they avoided bright lights, something Jerry thought they might want to install if they made it through this day. Katie had told him how the zombies had attacked in heavy overcast, but mostly they hunted for food at night.

Jerry never expected them to attack this far away from a city. They'd prepared their defenses for humans, not thinking zombies might attack. He hoped the people here could adapt.

The zombies were not stupid beasts, but they were driven to eat. No one knew how long they could go without food, but it had been months since the fall of civilization and the virus which had killed most people and turned half of the people left alive into these monsters. It had been more than five months since the hurricane which undoubtedly killed many more.

Fresh dead bodies for food were probably running low so the zombies were more of a danger to anyone still living and breathing, like the many people on the farm.

~ ~ ~

GETTING OFF THE INTERSTATE, AND A LITTLE AFRAID OF WHAT she might find, Amanda stopped to re-fuel the truck from a semi that was sitting on the side of the road. The temperature had risen to the mid 50s and the sun was warm.

As she drove into the town, she passed a number of buildings that had been ransacked by the wildlife. Fires had claimed many others. A bank stood in solitude, looking much like it had two months before, she assumed.

Amanda saw a clothing store in a commercial area that didn't look like it had taken much damage. Needing more clothes, she pulled into the parking lot and turned off the truck.

Rolling down the window of her truck, she listened to the silence. She heard animals fighting and birds making noise, but no sound of humans. There were no cars honking horns or brakes squealing. Without someone with her, Amanda felt more alone than at anytime in her life and it frightened her.

She was anxious to get away from here and to find out what happened with her mother. She listened for another minute before reaching for the five-shot shotgun. She made sure it was loaded and got out of the HUMVEE. Every sound she made echoed eerily to her ears.

The clothing store's front windows had been shattered and there were no lights, but Amanda could see winter jackets and clothes inside. She stepped across the sill and sat her gun down against a display and looked through the racks. The clothing felt damp and on two of the racks she frightened mice from their homes.

She found two winter jackets and enough clothes to replace all she had left behind back in Canada. She'd miss her field jacket most, but the replacements were well-designed and fit her, so she liberated them from the boutique. She turned the truck on and the heater to full blast while she looked for other clothes she might need. The heat dried the jacket and outwear, but left the truck smelling musty.

Amanda was returning to pick up the shotgun, after finding a good pair of work boots and underclothes which she threw into the truck, when she heard a low growl that was out of place. She stopped, one foot in the store's front display window, the other still on the sidewalk. The gun was three feet from where she was standing. It was loaded, but with the safety on.

She heard the growl again. It was a low growl, deep, feral and foreboding. Amanda swiveled her head until she saw where the growl was coming from. Down the street, maybe 25 feet from her was a large American Bulldog. It looked feral and ready to attack. It had huge paws which held up its 90-pound bulk. It was a muscular dog and its shoulder muscles rippled.

It was stalking her, head low, padding one paw in front of the next with careful precision. Its white and black spotted ears were flopped back against the skull. The animal's short fur had seen a few fights and she could see the dog had scars around its muzzle.

It was moving closer to her at a steady walk. It looked like it was waiting for her to run.

As much as Amanda hated to do what she was going to, she lunged for her shotgun. As soon as she moved, the dog ran at her full speed. Amanda grabbed her gun and was clicking off the safety in one smooth motion as she rolled to one knee and spun to face her attacker. A round was already in the chamber as she turned to where she knew the dog would appear outside the display window.

The dog ran at full speed, hind legs propelling it in five long gallops to where she had stood a second before. It ran across the front of the display window almost too fast for Amanda to see and then it was gone.

The next thing she heard was barking and growling and a dog fight that was in full fury.

She looked out from the display window and saw a German Sheppard, a Husky and two mongrel dogs fighting with the American Bulldog. The big animal hadn't been coming for her, it had been stalking the other four, maybe defending its territory.

Amanda knew the smart thing for her to do would be to get in the truck while they were fighting and leave the area as fast as she could.

But something about the way the big dog had acted made her stop. It would lose a fight against four dogs, but if it hadn't been for him, the four other dogs could have killed her.

She was going to repay the favor. Raised as she was on a farm, she had respect for animals and her dad had taught her to be kind to them. But he had also showed her how to hunt and explained that sometimes you had to put an animal down. As she pulled the gun to her shoulder she remembered how she cried her eyes out when her dad had put down a calf that had been born defective. It was the merciful thing for him to do.

Now, Amanda was going to be merciful to the bulldog.

Her first shot dropped the Sheppard. It was a clean kill through front of the dog's neck and out the back. The dog didn't even utter a final yelp as it fell to the pavement.

The three remaining dogs stopped fighting at the sound of the gun for just a brief second. One of the mongrels ran off, another nipped at the bulldog's hindquarters causing him to re-enter the fight. The big white and grey Husky looked directly at Amanda and charged with all his speed. His gait ate up five yards with every gallop. Amanda ejected the spent round and chambered a second as quick as she could.

The dog was three leaps away when she pulled the gun onto target and she loosed a second round. She must have hit the breadbasket because the dog yelped and was thrown off his gait. Amanda chambered another round and put him out of his misery.

The American Bulldog had the last mongrel, what looked to be a mix between Black Lab and Irish Setter, in a death grip with its jaws. Amanda watched in sadness and fear as the mongrel was killed by the black and white spotted bulldog. She should leave but something held her there. She watched the bulldog. It dropped and backed away from his kill and looked at it and straight at her.

~ ~ ~

SIX OF THE ZOMBIES WENT IMMEDIATELY TO THE MOUND WHERE Danny had buried the bodies of the brigands who'd attacked the farm. They dug into the dirt with bare hands until they got to the bodies.

When they got to the corpses, they started rending rotted flesh from bone like hungry jackals.

Two others headed for the burial spot of Rusty, Mike and Boomer.

It was difficult in the early morning darkness for the defenders to pick a target, even with the advanced scopes, but once their eyes adjusted to the dark they opened fire.

There were six zombies by the house and three men from the farm had high-powered rifles.

It should have been a turkey shoot.

It wasn't. The men were shooting 7.62 military rounds and hitting their targets more often than not, but the zombies didn't go down. The zombies were never still enough to get a good shot. Danny hit one in the thigh with his Dragonov and instead of falling to the ground in agony, it looked up at his position it ran at him, still chewing on the body part from one of the dead men. The beast covered 50 yards, half the distance to Danny, in less than 10 seconds. Danny put two more rounds into the beast, but it was stopped only when Cleve took the thing's spine out from the side with a round from his DSR-1 rifle.

Jerry, whose position was 250 yards from the zombies had a little better luck. He was shooting from the prone position with a bipod on his H&K PSG1. He had four five-round magazines and was picking his targets.

His first shot hit low taking most of the leg off a zombie. The beast fell, but got back up, looked in his direction and started running in a low loping gallop using his hands to propel itself at a ground-eating pace.

It took the rest of the magazine, but eventually Jerry got

the shot which took the top of its head off. He switched magazines and killed his second zombie with a lucky perfect shot through its temple with the third round. The big 7.62 round entered as a small hole and exited with the left side of the zombie's head.

The zombie didn't die straight away like a regular man would have, but turned toward Jerry, dragging it's right foot and moved about 10 feet before having the good sense to die.

Jerry, Danny and Cleve fired another 35 or 40 round before finally killing the other three zombies. Even head shots were not always a guaranteed kill. One of the zombies got within 15 yards of Cleve's position with half its grey matter hanging out of its head. Only when Danny blew its leg completely off at the hip did the zombie go down.

Buff killed the two zombies that had gone for Rusty's grave with two shots. The first shot, from less than 100 yards, blew through the beast's chest taking its entire spine out. It dropped.

His second shot at the remaining zombie took everything above the neck off in a fine spray. There was three minutes of silence before Jerry heard Kellie in his ear. "There's no movement anywhere Jerry. I think we got them all.

Jerry relaxed. The zombies had scared the hell out of everyone. There was no need for coffee as the adrenalin was still pumping through everyone as they gathered for an early breakfast.

When everyone got together in the control room with the Padre, they discussed how they could change things so they weren't caught unprepared like this again. Some of the things they would improve on were no more burying bodies on the property. "They must have smelled the bodies we buried," Jerry told them. "Either we burn the bodies like we did before or bury them elsewhere, far away.

"Also, bright lights that can be turned on and aimed should be installed if we can find some, maybe from that stadium where the PA system was found." Everyone agreed that the lights would have helped against the zombies, but the speed with which they tore through the gate was of more concern.

The gate had been heavy duty chain link with welded hinges, 3/8th's-inch chain and heavy duty lock and the zombies tore through it like it was a snow fence at a college kegger. It hardly slowed the beasts down.

Tony said he could electrify a wire around the perimeter if they could get some more of the same type batteries they used for the electrical grid for the shelter and motorhomes. "I'll draw power from the second paddle wheel generator to keep the batteries charged.

"Maybe a chain link fence won't stop zombies, but 15,000 volts at 20 amps will shut their ass down. I'll start on that tomorrow." Jerry nodded to Tony and told him to take anyone he needed to make sure it was finished as soon as possible, then turned to Buff. "Buff, you got two kills with two shots and it took us more than 30 rounds to kill six. How?"

"I used that rifle the brigand used to knock out the SWAT truck. It's an M-107 .50 caliber rifle with armor piercing rounds. It still had two rounds so I thought I'd give it a try. It kicks like an ex-wife, but it blew the shit out of those zombies," Buff said with a small chuckle.

"Tia mentioned Ft. McClellan earlier and I didn't give it much thought because last I knew it was a training base, but if I remember right, they used to repair heavy equipment near there, didn't they?" he asked, directing his question to Tia.

Tia's husband, an Army major, had died on the base and she spoke up after thinking about it for a moment. "You know, I do remember my husband saying something about the Anniston Army Depot. It must be near the base."

"I think we ought to visit the place," Buff said, favoring Tia with a smile, "and see what we can find by way of military weapons." Jerry nodded in agreement.

Tony, who had returned to his motorhome, interrupted the conversation over the walkie-talkie. "Jerry, you better get over here. Keith from the Smith Compound is on the radio and he's got quite a story."

~ ~ ~

THE DOG WAS A KILLER, AS AMANDA HAD JUST WITNESSED, AND it was just feet from her. It was bleeding from a new injury to its muzzle and limping from a bite on its back leg. She wondered if it would attack her next so she slowly chambered the fourth of five rounds in the gun, just in case.

With the round loaded, she let the barrel drop a little. The bulldog looked at her then back at the dog it had just killed, then back at her.

It sat down.

"Good dog," was all Amanda could think of saying to the dog. He wagged his tail.

"Good dog," she said again, this time with more feeling. The dog wagged his tail even harder.

"Who's a good boy," she said sweetly, lowering the barrel of her weapon a little more. The bulldog stood up and started walking toward her, tail wagging side to side so hard, she thought it might fly off the dog's butt. Its entire hind quarters seemed to wag and his ears were perked up.

As a farm girl, Amanda could read a dog that was happy. The bulldog was happy. Keeping the gun ready, she held out her hand, palm up and the dog came to within a few feet of her and sat down again. It leaned forward hesitantly, first sniffing her hand, then licking her palm.

Amanda slowly kneeled down and the dog didn't move. She looked it his eyes and his tail wagging started all over again.

"Who's a good boy?" was all she could think to ask again. The dog seemed to know he was the good boy and licked her outstretched palm again. She petted his head and the dog closed its eyes in joy as she scratched the places his paws didn't reach.

"Do you have a name, boy?" she had already checked and the dog had no collar. She continued to pet him as she looked at his injuries. They had already started clotting and were superficial at worst. He'd obviously been in much worse fights and survived without medical treatment, so she decided the best thing to do was to do nothing and let the wounds heal themselves.

She petted and scratched the big dog for a few minutes. She wondered if he'd follow her so she walked back to the truck and opened the back. She pulled out her mess kit which was still in her ruck sack. She put it on the ground and poured a bottle of water into the lid. The dog drank it quickly and looked up at her as if asking for more.

She pulled out on of two 5-gallon water bottles and kept pouring until the big dog's thirst was quenched. She had no food for him, but the gas-n-go across the street might have something so she walked over to the store. The dog followed her, walking on her left, just like he'd been trained by someone.

He sniffed the air and the ground and was always searching around him.

The windows of the gas station were broken just like the boutique she'd been in. She could see inside and near the door there were 20-pound bags of dog food, just like she'd hoped to find. There were four different types, but three of them had been infested or broken into by some other animal. She reached through the door and unlocked it. The dog growled and barked a single bark. Some wildlife that had already encroached on this find scampered back into the darkness, far from the door.

Amanda pushed the four top bags off the first stack. Rats ran from the bags. Two of the bottom three bags were still in pretty good shape. She could see no place the rats had gotten into them and they hadn't drawn moisture from the floor.

She took them over to where her mess kit was still on the ground and nipped off a corner of one bag. She poured the dish full. The dog ate with gusto. Within a minute, she had to pour more. Then she did it a third time.

Amanda scratched the dog's head as he ate. "I'll be right back, boy," she said to him as she poured him a fourth bowl of food. "You need a bigger bowl or we'll be doing this for the next hour." He looked up at her. "Stay." She ordered him, wondering if he would understand. He sat down and stuck his big nose into his food.

She sat the bag of dog food down and walked back to the gas station. She was able to get three more good bags of food, having already decided the dog was going to stay with her. There were no dog bowls, but there were empty 5-gallon water bottles, so grabbed two and used her knife to cut the bottom six inches off. The bottoms were easily big enough for the dog. She also picked up two more five-gallon water bottles that were full and put them in the back of the truck with the food. She was now feeding two.

She went back for a last load of comfort food for herself. Much of it had already been gotten into, but she found some potato chips and candy that hadn't been touched. She could see the wall coolers covered with mold so didn't even open them.

As she was walking out, she looked at the counter and saw four GPS units under the glass. She didn't know if GPS still worked, but she'd give it a try. She went behind the counter and the key was still in the lock. She opened the door and pulled out the four units. They didn't look like display models so she took them all. She also grabbed chargers that were on a display rack.

Back at the truck the dog was finished eating his fill. He saw her coming and stood up, but didn't run over to her until she said "come here, boy." He then romped over to her, still favoring his back leg. She pet him on the head and asked him if he wanted to go for a ride.

He did.

She closed up the back of the truck and opened the driver's door. The big dog jumped in and sat in the driver's seat. "Get over you big lug. I'm driving." The dog looked at her and didn't move until she pushed him. He then moved into the passenger's seat and Amanda got in, rolled the dog's window down a couple of inches and started the truck.

She plugged the GPS charger into the power port of the truck and plugged into the Garmin Nuvi. The unit powered on and after a few moments showed her position on the screen. It looked accurate so she put her destination into the unit. The default voice was a man and she changed it to a woman's voice. She didn't know why, but it sounded better to her. When it spoke for the first time, the dog growled then licked the unit. It must not have tasted good because he went back to looking around and sniffing out the window.

Amanda's next stop would be her mom's place. The GPS told her the drive should take about 12 minutes from her present location.

As she drove away from the boutique, she had to drive around the dead dogs. They were three more bodies in her wake. First had been the ones at Ft. Wainwright, then Spec. 4 Johnson and her friend Shep who was killed in Canada. Now it was three dogs. Her gut told her she was not to blame for what happened, but the fact remained the dead were dead.

As she drove, she petted the dog in the passenger seat. It had started panting a little and drool was dripping onto the floor. Having the dog with her made her feel better, and right now, as she was driving through the suburbs, following the directions given to her from the GPS, she needed his friendship.

She saw bodies that were in advanced decomposition along the roads. Houses were burned to the ground and cars and trucks wrecked. Small animals scurried at the sound of her truck.

"I guess I should call you something besides 'dog,'" she said to him. "I think I'll call you Chopper."

The dog looked at her and licked its muzzle. "You like that name, Chopper?" she asked him, scratching behind his ears. His tail thumped against the seat. She didn't know if it was the scratching or the name, but "Chopper" seemed to like the name well enough.

She talked to the dog to familiarize him with her voice until she heard "You have reached your destination," from the GPS. Amanda pulled to the side of the residential street. The house in which her mom and step-dad lived was still standing. It hadn't been consumed by fire like many of the others. She got out of the truck and was followed by Chopper.

The yard was overgrown and debris scattered about. Houses on the entire block were the same. She walked around the house to see if it had been broken into, but the windows and doors were all locked. She could easily break in and find out for sure, but she could tell, there was no one alive in this area.

Chopper stayed by her side and nuzzled her hand as she stood on the front porch. Amanda knocked and knew she wouldn't get an answer. But she had to knock. She heard something, but it was only a small animal scurrying from under the porch. Chopper started to chase it, but Amanda said

"Chopper, no!" and the dog stopped. He looked at her, then at the animal that was getting away, then back to Amanda. He stayed with her.

Amanda walked around the house one more time, double checking every door and window. All were locked. One window, on the back side, had the blinds not all the way down. Cupping her hands, she peered through into the darkness inside.

Amanda could see two bodies in the master bedroom. One was in the bed, the other slumped in a chair beside the bed, holding the hand of the one in the bed. They had gone together.

"There's no one here, Chopper. Let's go," she said to the dog, who was sniffing the trail of the rabbit that had been frightened out from under the porch. "Have you ever been to Alabama?"

Amanda and Chopper got back in the HUMVEE and drove the rest of the day. She stopped every two or three hours to refuel when it was convenient. She passed off ramps, looking to see if there were any other vehicles, but she didn't see any.

Amanda thought a lot about her mom. She tried to remember all the good times she and her mom had experienced together and smiled at the memories.

Mom often made her famous banana pancakes for breakfast on weekends. She was always ready to read to Little Amanda when the girl had a bad dream. Mom was always the one to pamper Amanda when her knee was skinned or her hair wouldn't stay in position.

Mom was a good person who didn't deserve the end that came to her. Amanda could only hope the end came peacefully for her mom and what she saw through the window, her husband holding her hand was the best she could hope for. Tears welled up but a swift hand wiped them from her face before they could fall. It was an unfair world, but Amanda wasn't going to let it get the better of her. She was alive and she'd keep trying to stay alive.

During every stop, Chopper would climb out with her and run around, sniffing everything and marking his territory. Twice at one stop, he froze in place and growled. The short hair on the back of his neck stood up and he would pace in place, watching a building, but not going anywhere near it.

Amanda would call out, but no one ever came to her calls. She figured it must be some animal that got his hackles up.

The Rocky Mountains fell behind her that first day out from Spokane. She had hopes for seeing someone else on the highways, but it was void of live people. There were still bodies in the wrecked cars she saw.

Darkness fell just about the time she pulled into the outskirts of Bozeman Montana. They had a few more mountain passes to drive through the next day, but tonight she was going to find someplace other to sleep than in the HUMVEE again.

~ ~ ~

KEITH BENNETT, A RADIO MAN AT THE MILITARY COMPOUND located at Ft. Knox, was on the radio much earlier than his usual call time. His story brought back memories they'd put behind them months ago.

Unlike the Saunders's Farm, the Smith Compound was run like a military installation. There were more than 100 people on the base that was led by a former battalion executive officer.

Lt. Colonel Smith ran the base under his interpretation of martial law. Keith had told Tony of summary executions and strict adherence to following orders of those in charge. They'd all sympathized with Keith, but there was nothing they could do for him, even though they tried to keep his spirits up by letting him know if they found a way to rescue him, they would.

His story this morning, however, involved an old nemesis and interested Jerry, Randy, Kellie and Danny with an intensity that roiled their guts.

The way Keith had heard the story, two men had stumbled into the compound's sentries and been captured. They told stories of an encampment of 25 or 30 men east of Birmingham who were capturing anyone they could find. The men were killed or used as zombie bait while the women were used for breeding stock. The captured men told horrific stories of crucifixions and murder, burning at the stake and other tortures straight out of the dark ages.

Jerry surmised the men were two of the half-dozen brigands who had escaped with their lives after attacking his farm three weeks earlier.

"That's not the worst of it," Keith said over the short wave. "There's a woman who has been put in charge of the colonel's peacekeeping unit. She showed up about six months ago and said she was a captain assigned to Redstone Arsenal in Huntsville. She said she was company commander for some tech unit. The colonel talked to her for hours then assigned her to the peacekeeping unit as executive officer. A month later she was in charge of it and still is. Everyone is afraid of her because she kills like it doesn't bother her."

Everyone listening at the farm knew who the woman was. They'd hoped that they'd never hear from her again, but should have guessed, like a bad penny, she'd return.

Even as they were hoping she'd been captured by some other vigilantes, they somehow suspected the woman would have found a way to survive.

"Here's the kicker guys," Keith said over the radio. "Scuttlebutt has it she is going to mount a rescue of the women there because we only have 11 here. The colonel thinks, because he was told by these new men, that you have 20 or 30 or more women there being held hostage."

A cold shiver ran down Jerry's back. Cheryl was going to lie through her teeth to mount a mission to come here and destroy us. She probably thought we were done and that Kellie, Danny and Randy were dead, but the brigands who got away probably told the most embellished story they could think of to explain how we defeated them.

Jerry knew that she would be back with heavy weapons and military backing.

"Do you know when, Keith?" asked Jerry.

"Not yet, but I think soon because there's word we are moving the camp to Indiana in the summer. We have heard there's a military presence with a full bird in charge at the old Ft. Benjamin Harrison.

They say they have a thriving community going with people from all over the tri-state area. They have farms going and everything. We've got nothing but shit here and hardly any food and the colonel wants to move all of us there."

"Let us know if you hear anything, friend," Tony told him, and then signed off.

Jerry looked at the men in the room. Eddie, Cleve, Buff, Tony and a very angry looking Randy all looked at him.

Eddie broke the silence. "Shit's getting real. Let's get ready."

Jerry nodded solemnly.

~ ~ ~

AFTER ESCAPING FROM THE SAUNDERS' FARM, CHERYL WOVE A story of honor and duty, self-sacrifice and quick thinking on her part to Lt. Colonel Pendleton Smith. The colonel listened and questioned and listened some more.

Cheryl's story included fights with zombies and vigilantes, death and imprisonment and escape. She told about how everyone in her unit that had been on temporary duty at Redstone Arsenal, died while she stayed at her post as long as she could; told stories of how zombies had taken over, killing so many of others of those left alive.

She told her story just as she'd rehearsed it in her head during her entire trek to Ft. Knox. Randy had told her that Tony had made contact with a military base there and with her military background she believed they would accept her. She'd never been stationed at Redstone, but had done an article on the base when she was working at the public affairs office at Ft. Benning.

She remembered enough to make her story plausible.

As a woman, she would have been welcomed anyhow.

As a former Army officer, the colonel welcomed her aboard after just two hours and assigned her quarters. Food was mostly military rations and whatever animals the peacekeepers could shoot. There were no real farms or gardens like on the Saunders' farm so fresh fruits and vegetables were limited.

The towns near Ft. Knox had been burned after the tornadoes that had done so much damage, to rid the area of zombies without thinking ahead of the stores which had canned goods that could be used.

It had been a harsh winter for the area too, and farming hadn't gotten a good start. They had plenty of purified water, regular houses to live in, but a failing septic system, cars for use by senior personnel only, but because of the rarity of gas, were seldom used. The base had Abrams tanks and Bradley Fighting Vehicles everywhere, and Stryker vehicles that were being used for defense. The vehicles were only started if there was an attack, which they'd had six in the past nine months, because of the scarcity of diesel fuel.

The commander of the Smith Compound might have been a good military officer, but he wasn't good at running a community. His focus was on defense of the property and the safety of the 11 women and 93 men on his base. He didn't spend enough effort making the community survivable. He leaned too much on the stores on the base and the heavy equipment, big guns of the tanks and Bradleys. He had a military mind set, like he was waiting for relief or instructions from higher headquarters.

Smith assigned Cheryl, now referred to as Capt. Paxton, to Captain DenHarTog's peacekeeping unit. The captain was one of the few who had an unshared wife and was envied for it by many of the men on the compound.

DenHarTog did his best to keep the peace. To Cheryl, he was an honest man who worked hard and tried to take good care of the 15 men in the peacekeeping unit. The peacekeepers were responsible for the equipment, guard duty, and making sure fights over women didn't get out of hand.

If strangers were captured, they were interrogated to determine if they were vigilantes or just refugees from the bigger cities along the east coast. Vigilantes were executed.

Capt. DenHarTog was a former active duty officer before the fall. He was assigned to a military police detachment at Fort Campbell, KY. When the country fell, he was on temporary duty at Ft. Knox and submitted to the colonel's authority when the senior officer began setting up the camp.

One of the first women in the camp became his wife. He was lucky because she was only one of 11 on the base. The colonel had one, as did a few of the senior NCOs on the security force. The other women were in plural marriages of a sort.

DenHarTog saw Cheryl as just another peacekeeper and assigned her to patrols and guard duty even though she was his executive officer. She had more supervisory duties, but also had to man guard stations, break up fights, deal with prisoners and execute violators. The captain had only a few men to protect a lot of area and everyone in the unit had to pull duty. Cheryl hated it.

Even DenHarTog pulled guard duty as well as his command responsibilities. He believed everyone had a responsibility to do the boring jobs and the fun jobs, regardless of rank.

The house she was assigned, next to Smith's, was a lot nicer than the barn in which she was held captive for almost two weeks, but she had to fend off the men who wanted to have sex with her, some more insistent than others.

Four of the men on the peacekeeping were more aggressive in their suggestions and she shut them down, one with a knee to his groin and another with a knife. She wasn't punished. They had neither the prestige nor the power to get her what she was after. There were 93 men in the camp and only one had what she wanted and that was Col. Smith and it would take some real effort to wrest it from him. Her sex appeal wasn't going to work on him because his wife was a very pretty 26-year-old New Hampshire woman.

Smith had his camp set up as platoons of men. Each was responsible for a set of missions the colonel gave them. Cheryl's platoon worked in peacekeeping. The others in maintenance, engineering, communications, procurement and supply, weapons, medical, P.O.L. (petroleum, oil, and lubricants), engineers or part of his command platoon. Smith was a strict leader and merciless against anyone who stepped out of line.

Cheryl knew a week after being here it was a mistake to come. There were too many men loyal to the colonel, and the ones who weren't, were the dregs and not worth her time.

Now she spent her time devising a plan to leave the compound, something that would not be as easy as just walking away. The perimeter was closely guarded and anyone leaving had to have a pass signed by the colonel or be part of a scavenging party.

She also would need transportation, food and weapons. DenHarTog kept her on a short leash, not trusting her and knowing how someone like her could use men to do her bidding. He told her as much and warned her to act like an officer.

Cheryl knew that, even at 28-years-old, she was still pretty. She had smooth features, a slender, athletic body and light olive skin. Her eyes were dark brown and a man could get his soul stolen from a sultry look.

She was also intelligent and fearless and not afraid to murder. She'd done it before and would do it again without a qualm.

DenHarTog came up missing for first formation one day. His body was never found despite an extensive search by Cheryl and the peacekeeping detachment. Smith railed against everyone who was on duty that night and handed down punishments. Cheryl expected as much and took the criticism and discipline from Smith without complaint.

After 48 hours of searching by every member of the platoon who wasn't on duty, the Colonel called her into his office and told her his suspicions. "I think someone killed him for his wife. Find out who did it," he told her.

Smith never suspected it was she who had slit the Captain's throat as he returned from his morning run.

Cheryl had watched DenHartog for weeks and his pattern almost never changed. The morning she killed him it was raining, something she'd waited for because DenHarTog ran even in the rain. She put on her camouflaged rain slicker and hid in a spot where no one would see her or the murder.

DenHarTog finished his run, in the same place he always did and was walking the last quarter mile to his quarters. He had his hands on his hips as he walked. He tipped his head skyward, eyes closed letting rain fall into his open mouth when Cheryl came up from behind and slit his throat.

It happened fast. Cheryl used a razor sharp knife. Blood gurgled out of his mouth and he took four or five more steps, reaching up to stop the blood flow in vain, before he fell to the ground. The blood washed down the drain, just as Cheryl had hoped it would. His lifeless eyes stared up at her.

She dragged the body to where there were 55-gallon drums that had been emptied and stacked up. It took her two minutes to get the body in one and the top sealed. She was back in her quarters 20 minutes after she left.

From her quarters she could see when Col. Smith left for his office and she made sure she was in a clean, dry uniform when she met him on the sidewalk to walk with him, just like they had often done.

When given the order to find out what happened to the captain, Cheryl saluted the camp commander, did an about face and left his office without betraying any inkling that she had been the one responsible or that the colonel had just given her a way to advance her plan of taking over and putting the murder behind her.

It took a few days, but she found someone, an NCO about the right age, to take the fall. He was a man without a wife, a friend of DenHarTog's, but who was also loyal to the colonel. She made a show of "investigating" many of the soldiers, but she already knew the NCO was going down for the murder of DenHarTog.

It was almost too easy. She met with the sergeant near one of the security bunkers after dark and just before shift change. He had a side arm and an M-16 rifle and she had just the 9mm.

They were near a bunker, but out of sight of anyone. She pulled her 9mm and shot him in the heart before he could comprehend what was happening. She grabbed his gun and fired it in the air and put it in his hands before "help" could arrive.

The story she told was that while she was questioning him, he got suspicious and pulled his gun to shoot her, but missed when she ducked, at which point she pulled hers and shot him in the heart.

The next day, the captain's body was found and the bloody knife one of the soldier's found in the NCO's gear was all the proof the commander needed to put the matter to rest.

Her street cred grew as her death count increased by two, the sergeant and the captain of the peacekeeping force.

The colonel put her in charge of the security platoon the

next morning and for Cheryl, things were looking up. She was one step closer to being in charge of this compound.

CHAPTER 8

THE TWO NEWEST ADULT WOMEN TO THE FARM, KAREN and Natalie and the Florida man, Tim, did morning milking and farming chores while plans were hashed out in the shelter. The three were living together in the spare motorhome that had been acquired for their use and were still finding ways they could contribute to the farm.

The warning from Keith at the Smith Compound galvanized the Saunders Farm into taking extreme action to protect the farm. Jerry looked to Cleve, Buff and Tia for guidance at breakfast the following morning. Kellie and her assistant LT were there, so were Eddie, Randy, Monica, Nick and Tony.

Cleve cut right to the heart of it. "We need to get to the depot as soon as we can. We need to replace the SWAT truck which we can't fix and acquire get some military-grade weapons."

"We can't get anything we won't know how to use safely," Jerry warned. "It wouldn't do to have some big-assed gun only to have it break our arm when we try to shoot it."

"That's a good point. I am a Marine, but I was educated to be an astronaut and scientist. I wouldn't even think of trying to play with howitzers or tanks. I can set up defensive positions, lay land mines, call in air strikes and do reconnaissance, but I can't plan a battle."

"No land mines," Jerry said emphatically. "I don't want some innocent kid being blown to hell five years from now because we forget to disarm one." Hannah was pouring fresh coffee for everyone and she looked at Jerry. She was becoming quite the little executive assistant and Jerry had told her so, but she was also hearing the grisly details someone so young shouldn't have had to be exposed to.

"I think we should wait, at least until we get back from the depot, before making any more detailed plans. For all we know the place is destroyed or been scavenged completely empty.

"I think the sooner we get on the road this morning, the sooner we can start figuring out what we can and can't do."

Kellie spoke up for the first time during the meeting. "Something we might want to consider is finding some way to make contact with the Indiana group. Keith said there was a 'full bird' there?" Cleve told her a "full bird" was a colonel and would outrank the lieutenant colonel. "Maybe if the colonel has a growing community, he's not some despot and can tell the Smith Compound who they have on their hands."

"That's not a bad idea," Tony said. "Next time I talk with Keith I'll see what frequencies they're on and at what time and try to make some kind of contact."

"Can't hurt," Jerry agreed.

"Do we have time to make a secret tunnel?" asked Hannah, who had sat down next to Kellie with her coffee cup filled with chocolate milk. "Every castle has a secret tunnel."

Everyone looked at her and Hannah was afraid she'd said something stupid. She had a look of apprehension written all over her face. "That's not a bad idea, Hannah," Eddie said and the little girl's face lit up. "What do you think, Jerry? Do we have time to make an escape tunnel for the shelter?"

"Maybe not a tunnel, but we might be able to come up with something as an alternate escape route that Cheryl won't suspect. I'll give it some thought. Good thinking LT." Jerry said. The little girl beamed and sipped from her cup.

"Eddie, why don't you and Cleve ride with me, Buff and Tia ride with Randy. Nick, since you're the welding expert, can you start on fixing the gate? Josh will be here all day to help you." Nick nodded.

"Danny's going to dig up the bodies and re-bury them somewhere a long way away from here.

"Everyone else already knows their jobs and if they don't Kellie an LT can find something for them." He winked at both of them.

~ ~ ~

AMANDA PULLED OFF THE INTERSTATE, FOLLOWING THE SIGNS TO a rest area. The sun had set, but there was still enough daylight to see by. The lot was empty. She assumed most everyone in this area had gone to their homes before the great death. She saw one semi truck parked in the rest area and a body leaning against the driver's window, but there were no other cars around.

After finishing with the rest area, she went in search of some food. She was starting to run low.

She drove through the parking lots, but most of the businesses were specialty stores or restaurants, neither of which would help her. She did come across a mini-mart that looked to have been closed up with some forethought. There were weeds that had overgrown around the perimeter and in the parking lot, but the building still looked in good shape and Chopper wasn't growling.

She tried the doors and they were, of course, locked. She tried throwing several rocks at the door window, but it was made stronger than it looked. She thought about shooting the door open and walked back to the truck to get a gun, but then thought better of it. The sound of her shotgun would draw anyone within hearing distance. With the sun setting, she didn't want any attention tonight.

Chopper jumped in and Amanda drove the truck to the front door at an angle. She nosed in gently until the door broke away from its hinges. If the building still had electricity every alarm would have been set off. As it was, Amanda backed out and she and Chopper got out of the truck to inspect the damage.

The door was now open and Chopper ran in first. Amanda followed when the dog ran around the inside of the building and then came back to her like he was saying it was safe for her to come in.

Like the gas-n-go she'd been in earlier that day, she stayed away from the coolers with food in them. She grabbed a Poweraid that was stacked by the counter. She cracked one open and drank it, a little at first, then half the bottle. It tasted very good to her after drinking just water for the past month.

She loaded the Poweraids into the truck.

Looking through the store was getting harder as the sun was down and the lights from the truck only showed so much inside. She found a bunch of instant meals that needed hot water to make edible. She loaded them in the truck too. She saw hotdogs in one of the coolers just as she was leaving.

She reasoned that the hotdogs might have been in the cooler for 45 days or more, but once the electricity went off, the coolers quit working. But also without electricity, there was no heat in the building. It was still early spring so there was a good chance the hotdogs were still safe to eat.

She cracked the cooler door and sniffed. Inside the cooler it was much colder than room temperature. She didn't smell any spoilage so grabbed all 14 packages of hotdogs, sausages and cheeses that were in that cooler.

She couldn't live on noodles alone. She wasn't sure yet how she was going to cook them, but the thought of hotdogs over a fire right now made her mouth water. She also grabbed up cans of vegetables and fruits to fill out her diet. She stayed away from anything that was more than a month past its expiration date, but put enough in the truck to keep her fed for a week.

Now she needed a place to sleep for the night. She drove past the hotels and motels. They would be big and hollow and not someplace she wanted to sleep. She drove along hoping to find a house but instead she saw something that made her feel a lot better and would answer a lot of her problems.

Across from a strip mall was a Ford truck and RV dealership. She pulled in and drove through the lot. There were nice trucks, but the RVs, if they ran, were what she could use tonight.

All the vehicles were locked, so she drove her HUMVEE through the front door of the establishment and again it worked. She went in and found the keys all hanging on a board. They were numbered, but she figured if she took the first 20, one of them would work on one of the RVs in the lot.

Half an hour later she had one open. It was slow to start, but eventually a puff of diesel smoke spat out of the tailpipe.

The RV was six feet longer than her HUMVEE, but had a gas stove and a queen-sized bed. The propane tanks were stored under the stove and when she checked the dials. Both registered full.

It would do for the night.

She boiled some water and threw in four hotdogs. She took another one and broke it in half and tossed part to Chopper. The dog caught it in the air and gobbled it down. Amanda figured he could tell if it was bad and if he couldn't he'd throw it up in a few minutes anyhow.

The RV she chose was stocked with kitchenware, so she started another pot of water to boil for her instant meals. She found a can opener and opened up some creamed corn and peaches.

The RV was warm inside and the diesel engine was like white noise, very smooth and hardly noticeable. She checked and the fuel gauge read less than a quarter full. She used two of her spare cans on the back of her HUMVEE. That brought the gauge up to nearly half. She figured that would be enough if the truck was just idling for the night.

The RV must have been a display model because it had all the amenities. She turned the water on in the sink and it flowed and when she tested the toilet blue water swirled and flushed. She didn't know anything about the septic system, but for the night she was happy to not have to use out of doors. There was even a roll of soft toilet paper on the roll, neatly folded at the end, like in a hotel room. Towels hung beside the small shower and there were wash cloths in the rack on the wall above the vanity sink.

Her meal was simple and the hotdogs tasted good to her after eating MREs and snack food for the past three weeks. The macaroni and cheese instant meal with the side of corn filled her up. The peaches, while not fresh, were acceptable and washed down with more Poweraid. For tonight, it was a meal fit for a queen.

Chopper sat and watched her as she ate, so she flipped him the other half of the hotdog she'd given him earlier. When she was done, she put the dirty dishes in the sink and filled it with water. If she was leaving this RV in the morning, she saw no reason to do dishes. She'd leave it and a mystery to anyone in the future who might come across the RV.

She went back outside and let Chopper do his business while she brought the guns inside the RV. She then chose a change of clothes and the winter jacket she'd found earlier. It was cooler now and would probably fall below freezing tonight and in the morning Chopper was going to want to go outside, so she wanted to be ready.

Chopper came back to the RV after running around the parking lot while Amanda moved the guns, clothes, food and drinking water for in the morning to the RV. He must have run himself out because he came back with his tongue hanging out and drooling.

Amanda locked the HUMVEE and then made sure the doors to the RV were locked as well. She let the truck run to provide heat and set it so the two blankets on the bed would keep her warm enough.

She climbed into the bed and Chopper climbed up and lay beside her. She knew the dog was dirty and had mats in his short fur, but she thought if something bothered the dog in the middle of the night, he'd be able to wake her in time for her to get to her guns.

It was a race to see who fell asleep first, but Amanda thought she won.

~ ~ ~

THE ANNISTON ARMY DEPOT WAS IN SHAMBLES. STEEL BUILDINGS were ripped apart, heavy trucks smashed into tracked vehicles, passenger cars and trucks stacked up in corners where the hurricane force winds pushed them and collapsed administrative buildings.

Nature was doing what she could to reclaim the depot as well. Grasses had grown through cracks in the acres of concrete. Trees that had been fallen by the winds covered some buildings, the heavy rains and probable tornadoes rearranged the real estate, and flowers were starting to bloom on roofs that were now nearer the ground, covering the debris that used to be repair shops.

On the first drive through the depot, they had to navigate concertina wire that threatened to shred tires and foul the vehicles and the larger trees that had been felled. Jerry remembered Cleve telling him that the hurricane that had come through was actually two different storm cells that had met up in the gulf and headed northward. The circular storms moved with incredible speed starting with the panhandle of Florida, going north through Alabama and Georgia then headed east to the coasts of the Carolinas and Virginia. Even from space, Cleve had said they saw swaths of destruction left by dozens of tornadoes that were spawned from merged storm cells as well as the storm itself.

The depot had suffered as much as everywhere else in the south, but nature was taking back what man had once built. It might take years or decades, but she'd get it back.

Everyone dismounted when Jerry found a parking area that was large enough to give them room to park next to each other.

"Cleve, Buff, Tia, this is your area of expertise, we'll watch your back."

Two hours of walking around the area had gotten them nothing they could use for improving their defense of the farm. They avoided entering any buildings at first, zombies being something no one wanted to face after the terror and pure savagery they'd shown the night before. They looked for recent tracks from anything that might be a predator or other humans, but even those were missing. This place appeared to be deserted except for small wildlife and birds.

They found some equipment, HUMVEEs, 2-1/2 ton trucks, tanks and Bradleys, but they had all been parted out, buried in mud, or damaged beyond the party's ability to repair. They worked systematically through the equipment graveyard. It was depressing for all of them who thought they would find a cornucopia of weaponry when all they were finding was rusting hulks and useless steel.

Jerry was about to call the mission a wash. They'd found nothing of use and wasted a morning. He was walking back to the SUVs with the others and kicked a piece of debris. Underneath was a large sheet of textured paper and Jerry pulled at it thinking it was probably just another piece of paper from the mountains that every military unit spit out. The corner ripped off in his hand and he turned it over. It looked like the corner of a map.

Everyone else was continuing to walk back to the SUVs, but Jerry used a stick to dig out more of the piece. There was clear plastic protecting the paper under the debris and he was able to pry more of the map out.

He stood up after looking at the map for a moment. "Ahh, guys. I think we're looking in the wrong place."

It was a map of the installation. They were looking in the wrong place. The map showed bunkers, similar to how Jerry had built his, north of them but hidden by the trees and re-growth of nature. They'd been excited before so they reined in their enthusiasm. For all they knew, the bunkers were empty or flooded or whatever was stored in them was useless for defense. What good would and Abrams tank do without ammunition and no one knowing how to drive it? It would be a mobile bunker at best, but the fuel consumption would be too high to sustain the 60-ton behemoth that it would take 500 gallons of diesel to fill.

It took 20 minutes to weave their way through to the bunker areas. Jerry stopped and was disappointed by what he saw. It was all overgrown with weeds and looked just like the rest of the installation. They all walked up to the first bunker and it took everyone to move the fallen tree out of the way. The steel door was locked with a heavy-duty military-grade lock.

"Not a problem," Eddie said, going back to his SUV. He pulled out a portable plasma torch and generator and plugged everything in. "I figured this place may be secure so I brought this along just in case. That scrounger Jamal found it."

Eddie had the lock off in less than a minute and they waited until he shut down the generator to open the doors.

It was an Apache helicopter and it appeared to be in good shape. Jerry looked at Cleve and Buff. Both were pilots but fixed wing, not helicopter pilots. Jerry ran for the radio and called Kayla. "Can you fly a helicopter?" he asked when she answered.

"If you put wings on a washing machine I could fly it," she told them.

"Ummm, Kayla, dear. It's a helicopter. It doesn't have wings," Jerry said over the radio.

"I have more than 2,000 hours in helicopters. It'll do." She told him, shutting him up.

They found six more helicopters, but with only one pilot, the others were just metal paperweights and just as useful. They moved to other bunkers and found the tanks they'd expected to find. While it would have been nice to have one of these on the farm, its use was limited. The 120 mm main gun would likely do more damage than a hoard of vigilantes and no one really knew how to arm, aim and use the tank.

Other bunkers were empty and Jerry looked at his watch. The morning was gone and all they had for their trouble was one possible helicopter. He decided one more set of bunkers and then they'd call it a day.

Eddie cut the lock off the new bunker and Buff opened the door. The military men and Tia all smiled.

A Stryker vehicle was inside and it looked as pristine as everything else in the bunkers.

A Stryker is an eight-wheeled, 16-ton fighting machine that was designed for a fast-moving and mobile force in an urban environment. It was armed with the M-2 machine gun that could be fired from inside or outside the vehicle. It was armored and could drive almost anywhere and best of all, it drove just like a car. It had automatic transmission, a steering wheel and pedals just like the SUVs.

Another bonus was its diesel motor. Jerry had made note of the 5,000 gallon diesel storage tanks. He hoped they were full because if this Stryker started and ran, they'd need fuel to get one of them to the farm.

They found 14 Strykers and were able to get six started. All had been fueled and were topped off. Jerry had the group split up because, while the Strykers were cool, without ammunition, they were nothing but big armored trucks.

Tia found the ammunition bunker. It was filled with every type of ammunition they could hope to use. "We have got to come back tomorrow with a bigger truck and get as much of this as we can before someone else gets here."

Eddie suggested they spend the night here and have Kayla

bring the Ford and a trailer in the morning. Jerry agreed that now that they had the locks off the bunkers, especially the ammo dump, they'd best not let it fall into someone else's hands, no matter how long the odds of someone finding it.

Jerry called the shelter and told Kellie their plans and asked for three more drivers and Kayla to bring the Ford and a trailer. The group at the Depot spent the evening finding the right ammo to stock in the Strykers and the main gun of the Apache. They had no idea what the rocket pods used for ammunition so left them empty. Buff did find an AVGAS tank and topped off the helicopter with aviation fuel and charged its batteries. He hoped it worked and Kayla could fly it.

They set up a make-shift camp for the night and talked of strategies. They looked through more bunkers. They found one that wasn't locked and inside were MREs with the skeleton of a soldier nearby. It was clear the soldier had taken his own life. They didn't disturb the body, but took the MREs and closed the door to the bunker.

That evening, they told stories around a campfire like people had done for hundreds, maybe thousands of years.

They told stories of friends and families in their pasts, of people who had influenced them and famous people they'd met.

"I was six years old when I knew what I wanted to do," Cleve told them. "I met Colonels Jack Lousma and Gordon Fullerton that year." The others sitting around the campfire had no idea who those men were.

"I'm not surprised you don't remember their names, but to me, they were gods.

"My dad was an Army sergeant assigned to White Sands Missile Range back in 1982. He was with the 259th Military Police Company as a platoon sergeant. None of you probably remember, but STS-3, the space shuttle Columbia had to land at White Sands for some reason and my dad's platoon got to work with the traffic control.

"My mom and I saw the Columbia come down through the mountains and land. I was using my dad's binoculars and it was the coolest thing that I'd ever seen. I remember the dust it kicked up on the runway and the parachute that came out of the back of it.

"I don't know what strings were pulled, but dad and his men got to meet the pilot and commander of the shuttle. He took me with him and when I saw the two Air Force men in their flight uniforms, I felt like I'd been given an extra Christmas. Mom and I had to sit apart from the soldiers when the spacemen came in, but I was no less awed.

"I watched as my dad shook their hands and I knew right then I wouldn't become an Army man like my dad, but an Air Force officer so I could fly in space just like those men did.

"My dad was pleased when I got into MIT and did undergraduate work in electronics before joining the Air Force. I flew more than 400 missions during the first Gulf War before becoming a test pilot at Wright Patterson.

"After six months of that, I was accepted by NASA and they helped pay for my Masters Degree at MIT. I had hoped to fly on the shuttle, but it retired before I got the chance."

Eddie was chuckling at some memory.

"Something about that tickle your funny bone, Eddie?" Cleve asked the young man.

"Sorry, Cleve, but for some reason I pictured you as that guy Walowitz from that show *Big Bang Theory*. His character designed the Walowitz Waste Disposal System aboard the International Space Station and had a Masters from MIT," Eddie told them.

"Oh, yea, I heard about that. Well, I didn't work as a space plumber, I worked mostly in the Harmony Node, completing the cross connecting of the European Columbus and Japanese Kibō laboratories and troubleshooting the electrical issues the station had been suffering because of the poorly constructed solar panel connections."

The smile Eddie had on his face flattened out as Cleve, who never flaunted his intelligence, made it clear he wasn't just a fly boy. Eddie's level of respect for the man went up several notches.

There was a lingering silence as everyone thought about the station that continued to orbit above them and the last man there, Col. Rustov.

"I met someone famous," Buff said. "I met the former

vice-president of the United States."

"What was he like?" asked Jerry, knowing to whom Buff was referring.

"Vulgar," Buff said, then smiled. "He was meeting some of us scientists who were going up to the space station at a buffet NASA was throwing for us.

"Now I'm a former Marine and I've heard course language all my life, but I thought the vice-president was out of line when the director said the buffet was open.

"Right after the director said that, the vice-president said 'let's git it and shit it.' I knew right then I'd never vote for the guy. After all, there were ladies present."

Everyone laughed. They'd heard stories like the one Buff relayed about the language politicians used in public and in private and how it was sometimes very different.

"I never met anyone famous," Jerry said. "But I did know a man who is responsible for all of us being here today."

Jerry shared the story of his dad, and how when other farmers in the area were selling out to big corporations, he refused large sums of money to move off the land he loved.

"I was eight or nine years old at the time. I was thinking it would be great to be rich and move to the city. I didn't like living away from all my friends and having to ride the bus to school everyday.

"But my dad really loved working the land and growing things. He and my mom talked about it for a long time. I don't remember how much they were offered, but mom said dad would never have to work again.

"I remember my dad saying 'I work because the work I do means something.'"

"That's when I knew I wanted to do what my dad did. He was a hardworking man who got up early every morning and worked hard every day.

"I still miss him."

There was moment of silence around the fire as everyone thought about their fathers.

Eddie seldom heard his best friend's dad talk about his parents. He'd seen pictures in the old farm house, but had never really looked at them. He had always been more interested in playing video games and having fun with Randy. When he worked for Jerry on the farm, he did a good job, but only because he wanted to continue working with Jerry and Randy, not because he wanted to be a farmer all his life.

He was seeing the man now as someone other than just Randy's dad.

"You know," Eddie said, "I knew someone like that, too.

"My dad was never around when I was growing up. To me he was just a name on my birth certificate. My mom had a lot of men come through the house, but none of them were thinking about being a dad to me.

"I guess I was 13 when I was first allowed to stay at a friend's house. My mom was going out of town for the weekend with some guy and my friend said I could stay with him. I really didn't want to because of the chores I'd have to do, but I sure as hell didn't want to stay in our trailer by myself.

"The first night, we had been told to move some cows from one pen to another. One of the cows wouldn't move and I punched it in the neck.

"My friend's dad hollered at me. He hollered at me because I'd lost my temper and he hollered at me because I was abusing his animals. I didn't even know he was watching.

"Later that night, my friend and I were sitting in a tent outside the house. We were talking about his dad hollering at me when we heard the old man come out of the house.

"He came up to us and told his son that his mom wanted him for some reason. My friend went in the house and I was there with this guy who had really screamed at me. I thought he was still mad and I was a little afraid of him and hoped he would go back in the house.

"Instead, the man squatted down so we were eye-to-eye and looked right at me. I can still remember what he said. He said 'Eddie, if you are going to be hanging around here, you're going to have to follow the rules here. My son seems to like you and I don't choose his friends for him. On this farm, we do what is right, even if no one is looking and we don't abuse animals.'

"I was a little shocked," Eddie continued, "because I thought the guy was going to tell me to get off his property right then and I wouldn't have come back. But then he said 'You're welcome here, but be prepared because I'll treat you just like I treat my own son.'"

"After that, the man went back inside. I sat in the tent by myself thinking that he was the kind of dad a kid needs.

"I kept coming back to that farm. Jerry never tried to be my dad, but he was always a father figure to me. He's the reason I'm here now."

Other stories were shared, mis-steps made during childhood, bad decisions made while growing up and funny stories about friends and family.

It was a good feeling, Jerry thought, to have people of this caliber with him. He knew what type of personality of man was drawn to people like Cheryl and he told himself he'd take any one of these people for any dozen of the kind who would follow Cheryl.

~ ~ ~

THE RV WAS STILL RUNNING IN THE MORNING. AMANDA SLEPT A dreamless sleep and only woke up briefly when Chopper moved positions. She got out of bed and looked out the windshield. The sun was already up and she could see the desolation around her. The temperature gauge on the dash showed 38 degrees outside, so she put on her new clothes and jacket before letting Chopper out.

She walked around in the chilly air while Chopper went about his business. The HUMVEE had dew on the windows but nothing had been disturbed. There were birds overhead making noise, but otherwise the only sound she could hear in the parking lot was the RV. Feeling cold, she went back inside and sat in the driver's seat so she could watch for Chopper's return. There was an owner's manual and a sell sheet on the dashboard.

Reading the spec sheet, the RV she was in was considered a Class C mini-motorhome. She read that the reason for the two propane tanks was because it had a small furnace which heated the living area. It also had a refrigerator and small water heater.

Taking the manual with her, she walked around the RV and checked out all the accessories. This RV would be better suited for driving across the country than the HUMVEE. She hadn't given it any thought last night, but she would be driving on interstate in the states and not the rugged country of Alaska and she might as well take this instead of the HUMVEE.

She went back up to the driver's seat and read more through the manual. The HUMVEE had been a horse and she'd hate to leave it behind, but driving the RV would be more comfortable. It also had a 55 gallon fuel tank and according to the manual, this model averaged 14 miles to the gallon on the highway. That was about three times better than the HUMVEE and she would only have to fill up once a day at most.

She saw Chopper come running in a lazy lope across the parking lot. His tongue was hanging out and she could tell he found some mud. Where ever he'd been he'd been having fun. He ran around to the side door.

Instead of letting him in, she met him at the door. From the HUMVEE she got the two dog dishes she'd made him the previous day and filled one with food, which he dug into like he was a starving third-world dog, and then filled his water dish.

While he was eating and drinking she walked around the RV, checking tires and looking under the hood. It was brand new with less than 200 miles on it. She already knew the HUMVEE was a solid vehicle, stout and ready to go another 3,000 miles, but if she moved into the RV, she was taking the risk it might break down. While she could probably fix it, she didn't have any tools with her and she wasn't an RV mechanic.

She'd have no trouble driving the RV, in fact it would be easier. It wasn't as loud as the HUMVEE and it did have a nice CD player and sound system. She didn't have any CDs, but she was sure she could find some, probably in the store she'd broken into the previous night.

When she asked Chopper, what he thought, the dog looked at her and went back to finishing off his breakfast.

She left the door open for him when he was finished eating and started moving everything to the RV. She really liked the HUMVEE, but having an inside bathroom and a nice bed to sleep in every night was the kicker.

She fired up the stove again and tossed four sausages into a pan. While waiting for them to heat, she found a towel to wipe Chopper's feet when he climbed up the steps. Using a fork, she rolled the sausages around and moved her clothes and the food into their proper places in the RV. She wanted it to be orderly and nothing moving around as she drove.

When the sausages were well done, she sprinkled cheese over them and turned the heat down so the cheese would melt, not burn.

While she waited, she finished bringing in everything from the HUMVEE. The last things she brought in were the radios. She had to really work to get the Army radio out of the HUMVEE, but it had a small tool kit stored underneath the radio itself.

It took her less than 15 minutes to transfer the radio to the RV. Since she didn't use the passenger door, she ran the coaxial through the door frame to the antenna she bolted to the mirror and called it good. She wasn't sure why she hooked the unit up after her breakfast, but four of the people she knew who survived the plague had been military. This model of RV also had a 40-channel CB radio installed. Once she got on the road, she'd have to give it a try. There were three power ports on the dashboard, so the GPS and Army radio both had power when she turned them on.

She realized the M-60 machine gun would not be something she could reasonably use, so took the firing pin out and left it on the HUMVEE. She didn't want someone else using it.

The last thing she did was pump as much fuel as she could from the HUMVEE to the RV. She figured it was more than 35 gallons in total and that would allow her more than 500 miles before she needed another fuel up, but she'd try to fill up every other break just to be on the safe side.

She left the keys in the HUMVEE and a note saying she was traveling to Alabama. She didn't think anyone would ever read the note, so she signed it "A Survivor" and left it on the driver's seat. She kissed her finger tips and pressed them to the steering wheel and said "Thanks truck. You did good."

She closed the door and she and Chopper boarded the RV and got back on the road.

She wasn't in a hurry; there was no time-table she had to meet, so she stopped one more time before getting back on the highway at the mini-mart she'd broken into the previous night. She and Boomer went inside, this time scaring some small furry critters. Amanda went to a circular rack and grabbed all the CDs, even the ones of artists she'd never heard of. She also loaded more dog food into the RV and the three remaining five-gallon water bottles they had in the store.

Behind the counter she found a new 17" laptop setting on a stack of milk crates. She picked it up and put it in the truck as well. She liked to write and even if there wasn't an internet anymore, she would enjoy writing again.

On one more look before getting back on the road, she found travel-size toothpaste and tooth brushes. She was brushing her teeth before she even left the building. When she was done brushing and spitting, she told Chopper it wouldn't hurt if he tried brushing more often. The big dog just looked at her and sniffed at the spot she'd just spit on.

The mountains were on both sides of her RV as she drove out of Bozeman and into the farming land of Billings Montana. The monotony was relieved by the CDs she was able to play. The temperature climbed to the mid-50s in the early afternoon and she turned up the sound system in the RV as loud as she could stand it. Her dad used to bitch at her and tell her she'd go deaf listening to music so loud, but now she didn't think it mattered anymore. She listened to a Taylor Swift album, followed by Lady Antebellum, Jessica Price and Adele. It was something to change what her brain was used to listening to.

She listened to a complete rap album for the first time in her life and then a classic hits collection. The miles seemed less dreary than her trip across Canada with the music playing. Chopper would spend time with his head out the passenger window until slobber was flying out of his mouth. He'd then pull his head back in and go back to the living area and lay down on the floor to nap.

The first day in the RV, she stopped every hour for rest

breaks for her and Chopper. She stopped the RV in the middle of US-212 and let the dog run until he was tired. He seemed good with it. Wyoming was as empty as any place she'd ever seen in her life. It was wide open space with low mountains off in the distance. She'd seen a few cars and semis wrecked along the way, but the music had her in the mood to just drive and not stop to refuel.

Amanda eventually stopped for the night in South Dakota. She came across a large truck stop in Belle Fourche. There were dozens of trucks and two cars parked around the station but she could see this was like all the other small cities and towns she'd passed through that day.

Dead.

There was a supermarket across the road from the station and she and her dog walked over to it in hopes of finding a wider variety of supplies. Halfway across the road, however, Chopper stopped.

Amanda encouraged the dog to follow her, but the hackles on his back and low growl made her stop. She looked at the store and couldn't see anything, but Chopper refused to budge any closer to the store. There were six cars in the parking lot, but Amanda didn't see any movement. Looking closer, she saw one of the front doors had been shattered outward.

Chopper had his head down, ears back and muzzle twitching, looking like he was prepared to attack. Amanda put her hand on his head and backed away. Chopper followed slowly, but kept looking back at the supermarket as if expecting something to come out.

Back at the service station, the station itself showed it had been locked up before the last man had left. She saw small animal prints, but nothing large enough to be a threat to her and Chopper. The dog stayed near her and sniffed at every print. She walked around the station twice before deciding to break in.

It was more difficult this time because she didn't want to damage the front end of her RV. She found a breaker bar in the saddlebag of one of the rigs parked at the station and a pair of work gloves. Chopper never left her side and he seemed on edge, but he wasn't as nervous as he'd been going over to the store.

Inside the convenience store she found more canned food and dry goods to supplement her food supply. She wished for some fresh food, like the steaks her dad used to cook on the grill with foil-wrapped baked potatoes, a nice fast-food hamburger with tomatoes and no lettuce and a side order of fries would have been good too, but the food she found wasn't terrible.

The electronics section of the store got her a splitter for the power ports on the RV. She remembered the laptop she'd picked up which she'd play with tonight. She was interested in starting her journal.

With everything she thought she'd need for the next week, Amanda organized the interior of the RV and re-fueled it from the semi parked in front of the gas station.

Chopper was fed and watered and stayed outside the RV and paced in front of the vehicle, always keeping a watch on the store across the road. There was something unseen over there that bothered him so Amanda chambered a round in the 30-30, but made sure the safety was on. She placed it on the dashboard.

The Valtro PM5 Shotgun had its magazine in but she didn't chamber a round because she kept it near the door and didn't want Chopper to accidentally knock it over and discharge a round. The Baretta she kept in the sleeping area.

The sun was just setting when Amanda finished her chores around the RV. She read through the owner's manual and learned about the septic system and how to maintain it. She emptied the water in the fresh water tanks and refilled them with water from the Culligan bottles in the store so she had good water from the sink. She had a quick shower just to test the hot water heater in the little RV and it made her feel 100-times better. The clothes she put on were all new, some still in the packages until she opened them.

Refreshed and everything put in its place, Amanda looked out at the twilight through the windshield. Chopper had lain down in front of the RV and Amanda could see the big dog was keeping a close eye in the direction of the store. There was something about it that fascinated or bothered him.

The sun was well below the horizon and reflecting off the clouds in hues of amber and maroon. After two minutes of looking, Amanda decided it wasn't even close to being as majestic as the sunsets in Alabama.

Not feeling tired she decided to install the CB and antenna. Like the Army radio she installed under the dash, she checked all the channels in vain hope of hearing anything. All she heard was static. After 20 minutes, she turned the squelch until the static was gone and tossed the microphone onto the dash.

She also opened the laptop and plugged in the charger to the power port. The laptop must have been new because there were no passwords and only the administrator log in. It had an open source Office Suite installed and a few other programs which looked like inventory and accounting, but it was the word processor program she wanted.

She started her journal, beginning with her flight from Fort Wainwright. She'd written about two pages, getting to the parting of destinations with the captain, when she heard Chopper's bark.

Amanda looked out the windshield, but in the darkness it was hard to see. She started the RV and the headlights came on.

Chopper was looking as vicious as she'd seen him this morning. He was angry and she saw in the distance what had upset the dog. Coming out of the store front were a pair of the ugliest looking people she'd ever seen. They looked in her direction and then hid their face, like the intensity of her headlights bothered them.

They came running in her direction, heads down, but with intent.

"Chopper!" she hollered at the dog. "Get in here!" With the dog standing in front of the truck, she couldn't drive away and she didn't think she'd get away backing up. The monsters were running with gound-eating speed she'd never seen except in cartoons. "Chopper!" she hollered again, glad she'd left her window open for him to hear.

The dog hesitated after the first yell, but not the second. He ran to the side door and was in the RV even as Amanda was putting it in gear.

The beasts coming at her were wearing ripped and tattered clothes. One had socks and she didn't know why she noticed it. They looked like malformed body builders with elongated arms, legs and foreheads. Amanda had seen enough movies and read enough books to know these things were coming for her and they didn't have her best interest in mind.

Not even waiting to close the side door, she accelerated out of the parking lot. Supplies that weren't stored securely crashed in the living area, but Amanda didn't care. She'd take care of them later.

She was out of the gas station parking lot and onto US-212 like a NASCAR driver headed to the checkered flag. Her foot was all the way to the floor and from the passenger window she could see the two beasts cutting across the parking lot. Their speed and agility were amazing but the RV wasn't made to accelerate like a sport's car.

With one hand on the wheel she used the other to grab the 30-30 from the dash. The beasts were beside the truck and reaching the door that was still open. With one eye on the road and the other in the rear view mirror, she could see one of the beast's hand on the frame. She aimed as best she could while driving and trying to watch the road and shot the thing in the face as it's head appeared. She could feel the rear duals as they drove over the fallen whatever it was.

She checked both mirrors and couldn't see what happened to the second beast. She hoped it had ceased chasing her and was pretty sure the damn things couldn't run at 70 miles per hour, the speed she dared drive the RV right now. She started to breathe normally again, but the hackles on Chopper's neck were still up and he was growling and barking at the passenger window. She checked her mirrors again and still didn't see anything.

Amanda put the rifle back on the dashboard and petted the dog's back. She jumped when the dog barked, as if startled. She wasn't about to stop the RV and close the door that was flapping in the slipstream, preferring instead to put a lot of miles between herself and those nightmares.

Chopper barked again and Amanda thought she saw something out the driver's side mirror. She wasn't sure, but there was movement where there shouldn't have been. She placed one hand on Chopper's back and slammed on the brakes of the RV. The truck's anti-lock braking system kicked in and from overhead, a body went flying off the top of the truck.

Chopper started barking ferociously through the windshield and Amanda gunned the RV. The beast had time to skid to a halt and get back to its feet when Amanda's front bumper caught the it just as it was crouching to leap at her.

For an instant Amanda saw the dead black eyes before it was knocked down in front of the accelerating RV. It skidded on the pavement, flesh scraping off and blood flowing from a gash in its side, but it was still trying to get up when the driver's side front tire ran over it, followed a heartbeat later by the rear duals.

Amanda continued accelerating until she felt safely away from the horrors. Her hands were shaking and heart was beating loud enough she thought the dog could even hear it.

Ten miles later she slowed the truck to a more reasonable speed and stopped just long enough to close the rear door. She had been scared, but between her and Chopper, who had stopped barking now and instead lay down in the back, they'd survived another day.

The GPS's voice startled her and she realized in her escape from the beasts, she'd gone off the route, but there was no way she was going to turn around so she drove on until she got to the intersection of US 79. She drove her RV in a big circle looking in the distance to make sure there was nothing out there, before parking in the middle of the highway for the night.

It took half an hour to clean up the mess that she'd made in the living area, but once everything was back in place, Amanda felt calm enough to get some sleep. She took Chopper out and he ran around happily, which gratified Amanda. The dog didn't seem afraid, so this would be a good place to stay for the night.

Amanda checked the damage outside the RV and there were blood stains along the one side, but the shot she'd taken missed the truck completely. In the front, there was a dent in the hood, but nothing she was worried about. She'd feared that she might damage the condenser or radiator, but there was only a small crack in the plastic grill work along with the dent.

Fortunately the headlights were still working.

Chopper found a rabbit to chase and was tearing off down the road, but he gave up when the little animal dashed off the road at a right angle. The big dog couldn't make such a turn so gave up the chase and came back to the RV. Amanda got down on one knee and ruffled the dog's big head. He tried to lick her face, but she kept his tongue at bay. "Good boy, Chopper. Good boy," she told him. "Now why don't we try to get some sleep?"

He followed her into the RV and she started turning off the equipment she didn't need. She left the truck running for the night, rather than use the heater in the living compartment. If Chopper woke her in the middle of the night, she wanted to be able to make a quick get away.

There was a CD player in the sleeping area so she put in a new CD before getting into bed. Chopper lay on the floor tonight, finding it more to his liking than the kicking from Amanda during the night. The two survivors fell asleep to Coltrane.

Amanda slept fitfully, awakening twice when Chopper got up to move positions. Amanda got up and looked out every window but saw nothing but stars and her own RV's headlights.

She was glad when morning finally came. She had parked so the sun coming up would wake her. The adrenalin rush from the night before made her feel stiff. She needed to stretch. The temperature read 42 degrees, which was cool, but better than Alaska so Amanda decided on a short run. She put on her tennis shoes and the loosest fitting clothes she could find in the clothing she'd picked up. She hadn't thought to find running clothes. A loose pair of jeans and a tee shirt would work for now.

Chopper was already by the door when she was ready. She started her run in one direction chosen at random and ran slowly for ten minutes before turning back. Chopper, who had to take care of business, was just catching up with her as she headed back toward the RV.

She was feeling like her head was clearing so she continued on past the RV for another 10 minutes before turning back. The cool air felt good and the dog running beside her made her feel as safe as she'd been since leaving Fort Wainwright.

She slowed to a walk and looked around her as she finished her run. It had felt good and her muscles had relaxed. She was parked in the middle of nothing where two highways crossed. She couldn't see any other cars or trucks and the only animals she'd seen were far off in the distance.

She felt both alone and comforted by the solitude.

Chopper nudged her hand, assuring her she wasn't alone.

"Good dog," she told him. "Let's get you something to eat before you start on my hand." She got his bowls from the RV and filled them both. For breakfast she made herself some instant coffee, something she hadn't had since the Army chow hall had closed, and some pears from a can. She also heated some water and made a passable bowl of oatmeal which she sprinkled with sugar. It wasn't a breakfast of champions, but it would do.

Taking care of a few other things which needed attending, Amanda was back on the road, headed south on 79 toward Sturgis, according the GPS. She set her goal for Rapid City by the end of the day. Rain was moving through but it didn't dampen her spirits. She had her music on, a happy dog in the passenger seat and a full belly.

The day went by as quick as the miles.

During a pit stop for the dog in the late afternoon, she played with the GPS and saw she would be driving near Mt. Rushmore. She'd never seen it and since she'd be in the area before sunset, she was going to see the monument before continuing.

She parked in front of the tourist attraction and looked up, as millions of others had done. She was awed by the workmanship and majesty, but after seeing it once, she was ready to move on.

Amanda refueled the truck and drove for a little while before stopping on the interstate near the town of Wall, South Dakota. She'd decided that until she needed to, she'd stay away from improved areas and truck stops. She drove under the I-14 overpass and, just like the night before, parked in the middle of the road. There was a water tower in the distance, but from where she parked it was all she could see.

"Good enough, Chopper," she said to the dog as he got out of the seat and ready get outside. She also got out of the RV, despite the light rain that was falling. It was a cold rain, but not heavy. It felt good for about two minutes before she went back inside and left Chopper to his own fun of romping after scents he picked up.

She fixed herself a dinner meal and looked at the map on the GPS. She hadn't gone a lot of miles this day, but she was still making progress. She figured by tomorrow she'd make it to Omaha or even if she pushed it, Kansas City.

She wasn't sure if she was in a hurry to find out if her dad or brother had survived or wanted to keep not knowing. Part of her wanted to hurry home, while another part wanted to never know and to perpetually dream about them being alive.

Chopper played outside after finishing his second bowl of food for the day. Amanda cleaned the dishes and put things away before settling in to write in her journal. It was comfortable in the front seat because she could write on her laptop, listen to the music she'd chosen and watch as Chopper played at chasing small animals, none of which he could seem to catch, but he didn't stop trying.

Amanda thought, at first, something was wrong with CD player when she heard strange sounds. She'd been listening to Luke Bryan while she typed and it sounded funny to her so she popped the CD out of the player.

That's when she heard a crackling voice. "Is there anyone out there," the male voice asked. "This is Dan Sullivan calling on channel 19, is there anyone out there." Amanda started shaking. It was a voice that sounded desperate, but Amanda was still reminded of the Canadians who had killed Shep.

After a moment's thought, she reached for the microphone.

"This is Amanda, calling Dan. Come in Dan, over."

There was silence on the CB, so Amanda reached for the squelch dial and turned it to just far enough, she could hear the static.

"This is Amanda, calling Dan. Come in, Dan, over," she

repeated and waited.

"Oh my God," the man on the other end said. "I'd almost given up hope of reaching anyone! Amanda come in! Are you really alive?"

"I am Dan, and it's good to hear another voice," she said, wondering if it was the truth.

"Sweet Jesus, Amanda. We've been alone for weeks now and had given up hope. Where are you and are there more people with you? We're in danger and we're all scared."

"Slow down Dan," Amanda told him, working out what to say. "I am not alone and I am in South Dakota right now. How many are there of you and where are you."

The vagueness of her answer didn't seem to bother him. "There are six of us holed up here in a house by the grain mill," he told her, assuming she knew where the grain mill was, which she didn't. "It's me and my daughter, three other kids and Audrey from the motorcycle dealership."

Dan talked like Amanda should be familiar with the area. She gave him the bad news. "We are headed to Alabama. We're not from around here."

"Please wait! Don't go. Please, you got to help us," he begged over the radio. "We're all a little scared. There were nine of us, but three guys who went out for food never came back. Jimmy, one of the older boys, said there was something in the buildings killing people. We're running out of food now. Help us please!" The desperation in his plea was evident.

"Hold on, Dan. Wait for me to talk with my partner. Don't go away." Amanda didn't want to be a liar, so she called for Chopper who was tracking still another rabbit that had outsmarted him. The dog looked up and ran toward the RV.

"Someone wants our help," she told the dog. "What do you think?"

Chopper wagged his tail as she pet his head and scratched behind his ears. Dan sounded desperate, but not like he was in any danger right now, so she thought it might be better if she waited until morning to make face to face contact. That'd give her time to think this out and prepare.

"Dan, this is Amanda, come in, over."

"This is Dan. Where are you? You've got to help us. We

only have enough water and food to last two or three more days. We're afraid to go outside at all. We don't have any weapons to defend ourselves from the monsters. Please, you've got to help us."

"Dan, slow down. I'm not going to leave you. Do you have transportation at all?"

"There are cars all over the place, but we're afraid to go outside. There's something out there killing people and we're afraid. We've barricaded ourselves in the basement of my house and we can hear something upstairs moving around."

That changed everything for Amanda. If the man was barricaded in a basement, the only way out was through the beasts that had chased down her RV. One of them had survived being thrown off the truck at 60 miles an hour and was still coming at her when she ran it over. If the beasts really wanted to, they'd find some way to get at the people barricaded in the cellar. It also answered the question of why he was talking like he was whispering, making it hard for her to hear him.

"Okay, Dan. You're going to have to tell me exactly where you're at and I'll see what we can do." She told him, hoping he didn't notice her use of pronouns.

"We're in the basement in my workshop, all the way in back," he told her.

"No Dan. I'm on the interstate. I need your address."

"Oh, sorry. I thought you were from here," he apologized and gave her the address of his house. It was ten minutes from where she was parked.

Amanda got Chopper back on board and turned the truck around, making up a plan even as she drove to the address. The sun had set, but it was still light enough to see, even without headlights, but they came on automatically so she left them on.

The house was on the corner lot in a residential area.

When Amanda arrived in the area, she looked first for an escape route that was as strait as possible for her to get away in the RV in a hurry. She kept Dan on the radio, telling him what she saw to make sure she had the right house.

She found out the room he was in had one small window, but it had security bars. He was a wedding videographer and did all his editing in the basement of his house, so had no tools to get out through the bars. He'd used furniture, the water heater and water softener tank to block the first door to the upstairs, and a full washer and dryer to block the second. So far the monsters hadn't even tried to get at them.

She drove by the house three times as it slowly got darker outside. She saw the window to his workroom with the bars. She asked Dan how he'd put them in and he told her they were in sunk in four inches of cement around the window.

"Could I pull them out with my truck and you guys escape through the window?" she asked him.

There was a long pause. "Yea, that will work Amanda. But I warn you, there's something upstairs and if it starts coming for you, you better be able to run."

"Okay, Dan. You get everyone ready to get out that window. I'll be back in five minutes. I have to go find something."

Amanda drove off and found a semi with a chain to pull the bars off. She hitched it to the front of her RV and laid it around the driver's mirror. When she was ready, she called Dan on the CB and told him what to expect.

"We're ready for you Amanda," he said, but there was something in his voice she didn't like.

"Dan, we're going to make this work. Just be ready because we're going to have to be fast," she reassured him. "Here I come now." Amanda circled the block so she could have as straight as approach and escape as possible. She drove to the window and jumped out of the RV, grabbing the chain and looping it through the bars. She was almost back into the RV when she heard a crashing inside the house. She put the truck in reverse and pulled the bars out of the ground and away from the window. Chopper was barking and growling.

Dan had the first kid out before she'd gotten stopped. The first was a little girl about eight years old and she started running for the open door of the RV, tears running down her face. She put the truck into drive even as the next three children came through the window followed by, who she presumed to be, Audrey. She'd told Dan that they had to be prepared for a fast get away and she'd stay with the truck and to remind the children to get in the RV and move all the way to the back.

Amanda grabbed the microphone and told Dan to hurry. Audrey, who looked like the kind of woman who would work at a motorcycle shop was grabbing up the last boy, who had tripped. They were almost to the truck when she saw the man struggling through the small window. He had just about gotten out when a hand grabbed at his leg through the window, then another and a third.

"Go!" Dan hollered at her. "Get out of here!" he screamed kicking at the monsters that were pulling him back in. The kids were all in the truck now and screaming and crying. "Hurry, before they get you! Go!" Dan screamed.

Chopper was barking through the windshield and in the space of time it takes for eyes to blink, Amanda grabbed the 30-30 from the dash while throwing the truck into park.

She was out of the truck, glad she hadn't put her seat belt on after putting the chain on the bars. Dan had been pulled partway back into the cellar, and he was screaming from the worst pain she could imagine. She ran up to him and started shooting into the heads she saw in the window in the bright lights from the headlights. She shot until the gun was empty and then grabbed Dan by his shirt's collar and pulled him away. His left leg was a bloody mess, she saw bone, and pants were ripped and he was still screaming. She was able to pull him free of what was in the basement, even as the hands were reaching for him again.

Dan was a portly man and Amanda helped him to his feet, Audrey coming back to help, before the mutants could regroup and come after them.

Amanda shoved the man through the side door of the truck and told Audrey to take care of him. She ran back in front of the truck to remove the chain from the bumper of the RV. If she didn't unhook it and the truck ran over the chain it could cause the truck to wreck or be damaged so none of them could get away from the hell that was coming through the window.

It took Amanda the count of three to get the chain unhooked. She was going to pull it all the way off, but the first of the monsters was now in the window. It was struggling getting its hips though the hole, but it was making progress. She could see the blackness of its eyes and the desire to consume her. Its jaws were snapping open and closed and dripping with blood from Dan.

She couldn't wait any longer and she had to go.

Swinging back into the driver's seat she had the truck in drive and foot on the gas pedal even before her door was fully closed. She saw the first monster just clearing the window as she got on the street with the RV. From there, it was a straight drive for Amanda and she watched for pursuit in her driver's side mirror.

She almost had to laugh when she saw the chain that she had unhooked, finally worked itself free and hit the monster that was chasing them.

They'd made it.

With the children in back crying and Audrey tending to Dan, Amanda focused on getting out of this little town as quickly as possible. It had been a close escape and she hadn't taken time to process what she'd done. Driving now, safe for the moment she felt her hands shake.

Chopper, who hadn't stopped barking, was still sitting in the passenger seat. He looked over at her. His face reflected the glow from the instrument cluster and headlights. He was panting from the heavy barking, but his tail was wagging.

Somehow, Amanda knew the dog understood they'd done a good thing today. His happiness calmed her.

Amanda finally stopped the RV on an overpass about 20 minutes after leaving Wall. There was nothing to see in the dark and she drove in a circle just to make sure there was nothing as far as she could see.

The children in back had stopped crying and Chopper was acting like he needed a break. She needed one too.

Dan was the first to speak to her and told their story. When people started to die, he and his daughter had supplied their basement as best he could. He found Audrey walking the streets one day, looking for food for the three kids she'd found and taken in. They had been in the church and she'd heard them crying and promised to care for them.

Dan had been able to contact three truckers who were running in a convoy to Ft. Carson Colorado. They'd heard of a military base there where survivors were gathering. Dan said the truckers had heard their call on the CB and stopped in. "That was before we knew about the monsters. They went to the store to get some food and we were going to have a big meal here before setting off.

"Andy," he said pointing to the oldest boy, who looked about 14, "went with them. He came back about 20 minutes later, screaming about the monsters. He came running in the house yelling that the truckers were being eaten.

"I shined my flashlight out the front door and there were two running down the street, coming right at us. That was when we barricaded ourselves in the basement. It was five days ago and we had been trying to get someone on the radio ever since."

Dan didn't know why the monsters hadn't broken though to the basement hide-away. He was just guessing the monsters were waiting until they were hungry again, but he didn't know. They were too afraid to try escaping though the house because of what Andy had told them about the monsters eating the three truckers.

Audrey, who was probably in her early 30s, had short dark hair that was a mess, tattoos on her neck and arms, stood up from the couch in the living area. She hugged Amanda. She had powerful arms. "Thanks to you, we didn't have to do what we were thinking." Amanda didn't ask what that had been.

Dan introduced his daughter Lisa. She was a red-haired girl about eight years old. She, like the rest of the group was dirty and had tear-stains on her face from crying. Dan was sitting on the floor, with his lower left leg bandaged with material from Amanda's Army first aid bag she'd kept with her. Audrey said bones were broken but she'd gotten the bleeding stopped. There were several deep cuts, probably from teeth, but at least he was alive and for that he was thankful. It was the best she could do.

Audrey introduced the other kids. "This is Andy and this is William," she said pointing to the two boys sitting on the bed, "and this little girl is Beth." Beth was a dirty-faced little girl in a blue dress she'd probably been wearing for days. She was holding to Audrey's arm, looking scared and tired of crying. Amanda nodded to the boys and knelt down to be at eye level with the little girl. “Well hello Beth. My name is Amanda. How would you like something to eat? You’re looking a little hungry.”

The little girl snuggled in behind Audrey shyly and nodded. “Okay, let me get things squared away in here, and I’ll fix everyone something warm to eat.” Amanda showed Audrey where everyone could wash up. She turned on the propane tanks under the sink and told them it would take a few minutes for the water to heat up. She pulled the four towels out from the cupboard and handed them to Andy.

Amanda put together a meal of soup with hotdogs, plenty of crackers, a side of peas and peaches for dessert. She apologized for the simplicity of the meal, but Dan told her it was the best food he could remember eating.

Their evening was spent with stories of how the end of civilization had affected them all. Amanda told of her exodus from Alaska, skipping over the suicide of Spec. 4 Johnson and murder of Pvt. Sheppard. She edited the story, saying they had gone their separate ways. She figured she’d save the kids from further nightmares, but Dan and Audrey probably guessed what had happened.

Once the kids were fed and clean, Audrey asked if, for the night, they could sleep in the bed. Amanda said of course and helped Audrey tuck them all in. She could still see they were afraid, but they were so tired. They were asleep in minutes.

Dan was on the couch, leg elevated. He had his arm over his eyes and thanked Amanda again for all she’d done for them. Amanda smiled and told him it was the right thing to do and he’d have done the same for her.

Chopper was sitting by the door and Amanda said she was going out with him. Audrey followed.

Chopper ran off to do what he needed to do. The rain had finally stopped and the sky was clear. The stars above were brilliant and the moon still below the eastern horizon, giving the whole world they could see a peaceful glow.

A flash from behind Amanda made her jump. Audrey was lighting up a cigarette.

She blew the smoke skyward. “Oh that feels good,” the woman said. “You want one?” she offered Amanda. “No thanks. I don't smoke."

"I'm sorry," Audrey said, stepping further away.

"No reason to be," Amanda assured her. "Some of my best friends were smokers and as long as we're outside, I don't mind at all. Although I hope you won't light up in truck. If it were just me, that'd be one thing, but with the kids there…."

"That's funny," Audrey said. "That's what Dan said in his basement. I had to go five days without. Another day and I might have gone upstairs and kicked those monsters' asses by myself for a smoke." Amanda smiled. She'd never been a smoker, but some of the soldiers in her squad were and they could be sneaky when it came to needing a cigarette.

After a few minutes, Audrey asked what Amanda's plans were. "I've been thinking about it and Dan said there was a gathering at Fort Carson. I was thinking we might head down there. If we leave early we can be there around sun down tomorrow. If there is a camp there, we might find a doctor for Dan."

"I think that's a good idea," Audrey said, lighting up a second cigarette. "His leg was pretty torn up. I stopped the bleeding, but there's bound to be an infection and you don't have anything in the first aid kit for that."

"So, Fort Carson it is," Amanda said, kneeling down to intercept her on-rushing dog. "Oh yes, big boy," she said rubbing his head. "By the way Audrey, this is Chopper. I picked him up yesterday and he saved my ass twice already. He can sniff out a beast, what you called monsters, from 200 yards away."

"That's a good kind of friend to have," Audrey said, reaching down to pet the big dog. He lapped up the attention. Amanda got out his bowls and fed and watered him. He ran off one more time when he was finished. Amanda picked up his dishes and stowed them.

She found Audrey a spare blanket and she used one of the towels as a pillow. She said she was comfortable on the floor and would be able to tend to the children if they woke up in the middle of the night.

Amanda stretched out in the driver's seat. She used her jacket as a blanket. It wasn't as comfortable as she'd been the previous night, but as she drifted off to sleep, she wasn't unhappy with why she was doing it. Chopper climbed into his place in the passenger seat and everyone in the RV was asleep before the moon was fully above the distant horizon.

~ ~ ~

CHERYL'S PEACEKEEPING PLATOON GREW TO 19 MEN AND SHE made sure they were well provided for. Some of the platoon's previous members had been forced out and replaced by people she could better manipulate.

Lt. Col. Smith gave her wide autonomy as he was busy trying to make the compound more survivable. As long as she kept the area safe, he left her alone to do as she pleased.

The commander's comm officer, a pimply faced teenager, had contacted two other groups, but they were too far away to try merging with Smith. He was hoping to locate another military installation that survived so he could move his command to someplace more hospitable.

Most of the east coast, including the DC area was silent and refugees from that area told of widespread destruction from a storm that had walked up the east coast, vigilante groups, death, destruction and other horrors.

Vigilantes were roving and living off the land, killing and capturing what they wanted, causing terror and keeping viable camps from flourishing. Women had a chance with the vigilantes, if they were willing to subjugate themselves to the will of the men in charge.

Men and children had less of a chance.

The worst were stories of packs of zombies attacking camps and eating every human body they could reach. Entire camps were wiped out from the beasts. The survivors had been in groups of sometimes as few as six or seven, but some stories saying as many as 30 or 40. They surviving day to day, having outlasted the storms and the fall of the world.

Anything east of Kentucky was a waste of time Smith decided. He was hoping something west might be possible.

Two men were captured by Cheryl's peacekeepers. They were ragged and hungry and surrendered quickly after one of her men rattled off 10 rounds from an M-240 machine gun aimed five feet to their left. They were captured while walking north on I-65, headed toward Louisville.

Smith insisted on interviewing anyone who was captured. The men told the story of being attacked east of Birmingham by a group of 40 to 60 vigilantes. Their story was that they were a peaceful group of 30 refugees from Florida working their way to Texas in hopes of finding a safe haven and settle down. They told of being attacked, their women captured and the men killed. They said they were fortunate to be alive.

Smith had heard similar stories, most recently from Cheryl, but what got his attention was the women. Smith had just 11 women in his compound and almost 100 men. It was not a survivable situation and fights often broke out.

Cheryl listened to the men tell their story to the colonel. She asked how many women were captured and the men told her they'd lost 17 women to the vigilantes. One of the men told of others who had lost women in that area as well. The colonel interrogated the men for an hour and afterward assigned them a house in which to live and a small amount of rations.

Cheryl and the colonel spoke afterward. She pleaded that the women must be saved from a life of torture and rape; that they couldn't be left to the vigilantes. The colonel disagreed, saying he couldn't spare the manpower or the fuel, but Cheryl laid it on thick. She made up stories of indignations suffered by women in past wars and how she and a hand-picked team could go in and use a military surgical strike to take out the vigilantes and save the women.

"If they captured 17 from that group of refugees, they might have as many as 50 to 100 women held captive. I won't be able to sleep at night knowing there are 100 women being raped and tortured by those heathens who have no respect for human life," she pleaded with the colonel, a crocodile tear starting to run down her face.

The men's stories had been an embellishment at best, outright lies most likely, but even if just part of their story was true, that there were women being held against their will, the lieutenant colonel couldn't go home at night and face his wife in good conscience.

If just half of what the men said was true, there might be women needing rescuing and Smith finally agreed to let Captain Cheryl Paxton lead a team 300 miles south to check out the stories the men had told in such detail.

"You can take six HUMVEEs and 20 men, but not more than half the peacekeepers. See Lt. Daniels for armament. You leave in two days," he finally told her. "That'll give you time to find fuel, interrogate the men for intelligence of what you'll be facing and get everyone packed up.

"Down and back in six days, no more, captain. I still need you and your men here. We have a lot of work that needs to be done."

"Thank you, sir," she said sincerely and stood up, saluted and left his office.

She knew without a doubt the men her team had captured were lying because she had been held captive exactly where they'd come from some months earlier. She knew the "vigilantes" they spoke of was a simple farmer, several middle-aged men, a couple old women and some kids, who lived in campers and scratched out a life. They'd be no match for an armed platoon.

They might have brought back some astronauts from the coast, but she recalled Randy telling her the chances were less than a 10 percent. Cheryl couldn't see the farmer and his clan rescuing anyone with a beat up truck and a police van. She figured the spacemen had died so she discounted them.

Cheryl recalled how her quick reflexes had saved her during her escape. Her last action on the farm was killing some guy who ran through the door by shooting him in the head. She wasn't sure if she'd killed Kellie, but was pretty sure the iron bar she'd hit Randy with had crushed his skull. There was a lot of blood on the floor when he was hit so she was certain he was dead.

She'd shot Kellie in the gut and there was no one on the farm who could have bandaged up that wound. If the woman lived, she didn't live long and died painfully, hopefully in the arms of Farmer Jerry, the yokel who had built the shelter, made her wear a dog collar locked around her neck at night, and secured her with leg irons during the day.

Cheryl talked to the men some more later in the day when they could be alone and told them she didn't believe their all of their story. She pulled a gun and said they better start telling the truth or else someone was going to be shot trying to escape.

The older vigilante talked quickly of the attack on the farm and how it really went down. He told her how 14 of 20 men had been gunned down by snipers and machine guns. He wanted revenge because his brother had been killed by the farmer, shot in the head.

When she told him she was taking a team to "rescue" the women there, she asked if they'd made up that part of their story. The man told her he killed at least one and probably two but wasn't sure. "The place was a working farm with a lot of people on it. They had an armored truck we stopped with armor-piercing rounds and killed the driver, but some guy with a machine gun mowed down six of my men."

Cheryl told the two vigilantes they were going with her as "advisers." The one whose brother had been killed, used to be a meat packer and the other worked for a printing company. As advisers, they were pretty useless, but they wanted revenge too and she didn't want them staying here, changing their stories.

Their lives were in her hands and she'd eliminate them when the time was right.

The rest of her team was made up of 10 of her most loyal men from her platoon, some with wives, giving them reason to want to come back alive. She wasn't really concerned with the compound here. She knew she wasn't coming back when she left, but she didn't tell the soldiers that. They'd either be eliminated if they caused problems or move their wives to the more comfortable farm when she was done.

Cheryl also picked 10 other men she could trust who were not peacekeepers and wanted women badly. After many months here, she had found out who she could trust and who were posers and not worth her time. They'd be along as fodder for her planned attack on the farm. She didn't tell them that. They thought she'd chosen them for an important mission and were enthusiastic about it.

When she was done with the Saunders farm, she would own it. She had thought about eliminating Smith and taking over his compound, but Saunders' farm was in a better location, had fewer people, more fuel and warmer weather. Taking the Saunders farm was a much better option than trying to take over this camp.

She ended up with seven fully-fueled HUMVEEs and 22 men for the mission. Five of the HUMVEEs were armed with the M-2 heavy machine gun, one with an M-134 mini Gatling gun and the seventh had a small M-240 machine gun and the radios with which Cheryl would command her platoon.

The HUMVEEs were diesels so they could scavenge fuel on the way. They had manual hand pumps in each of the military trucks.

Smith met her as her platoon was loading up to leave. He told the captain her primary mission was to reconnoiter the farm and form a plan of attack that would allow minimum casualties to the soldiers going with her, rescue the women and withdraw from the area.

If things went well, she was to further scout Ft. McClellan and Anniston Army Depot for more equipment and supplies. She assured him the weaponry she had included for the "rescue mission" would be more than enough for what the two men had told her to expect.

"Once we've rescued the women on the farm and neutralized the threat to others, one squad will escort the women here to safety while I take two others to scout the surrounding military installations, sir." It was a lie to keep the lieutenant colonel from changing his mind. She saluted and the convoy headed out of the main gate of the compound.

Smith turned to Keith, his pimply-faced communications expert who had come out of his commo shack, and told him the woman was "a real soldier." Keith had tried to tell the colonel the people the captain and her platoon were going after were just a peaceful group on a farm with whom he'd been talking for the past six months, but the colonel hadn't listened to him. The communications "nerd" wasn't military, but was the only one on base who knew how to use what few radios still worked. The problem was there were few people to contact and the colonel only wanted to hear about other military bases. He wasn't interested in farmers and refugee camps.

Ever since that woman had arrived on post, the colonel had become even less genial toward Keith.

~ ~ ~

KEITH HAD SURVIVED THE "GREAT DEATH" AS IT HAD BEEN called where he lived. He was the only one he knew of to still be alive from the town of Dry Ridge, KY. He left the empty town on a bicycle because he didn't know how to drive. He was intercepted on I-65 by one of the major's scouting parties and taken to the post.

After interrogation, he was offered protection and food by the camp commander, Lt. Col. Smith. He was given the responsibility of getting the communications gear working when he wasn't on guard duty or working in the kitchen. Keith was envious of Tony and their fresh food, fresh meat and better weather. The two had become friends over the radio and Keith hoped one day he could escape this camp and work his way down to where Tony lived.

The woman arrived a few weeks after the storms that destroyed so many towns near the base. The storms had been part of the hurricane that ravaged the south and his friend Tony's area.

Capt. Cheryl Paxton had pushed the base commander into a more militaristic bent. Keith, having never served in the military began being left out of the colonel's plans.

As Cheryl and her platoon pulled out, Keith again told the colonel of his misgivings about the stories told by the men they'd captured and just sent off on a mission to "rescue" women.

The colonel looked at the young man with derision. "Why don't you shut the hell up and do your job. This is a military operation and you're just a geek with a radio. And just to keep you from warning the farm, you're restricted to quarters until the captain returns."

Keith hung his head and turned away from the colonel.

Tony was his friend and he trusted him. With the weapons and vehicles that Cheryl had taken with her, he was sure the farm wouldn't be able to defend itself. He started walking toward his quarters, not seeing the colonel watching him.

The radio shack with the equipment he used to contact Tony was not far from his quarters. If he'd looked back, he'd have seen the colonel talking with one of his lieutenants.

Halfway back to the radio room, he took off at a run to the shack. He'd try to get a message to Tony before the colonel stopped him.

As the only radio man he figured the colonel might stop him, break his radios, maybe imprison him or even expel him from the base. But at least Tony would know the woman was coming for them.

~ ~ ~

MORNING WAS A RUSH TO THE LITTLE BATHROOM IN AMANDA'S RV, for everyone including Chopper. The sound of kids talking woke Amanda and she felt surprisingly refreshed. Audrey apologized, but Amanda said it was fine. Dan was exiting the bathroom, looking sweaty and drained. He put on a brave face, but Amanda could tell there was something wrong.

There was nothing she could do, so as soon as she and Chopper were finished with their personal needs, she put Fort Carson into the GPS. The numbers came up for a nine and a half hour drive. Amanda knew she could do it with just one stop, but the kids wouldn't be comfortable with it. She handed some CDs to Audrey when the children had been fed and cleaned up so they could listen to some music.

Andy came forward after a while and asked if he could play with her laptop. Amanda knew her journal was still open and she didn't want him reading it, so she said they could after the first rest stop. She heard Audrey sing to some of the Taylor Swift songs and she had a beautiful voice. The kids clapped for her.

Every once in a while she'd look back at Dan and he was looking worse. The towels wrapped around his foot were soaked in blood and had to be changed regularly. His pallor had turned pasty and his breathing more shallow.

Audrey gave him lots of water and his daughter, who had found a note pad, was playing a picture game, where she would draw something and her dad would guess what the picture was.

The activity in back made the miles go by quickly. At the first rest break, Chopper went outside and the kids did too. Amanda checked on Dan and he had a fever coming on. He said his stomach hurt and he had a headache, but he would be fine once he got some more rest. Amanda knew he wasn't going to get better with rest. Blood was soaking through the bandages on his foot too often, so Amanda and Audrey wrapped more towels around it.

She closed and secured her journal and gave it to Audrey for the kids to play games on during the next drive time.

Another three and a half hours on the road and Amanda pulled over so everyone could eat and she could re-fuel the truck from a semi that was parked along side the road.

The kids played outside, throwing a pair of knotted up socks for Chopper while Audrey fixed lunch. It became quite a game for them and allowed them to release some of their pent up energy from hiding in the basement for five days, then another day inside the little RV.

They had tomato soup for lunch with the crackers. Audrey found some fruit cocktail to finish off the meal. Dan was able to keep the soup down, but she could tell it was getting harder for him. His fever was getting worse.

It was about three more hours to Fort Carson and Amanda decided to drive straight through. If there was a doctor there, Dan needed antibiotics and more care than Amanda or Audrey could provide.

Audrey suggested a quick stop for clean clothes for everyone, and Amanda agreed, hoping to find some better first aid equipment. They pulled off the highway an hour north of Cheyanne, but Chopper was displeased so Amanda didn't stop and got back onto the highway. She waited six more exits before trying again. While Amanda fueled the truck and tended Dan, Audrey and the kids found clothes, then it was back on the road.

As they were passing through Cheyenne Wyoming, Audrey put all the kids down for a nap after showers and a change of clothes. She'd been keeping them busy with games on the laptop and cleaning, keeping them from being bored. Now they were all tired out and in the bed. Chopper had gotten tired of hanging his head out the window and went back for a nap beside where Dan slept fitfully.

Audrey came up to sit in the passenger seat. Amanda could tell the woman was being taxed with keeping the kids busy. Amanda looked behind her and saw all the kids were sleeping. "If you want to roll the window down, feel free to light up," Amanda told her. "You look like you need it."

"You sure you don't mind?" she asked, pulling a hard-pack from her denim vest pocket. "I never knew how much work being a mom could be."

"No, go ahead. The kids are asleep and the smoke will be drawn out the window. You're good," Amanda told her. "To be honest, I'm glad you came up front. I can use the company."

Audrey lit up the cigarette with great relish and blew the smoke out the window. She held the cigarette in her right hand so the smoke was drawn outside and she could flick the ashes out. "What up, buttercup?" She finally asked.

Amanda really liked this woman's attitude. "You can start calling on the CB to see if there is anyone around. We're about 45 minutes from Fort Carson, but we don't know if what the truckers told Dan was true or just a rumor.

"Hopefully, we can reach someone on the radio."

Two cigarettes later, Audrey heard a faint reply to her call on the radio. She handed the microphone to Amanda.

"This is Sgt. Amanda Saunders," she said into the microphone, using her military rank, hoping it still had some weight, "of the 52nd Aviation Regiment. Can anyone copy, over?" she released the microphone.

"Sergeant Saunders, this is Sergeant DeBusk from Fort Carson," Amanda heard a man say. "How can we be of service, over?"

"Yes sergeant, we are a party of seven in need of medical assistance. Can you help us, over?"

"Yes we can sergeant. Are you on foot or mobile, over?"

The question struck Amanda as strange – who would be talking on a CB while walking?

"We are mobile, sir. We are currently southbound on US-25, south of Cheyenne, over."

"Very good, sergeant. We are at mile marker 269, southbound to Fort Carson. We have a medic with our convoy. We'll wait for you, over."

"Roger that, sir. We should be there in 20 minutes, out." Amanda put the mic onto the dashboard. Audrey was smiling. Amanda was too, but she was also hiding a little fear because of the Canadians she'd run across. She didn't share her fears with Audrey because Andy took that moment to come forward.

"Are we there yet?" he asked.

"We'll be coming up on a convoy in a little bit," Amanda told the boy.

"Why don't you go wake up the other kids. They'll want to be awake for this. There's other people ahead and maybe some other kids," Audrey told him.

As promised, there was a medic waiting when they came upon the convoy of six military HUMVEEs. There were also heavily-armed guards in uniform. The sergeant, the one obviously in charge, came up to her window.

"Are you Sergeant Saunders?" He asked.

"Yes, and we have an injured man inside. He was attacked by some beasts," she told him, getting out of the truck. She was still wearing the same loose jeans and tee shirt from her run the previous day. The sergeant, who appeared about her age, maybe a few years older, looked at her.

Amanda reached back through the window and pulled out her wallet that she had on the dash. Chopper, who had jumped up into the driver's seat licked her arm as she reached in. She flipped it open to she her military ID. The sergeant looked at it, then back at the medical personnel. "Okay guys, get in there," he told them.

She and the sergeant, who slung his rifle over his shoulder, walked around to the side of the RV, Chopper jumped out of the truck and followed. "He has a daughter in there as well. She's eight. She'll want to stay with him. They've been through a lot of hell."

"It looks like you have as well, sergeant. That looks like blood down the side of your RV."

"Yea, I had one of those beasts try to catch a ride with me. He couldn't hang on anymore once I shot his face off."

"I can't wait to hear the whole story. I'm Sergeant DeBusk, Robert DeBusk," he said as Dan was brought out on a stretcher and taken to the Army truck with a red cross on the side. "You'll be debriefed by someone on the base. You'll probably want hot showers, clean clothes and some food." The kids who piled out of the RV nodded to the soldier.

Audrey was the last one out. "Damn, I love the sight of a man in uniform," she said as sultry as Amanda had ever heard a woman talk. Sgt. DeBusk blushed. "My wife says the same thing, miss," he told her. They stood around and waited for word from the medics. Chopper played with the kids to keep them busy while the sergeant filled Amanda and Audrey in on the base that had been set up at Fort Carson.

"General Angela Parker is the officer in charge of the base. She was a staff general for the Secretary of the Army before Armageddon, that's what we call it. She was on Fort Carson when all the people started dying and when she didn't die, she thought there might be more who didn't, so she started calling out for them.

"From what I was told, there were seven people who were still alive on the base when people finished dying, another 100 or so in Denver, where I was on leave, a few dozen from Colorado Springs and stragglers coming in, like you, show up every few days.

"Parker, who had been a surgeon, and the five soldiers who stayed with her started collecting food and supplies and preserving as much as they could. When people started showing up, Parker made it a community. The more people she got on base, the more resources she had to search out for more people in need.

"Now we have more than 300 people living there, and despite the hell everyone has been through, we hear stories that there are worse places to be," the sergeant said. "You guys have already run into the mutants. You're lucky to have survived. Some people here have lost most of their party to mutant attacks."

Amanda was about to ask about them when the medic came out of the back of the truck and came up to them.

"Well, he's doing better," the medic, who was wearing captain's bars and the Caduceus of the medical field on his collar. "I'll have to take the foot off just above the ankle because of the damage, but the anti toxins have already started working."

"Where's his daughter?" Amanda asked, concerned that the eight year old might have gotten misplaced in the rush to save her dad.

"Private Donnelly and she are playing on a laptop in front truck. Donnelly is just a kid himself and has a lot of games to keep her entertained while her dad is out of it," the doctor told Amanda. "I think we'd best get back on the road sergeant. We've got another two hours before we get back to camp and I'm sure these people would like a nice shower and warm bed."

Soldiers and civilians who were standing around got back into their vehicles at the sound of Sergeant DeBusk's whistle. Amanda, Audrey and her three kids got back in the RV. On the CB, Sergeant DeBusk asked them to fall into line in front of his HUMVEE. He had a Gatling gun mounted on top and was the rear guard for the convoy.

The next two hours were a pleasant but slow drive. Andy and Will played games on the laptop while Beth used Amanda's hairbrush to brush the dog. He didn't move as the little girl brushed him for nearly 45 minutes before falling asleep on the floor with him. Audrey picked her up and put her on the couch and covered her up.

Amanda and Audrey spoke quietly about their histories and what they hoped to find at Ft. Carson. They shared potato chips and Poweraid when the boys fell asleep a half hour out of Ft. Carson.

The sergeant from the convoy had called ahead and housing had been prepared. Gen. Parker made it a point to make sure those coming onto base were made as comfortable as possible to help ease the stressed nerves of the new world they were entering.

The convoy pulled up to the main gate of the base and the second truck in line, an older Army truck, and Amanda's RV were motioned to the side. There must have been a generator running because this gate had high-intensity sodium vapor lights. Two soldiers from the gate came to the RV and politely asked the two women and three children to exit the truck. They did so and Amanda introduced herself and Chopper to the soldier in charge of the gate. "We're glad you're here, sergeant, we really are," the specialist said as the other soldier walked around the truck. "We just have to be careful. Do you mind if we go inside and look around?"

"What if I say no?" Amanda asked, a little off put by her treatment.

"That's fine with us sergeant. If you want to continue on base, you can park your truck over there," he said pointing to a distant parking lot, "and walk on post."

"No, that's okay, specialist. I was just wondering. Feel free to look around," Amanda said.

"I know this probably feels like an invasion of privacy, but we had a couple of incidences with some people who aren't as law abiding as we are. We're just trying to be careful," he told her. "Does your dog bite?" he asked, looking at Chopper who sat beside Amanda.

"When properly motivated," Amanda told him. "He saved my life in Spokane by attacking another dog, and he saved me from the mutants in Montana. He can sniff them out from hundreds of yards away."

"The general will love to hear about him, sergeant. Those sons of bitches have killed a lot of our people and the stories of people coming here have been terrible. Be sure you mention your dog to her."

The private who inspected the interior came out and told the specialist it was clear.

"You're good to go sergeant," he said, putting a sticker on the inside of her windshield. "This will allow you in and out of the base without as many problems.

"Just go inside and take the first left. There's three quarters that have been readied for you and your friends. Someone will be by in the morning to help all of you get settled in if you decide to stay."

Amanda thanked the specialist and followed the Army truck into the base. The truck turned right at the first intersection and followed the rest of the trucks in the convoy. Amanda turned left and drove down to the end of the cul-de-sac. She saw signs out front with "Sanders" written them. Amanda assumed these were the quarters prepared for them.

Amanda and Chopper led the way. Audrey picked up Beth and carried her in, followed by the boys. They found keys in the door locks so Amanda wished Audrey and the kids pleasant dreams. Her quarters were fine for tonight, but she was more interested in moving on to Alabama. She looked through the kitchen and found fresh food in the refrigerator and freezer. Not much, but enough to make a decent meal with meat and potatoes.

While her steak was in the frying pan, she let Chopper out into the fenced in yard and went to the RV to get his food and a change of clothes for after her shower. She also grabbed her laptop and some CDs to listen to.

It felt good to settle in for the evening. She felt safe on the military compound and the food made her sleepy. She didn't make it to her writing or even put the music on. She was surprised she even remembered to let Chopper in and feed him.

Amanda fell asleep with the kitchen light on and dirty plates on the kitchen counter. The shower would have to wait until morning.

She slept long and dreamless.

Chapter 9

Tony was monitoring the radio when he heard Keith's call. "She's coming for you! She...." was all he heard before the gunshots. Tony tried for five more minutes to reach Keith, but with no success.

The silence told the story. He called for Jerry who had returned from the depot 10 days earlier with all sorts of cool Army equipment, including radios.

"I think she's on her way, Jerry. And I think they killed Keith. I heard gunshots then nothing."

Jerry hung his head. He'd hoped for more time to prepare the farm, but now he had to expect Cheryl within a day or two and he didn't think they were prepared enough yet.

Danny had dug up and re-buried the bodies of the brigands far outside their farm. Tony had tested his electric fencing by putting up a strand around the burial plot. When they checked the area the next day through the telescope, they saw four dead zombies, but the burial mound had been dug into and bodies were littered about.

The fence would work to a point, but it wasn't foolproof.

The team had brought back six Strykers, fully armed and fully loaded with fuel. The farm wasn't so large as the vehicles could be hidden very well. Danny, Jamal and Nick built earthen berms so the vehicles could shoot from improved positions.

The kids found ways to camouflage the bunkers and Randy and Kellie gave awards to the best job. Since they had so few people at the farm, two of the armored vehicles were held in reserve near the motorhomes while three others were stationed nearer to the perimeter in the rear, more open area of the farm to give them a larger field of fire. They'd also been positioned so they could with minimal movement protect the shelter entrance.

The sixth Stryker was hidden behind Buff's bunker and would be used to defend the southwest side of the farm. In a fight around the front of the farm, the big vehicle would be limited in its movements because of the limited space.

Kayla, who immediately fell in love with the Apache, got the 30 mm cannon armed and tested. She didn't know enough about the Hellfire missiles, but figured they wouldn't need them against the kind of force Cleve said they could reasonably expect. She was also concerned about contamination of the AVGAS, but when she started the attack helicopter, it ran up to speed without a cough.

She flew it to a spot cleared out near the farm, but because there was no place to hide it inside the fence, it was hidden outside the fenced in area and a trench was dug so she could get to the machine and take off and be in the air in less than six minutes from first call and three minutes if she was sitting in it.

Buff had found both regular and armor piercing rounds by the ton and it took three trips to fill the ammo dump they'd built on the farm. They got all the ammo they wanted.

Eddie and Randy, with help from the military men, took great joy in blowing up the ammo bunker at the depot. Everyone outside on the farm heard the echo of the explosion.

Each bunker now had a weapon that could crack an engine block, but the problem Jerry was finding was not enough people to shoot the heavy weapons. They would make do, he told them. They had what they had and no amount of wishing would change that.

Juan, Josh and Josh's daughter found a pallet of green plastic bags and filled them to use as sand bags around the top hatch of the shelter. Jerry said this was where he'd be and no one wanted the man who had brought them so far, to be hurt.

Kellie and LT practiced escaping from the shelter with the baby, younger kids and Cindy, through the new passage from the cellar of the shelter. They couldn't work a tunnel, but they had enough wood and equipment to dig and camouflage a trench that went from the cellar of the shelter to behind the motorhomes and beyond the fence to a trio of SUVs that were fueled, packed with food and water and well hidden. If things went bad, those who could escape were to head to Indiana and Ft. Benjamin Harrison and ask for sanctuary.

The option to run was raised for the farm to avoid confrontation with Cheryl. It was voted down by everyone who had a vote. Jerry had not meant to create a thriving community where people cared about one another. There was food and water, shelter and friendship. It was hard work, but it was worth it and no one wanted to give up without trying. Everyone knew the risks, but they believed in Jerry and the rest to protect them.

This place had become their new home and they'd not be pushed off it by some vengeful crazy woman.

That evening, when the sun had set and all work had been completed as it could that day, the "command group" met in the shelter's kitchen. There was one person in the control bunker, monitoring the perimeter and one person in a "crow's nest" Nick had welded to one of the wind mills. The crow's nest allowed a 360-degree view of the surrounding area and someone was in it all the time now with binoculars or one of the night vision scopes.

Jerry laid it out for them. He had spoken with Cleve and Buff extensively over the previous few days. He wanted as little bloodshed as possible and the safety of everyone was of paramount importance.

Cleve said an attack would most likely happen in the early morning hours if they had night vision gear. The farm now had the same type of equipment at every bunker. If it didn't come at night, then it would probably be in the early morning.

As far as Cheryl knew, they weren't expecting an attack and her surprise would be a farm armed to the teeth and ready to defend itself.

"We don't know who she's bringing or what they have been told. We don't want to kill innocent men and women who are just following orders to shut down what they think is a violent and lawless encampment," He said as they finished up for the night.

"If we can find some way to communicate our peaceful intentions we will, but if they come in here guns blazing, our first priority is defending ourselves and the people here."

Everyone nodded. They'd all talked about what they would do if attacked and all knew what their individual missions were. They also knew how they fit into the big picture Jerry had laid out for them.

Jerry sent them all off to bed. He didn't know for sure, but felt with Keith's warning there was an attack coming soon and he wanted everyone rested as best they could. As they all left the shelter, Jerry noticed Eddie take Monica's hand. He was happy for them and hoped the next few days went in such a way they could have a happy life.

Kellie watched as Hannah headed back to her mom's motorhome. She had her tablet with her and was reading something on it as she walked with the adults. For a nine-year-old, she was acting very adult and Kellie loved the little girl.

Jerry and Kellie watched until all were safely in their homes. Kellie took Jerry's hand and leaned her head on his shoulder as he looked skyward. He saw the ISS as it passed into the shadow of earth and thought of the Russian commander who died alone in space.

"I was never afraid to die alone," Jerry said. "What scared me was dying and no one caring. He," he pointing to the sky and referring to Col. Rustov, "died after doing everything he could to save his friends. At the time, I thought it was the bravest thing I'd ever heard of. Those guys and girls who just left showed me that bravery comes from all sorts of people."

The two walked back into the shelter, closing but not locking the door. If there were an emergency, everyone knew the escape route for the children went right through the shelter.

Kellie left her surveillance equipment powered on in expectation of the attack.

Jerry already had a loaded sniper rifle, an M60 machine gun with 150 rounds and two radios ready at his position at the top of the shelter. Kellie had Mini-Beryl 96 close assault rifle loaded and sitting next to her desk. The shelter was possibly the most secure area of the farm, but no one was taking chances.

They turned the lights off and went to bed. Both were tired from the long days of preparation, but knew they'd have to at least try to get some sleep. Jerry loved their bedroom as much as Kellie did. It was simple and austere but still had warmth about it.

Molly got on the bed first and Kellie shoved the little dog to the side. Tonight she would lie beside Jerry and the dog be damned. He turned off the light on his nightstand and pulled the blankets over him.

"I love you," she whispered and kissed his neck. "I love you, too, Kellie." He stroked her hair, hoping this was not the last night he'd be able to.

~ ~ ~

CHERYL'S PLATOON MADE GOOD TIME. AFTER A DAY OF DRIVING at 30 miles per hour, she allowed everyone six hours of sleep. She wanted them rested for the next day. The men had brought tents for the overnight. No one wanted to try to clear any buildings in the dark. They found a level area far between any towns and with a good view all around for the sentries Cheryl ordered to stand guard in one-hour shifts through the night.

Her senior NCO and driver, SSgt. Leo Byers, woke her up just before 0500 and gave her 10 minutes of privacy before waking everyone else up. By 0530 the seven-vehicle convoy was back on the road.

She had one of the vigilantes who had attacked the farm in her truck and she questioned him extensively. She learned the farm hadn't improved their defensive posture much since her escape. She believed they were still living in the hope everyone would leave them alone to live in peace and contentment. She did learn about where the farm had its defenses set up from the man when he and his band of thugs had attacked.

She remembered the layout the farm well from when she followed Randy around in those damned leg irons and was sure the simple farmer and his people would have the same defenses that had worked for them before.

Sure, they might have improved them with barricades and maybe some camouflage, but she had the heavy machine guns and M-134 mini Gatling gun which would tear through their wooden barriers they set up.

The more Cheryl thought it over, the more confident she became with her plan. There'd be refinements and she'd have to improvise, but she could do that. The trick was to make sure the soldiers with her didn't realize her real plan wasn't the one they thought they were on.

Cheryl wanted the farm and complete control of it. She wanted Farmer Jerry dead and if things worked out, the fat girl who shot and killed her brother's friend put in the leg irons for a while. After a few weeks of starving her, she'd turn her over to some vigilante group who knew what to do with young women.

With herself in charge of the farm, she could set up real defenses and build a real army, not like that joke Lt. Col. Smith had set up, but a real army of men and women. She'd be in charge and only her most trusted people would be her lieutenants and they'd remain loyal because she knew how to take care of soldiers. The president had declared martial law, which gave her the authority to be the law.

They arrived just north of Birmingham an hour before first light following their breaking of camp. They were able to re-fuel from a tanker truck they'd discovered at a truck stop that had been destroyed and burned. The tanker still had enough diesel to re-fuel all her HUMVEEs.

It was Cheryl's idea they pull the front of a building down using the winch on the front of one of their HUMVEEs. When they did, four zombies came rushing out. They were easily cut down by the four M-2s on the trucks covering the HUMVEE doing the winching. The .50 caliber machine gun could cut a car in half and made short work of the super strong mutant humans.

Inside the building, which had taken damage from the front facade being pulled off as well as the machine guns, the men found some canned goods and beer so they didn't have to eat just MREs. The easy kills lifted the spirits of the men and Cheryl allowed them to celebrate with the beer they found. She didn't let the men get drunk, but because beer was severely rationed on the base if she'd tried to keep them from drinking some of it now, she might have had a mutiny on her hands.

Their morale was as high as she could make it. She allowed them enough beer to feel good and then had the men store several cases for later enjoyment. They were excited about the mission and excited that by this afternoon they might be sitting around drinking beer with dozens of women grateful at being freed from capture.

With the trucks fueled and the men feeling better than they had in months, she laid out her plan of attack. On the ground she drew a rough map of the farm, just like the one the vigilante had drawn for her on a sheet of paper.

While she talked like a military professional with experience in setting up attacks on fortified positions, most of what she was really doing was feeding them bullshit. She'd chosen her men carefully, leaving out any NCO that might see through her lack of knowledge and experience.

Her driver, and the senior NCO of the men she had with her, had been a PFC in the regular Army before the Great Death, but he did have some training, a year and a half of active duty, and was promoted by the commander and Capt. DenHarTog.

Cheryl had served in the Army for less than four years and was given a dishonorable discharge at the end, but she'd edited that out of the story she told Lt. Col. Smith. She spun lies as easy as spiders spun webs.

The men she brought with her on this mission believed she was outlining plans on an invasion that rivaled the brilliance of Normandy with her use of military terms. "The first element will move into position here," she said, drawing the driveway of the farm and locations for the barn and garage.

"There will be improved positions here, here, and here," she said placing pieces of broken stick the ground. "These positions will be neutralized by HUMVEEs Number 1 and Number 2 of the first element. They will work as primary and wingman. HUMVEEs Number 3 and Number 4 of the first element will destroy a barn and garage and provide covering fire for the first element." She tapped the locations of two squares she'd drawn. "They are also tasked with destroying any vehicles, but not farming vehicles. We want to stop anyone from escaping, but not the ability to keep working the farm."

"HUMVEEs Number 5 and Number 6 are identified as the second element. They will enter the enemy base from here after the defenders have focused on the attention on the front of the farm." She pointed to where the back gate was on the farm.

"By the time the second element enters the farm, there should be little if any resistance. They'll be there mostly to close off any retreat by the farmers through the rear entrance to block any escape. Number 5 will stay by the gate while Number 6 captures the motorhome they have parked here.

"My HUMVEE will follow them in after they have put down any resistance. We'll attack the fortified shelter which is at the base of a rather tall hill, here." She made another tap on the ground. "We'll shoot out the door to the shelter and rescue the women inside, who are being held in the basement. We'll herd them into the motorhome and drive them out of there. Once we have them secured, every man who moves on that farm gets neutralized with extreme prejudice.

"No man lives after we get the women secured, even if they try to surrender. They've already shown what type of people they are and we don't need prisoners."

Her real reason was she didn't want any of the men on the farm correcting her story. The lie about women being in the cellar of the shelter was to keep the men interested in the mission.

The real reason she assigned her HUMVEE to attack the shelter was to make sure no one was left alive after the attack. She was sure there were only a few women on the farm and they would be fighting side by side with the men. They would die as well, but by the time the soldiers on the mission discovered this, the farm would be hers. Once the farm was hers, she could control the men and get them some women.

She knew how to control men.

The lies she she'd told the commander of the Smith Compound and the ones she was telling now would all crumble around her if anyone on the farm survived the day. She would make sure no one did.

Cheryl remembered the children being there and she doubted any of the soldiers would shoot kids. She'd allow them to live if they were able to survive. It had been almost six months since she'd been on that farm and for a kid, six months was almost a lifetime. She doubted any child would remember her from the brief time she'd been in the shelter.

"The farmers are armed with high-powered hunting rifles, but our HUMVEES give us a force multiplier, so I expect everyone here to be able to survive.

"They have cameras set up all around the farm, so watch for them and shoot them if you get a chance. They are located in these trees, on the barn, at the top of this hill and along this area," she said, pointing to the map on the ground again.

"We'll be taking back to camp as many as 50 women maybe more, who will be grateful for what you men are doing today. I think your lives will improve markedly," she told them. They'd all had just enough beer to have their inhibitions lowered and they cheered her and her bold plan. She'd whipped them into a fighting frenzy and dangled women in front of sex-starved men. It was the ultimate motivational force for these men.

Any decent NCO would have seen the flaws in the captain's plans. She was going in nearly blind and with no reserve force. She didn't think Jerry and his friends could have set up any type of decent defense or give serious resistance against seven heavily-armed HUMVEEs. She hadn't even requested a reconnaissance of the farm for improvements to their defense. She had one thing in mind and that was to finish wiping those people off the face of the earth.

Those people had captured her, killed her brother and a close friend and two other associates. Now she was going to repay the favor. If the farm survived, great, if not, she'd find someplace else to take, but she swore that no adult living on that farm was going to live to see the sunset.

The men broke up and headed back to their HUMVEEs. The vigilante who had been in her truck grabbed her by the arm. "I didn't tell you anything about a shelter or motorhomes. You've been there before," he deduced correctly.

"Take your hand off me you piece of shit or I swear to God you will wish you'd never breathed air," she said very quietly through clenched teeth. The man let go and she saw fear in his eyes. "Yes, I was there and I was held prisoner. There are some seriously sick bastards there and I intend to kill them all. People like them don't deserve to live. Now shut your hole and get in the truck."

She hated the vigilantes whose opinion of the farmers was exactly the same as her opinion.

~ ~ ~

General Angela Parker was everything Amanda imagined her to be and more. Amanda had been awakened by Chopper needing out before the sun was all the way up. While he was busy, Amanda found a jogging suit in the dresser along with clean socks. She took Chopper with her on a two-mile run. Other soldiers were out, most running in groups of four or five, doing morning physical training as well. They waved and smiled at Amanda running with her dog.

When she was returning to her room, she was met by a young soldier knocking on her door. "I'm already awake, soldier. What can I do for you," she asked as she and her dog walked down the hall to her room.

"Good morning, Sergeant Sanders," the private said referring to his note. "I'm from General Parker's office and she'd like to speak with you when you're ready."

"That's great and my name is Saunders. Can I get 10 minutes to clean up and change clothes?" she asked, unlocking her door so she and Chopper could go in.

"Oh yes, sergeant. She told Lt. Nila she saw you out running and he was the one who told me to come get you." The private waited in the hall. "I'm to wait here for you." Amanda could tell the private was nervous for some reason, probably because the dog weighed as much as he did. "You don't have to wait in the hall, private…." She couldn't see his name tag because of the rifle he carried.

"Private Sweet, sergeant."

"Private Sweet. Please come in. While I change, please make some coffee so we don't have to make the general wait."

By the time she was changed into new clothes, Sweet had

the coffee made, poured some cereal in a bowl and filled a glass with milk. He had also fed and watered Chopper.

"Thanks for taking care of him, Private Sweet," Amanda said, toweling off her hair and pouring milk into the bowl of cereal. "I hope he doesn't get upset having to stay in that fenced in area while I'm with the general."

"Oh no, sergeant," the private corrected her. "The lieutenant specifically said the general told him to make sure you bring your dog. He's out finding a leash and that's why he sent me."

Amanda finished her breakfast while letting Chopper out the back. She didn't want him making a mess in the general's office.

She hadn't tried putting a collar on him, but the way he acted, she assumed he'd been trained. She dug through the clothes she'd brought in the previous night and found a belt. When Chopper came back in, she knelt down and scratched behind his ears. He tried to lick her face when she put the belt around his neck. The dog had a big neck, but not as big as her waist so she took it off and used a fork to put another hole in the belt. When she put it on him, it fit loosely, but she didn't think it mattered.

Amanda locked up the apartment and she, Chopper and Private Sweet walked to the general's office. It was a nice morning, cool without being cold, spring breeze and clear skies. Chopper romped around the two as they walked, sniffing at everything, but not straying too far from Amanda.

They arrived at the office and Private Sweet saluted Lt. Nila who came out of the building holding a length of rope.

"Chopper, come," Amanda told the dog and he came over to sit beside her.

"You've got a well-trained dog there, Sergeant Sanders. If he doesn't need a leash, I don't see any reason to tie him up.

"I'm Lieutenant Nila, the general's aide. When she heard about you and your dog and his special talent, she was anxious to meet you. She actually wanted to meet you last night when you first got here, but Sgt. DeBusk told her you guys had come from the darkest pits of the worst hell and you'd probably want sleep more than you wanted to talk with some general."

"I appreciate it, sir, and the name is Saunders, not Sanders," she told him. "Someone must have got the spelling wrong.

"And this is Chopper. He's my superhero," she said patting Chopper on the head. He licked her hand.

"Sergeant Saunders it is. If you plan on staying in the Army for a while, I can have Private Sweet get you some uniforms, boots, the whole works. I can even make sure he knows how to spell your last name," the lieutenant said, eyeing the private. She knew who had made the spelling error now. She didn't think the private would make the same mistake twice.

"I don't really know what we're going to do, sir," she said as he opened the door for her and her dog and they all went inside and down the hall to the first office on the left. "I was headed to Alabama where my dad and brother lived, but I lost most of my clothes in Canada, attacked by dogs in Spokane, mutants twice and just spent the last month and a half staying ahead of freezing to death and the Grim Reaper. Last night was..." she broke off as the general came out of her office. Everyone in the room snapped to attention. Even Chopper, who sat next to Amanda's scratching hand, stood up.

The general had a warm smile and she used it on Amanda and her dog. "At ease, everyone," she said and the two soldiers behind desks in the office sat back down and went back to work.

"You must be the Sergeant Saunders everyone has been talking about," she said, reaching out to shake Amanda's hand.

"I am she, ma'am," Amanda said, returning the firm handshake, "but I don't know why everyone is talking about me. I just got here last night and haven't met anyone except these two since I got on base."

"Please, come into my office and let's get comfortable, unless you're in a hurry to get back on the road."

"Yes, ma'am. I mean, no ma'am," Amanda had never had to speak with a general before and Gen. Parker had her off balance. "What I mean ma'am, and as I was saying to the lieutenant, last night was the first time in a while that I slept without thinking I was going to wake up to some horror."

The two women went into the general's office and the dog

followed. The elder offered Amanda a cup of coffee which she accepted. Chopper lay down next to Amanda's chair. The lieutenant brought in a plate of fresh apple and orange slices and a rawhide bone for the dog and closed the door on his way out. Chopper looked at the bone, then Amanda, then the bone again. "Well, go ahead, Chopper. It isn't going to eat itself."

The general sat down behind her desk and laid it out why she was famous. "The man you brought in, Dan, told our medic a fanciful tale of how you rescued him and five others from certain death. He then went on to spin a yarn about how you drove down from Alaska on your way to Alabama.

"Sgt. DeBusk, our intrepid explorer who you met last night on the highway, told me a wild tale you told him about escaping from a pair of mutants, including shooting one that had gotten aboard your RV and running over another one with your truck.

"He goes on to say, you have a dog that can sniff out these mutants from hundreds of yards away," the general said, not reading from notes. Amanda listened and nodded but didn't say anything. The general hadn't asked any question so Amanda wasn't sure what she was leading up to.

Parker smiled at Amanda, who was looking uncomfortable with her story being unfolded in front of her. To Amanda, it sounded more impressive when the general told it, than how she remembered it.

Amanda remembered more about how afraid she'd been and how she broke down and cried twice in the same day.

"I'll give it to you straight, Amanda," the general said, showing just a glimpse of weary of the roll she was in, "We've lost 17 good people to those mutant bastards. Every time we go foraging we have to be so careful, and even when we are, we still lose people.

"Now, Dan and Sgt. DeBusk's stories seem too impressive and before we gone on, I want you to tell me they are exaggerations on your part."

Amanda looked the general officer straight in the eye and told her they were true. "Ma'am, I didn't do anything anyone else wouldn't do. Dan needed help and I helped him. As for the mutants, if Chopper hadn't stopped me, I'd've gone in that store and I'd be dead now. Chopper and I saved each other from a pack of wild dogs and we've been together ever since."

The general told Amanda she believed every word. When Amanda finished her cup of coffee the general refilled it. "Tell me about Fort Wainwright, Amanda."

Amanda told her about how everyone except for the captain and private had died on base and their decision to head to Anchorage. She told about meeting Johnson and his taking of his own life, the captain parting ways with her and heading off in search of his family, the murder of Shep by the Canadians, the entire story. She left out minor details, made no embellishments and kept to the major points.

The general listened without commenting or interrupting.

When Amanda was finished, the general asked Amanda if she'd like to go for a walk around the base with her. Amanda thought it was an odd request, but knew Chopper wouldn't mind going outside again. He'd finished destroying the bone he had been given.

"I'd like that, ma'am. I haven't had any time to enjoy a walk without worrying about something or someone trying to kill me."

The two women walked outside and Chopper immediately found a tree. They walked and talked about how the general came to command the base, and what she was trying to do to keep as many people alive as possible. They had fuel for generators, but that would run out eventually and they were working on other forms of power. They were scavenging from the air force base in Cheyenne and from Ft. Collins. Every bit of non-perishable food is being stored and we're working on a number of other initiatives.

"I'm working on building a self-supporting community, Amanda, but we need everyone to help, and that's the problem."

"I don't understand ma'am. From what I've seen, everyone seems to be working together, I see well-fed civilians and soldiers and you have electricty here. At Wainwright, we lost power even before everyone had died."

"There is a lot more going on than you can see, dear girl," the general told her. "There are roving bands of thugs who have attacked our rescue convoys. They've killed more than 30 people that we know about and captured seven women who were with them.

"That's why Sgt. DeBusk met you with loaded guns and ready for an ambush. Between the bandits and the mutants, we've lost 72 soldiers and civilians in the last three months.

"We have been working hard to keep enough food and water and we have a safety margin of 36 days right now. I know it sounds like a lot, but our first crops are 80 to 110 days away. We have a dairy set up and there's enough food for everyone right now, but next year, we will have a harder time of it, and the year after that. It's going to be hard. Making it harder is the refugees coming in from the south who need us.

"There was a hurricane that ripped through the south two months ago and we're still getting wanderers in. They need food and medical attention and housing. It's like we are an oasis in a desert with the only food and water available."

"I hadn't thought about it ma'am," Amanda told her honestly. "I'd only been thinking of myself and wanting to go home to see if my dad and brother were alive. I already know my mom didn't make it. I saw her house in Spokane. She died with my step-dad beside her." She hadn't told that part to the general and there was a hitch in her voice when she did now.

The general, who was two inches shorter than Amanda, put her arm around her. "I'm sorry, Amanda. That had to be rough."

They walked passed barracks and soldiers in uniform walking by saluted the general as they passed. There is some positive news, however," the general told her. "There's a colonel in Indiana who has a community growing like ours. We're able to contact him via shortwave a few nights ago.

"We heard about a compound near Travis Air Force Base in California that was nearly wiped out by a 200-foot tsunami. The Perry Compound survivors near Sacramento are attempting to make contact with them.

"The problem is we lost two full teams before we even knew the mutants were out there. We're more careful now, but still we lose personnel every week.

"I think you can help us."

"Ma'am?" Amanda asked.

"I'm not going to pretend to order you, Amanda. I know you've done more than your share already and you'd like to get home. I'll help you on your way with fuel and food whenever you want to go, but what I'm asking, is for you to stay here with us for a few months and help us before you go.

"You and your dog will be part of our scavenging team and I think the two of you will help save a lot of lives.

"In return, we'll provide you a nice house, food, water and power, with a big yard and repeal the leash laws for Chopper. I'll even give you a HUMVEE of your own to drive while you're here so you don't have to use your RV.

"If it would help, I will draw up paperwork for your honorable discharge so you won't feel obligated to stay here. I don't know how long you have left of your military obligation, but you seem like the kind of person who honors their commitment, even if there is no one to make sure."

Amanda saw that the general was good at reading people and had pegged her for exactly what she'd been thinking. She had introduced herself as "Sgt. Saunders" even though she knew there was a complete breakdown of civilization. Amanda had just extended her enlistment to get the advanced leadership training and maybe flight school before everyone started dying.

The two finished walking around the fenced in area of the camp. Amanda saw areas that were a hive of activity and places where there was nothing.

The general had given Amanda an out if she wanted it. She could leave the base, fully fueled and stocked with food. In three or four days she could be in Alabama, because she would have to stop in Mississippi first. She had promised herself when she was crying on the ground with Shep's head in her lap, that she'd attempt to find his mom and tell her how brave he'd been.

Amanda watched as Chopper loped around the area, tossing his head and picking up sticks for her to throw. The general had alluded to the hurricane in the south. If her dad and brother had survived the plague that had killed everyone, the hurricane, which the general told her had lasted for two full days and wiped out a number of camps up the east coast, had been as bad she said, it was doubtful her dad's farm was even left on the map. She remembered her dad telling her about Hurricane Frederick, a small hurricane that had nearly wiped out Gadsden before she was born.

Eventually, she'd want to go back home, if for no other reason than to pay her respects to her dad and brother.

"Ma'am," Amanda said to the general after walking in silence for several minutes. "I joined the Army to see the world. The world is now really different than it was three months ago.

"Like I said earlier, last night was the first night I slept without being afraid and I slept well. I think I am right on the edge of losing my mind sometimes and am going to wake up from a dream, but I never wake up.

"I know how you feel, Amanda. I feel the same way myself, especially when Sgt. DeBusk comes back from a trip with three fewer men than he went out with, like he did last night.

"We have farmers and electricians, mechanics and teachers, we have laborers and managers. What we need, Amanda, are soldiers." The general then shut up and the two walked while Amanda thought. It took a few minutes, but eventually the general had her answer.

"If I can get some uniforms and some gear, I think Chopper and I can be both physically and mentally ready for duty tomorrow."

The general, who had been walking close beside Amanda, slipped her arm around her once again, more as a motherly figure than the senior military officer in the United States Army. "Thank you, sergeant," she said and Amanda could tell the general meant it.

"I'll have Lt. Nila set you up with housing and you take the rest of the day off. Tomorrow morning about oh nine hundred, you report to his office and we'll get all the paperwork started."

"I already have an apartment, ma'am."

"I know you do, but it's not big enough for you and Chopper. You're in one of the apartments where we put all the new people. If you are going to be on permanent duty here, we have something with a much larger yard and a garage to park your RV in.

"In fact, if Lt. Nila is as good a prognosticator as I think he is, your house is ready for you now." The general pointed to a very nice two-story house with a two-car attached garage. "My house is the second one down. Lt. Nila and his wife live between us. I hope you'll be my guest for dinner tonight and we'll talk more about things then.

"I've got to get back to work, now sergeant, so I'll see you tonight around 1900?"

"Yes, ma'am. And thank you, ma'am." Amanda saluted the general, just as if she were in military gear. The general saluted back and headed off in the direction they'd come.

Amanda liked the looks of the house and Chopper didn't seem to mind either.

It wasn't home, but it was enough home for now.

CHAPTER 10

"DUST ON THE DIRT ROAD!" CAME THE CALL FROM the crow's nest.

Morning had broken and chores were finished on Jerry's farm. Everyone had completed breakfast and there were hopes the attack wouldn't come today.

"Looks like three or four trucks!"

The alarm for combat stations was sounding now. Everyone was moving quickly but without panic. The children, led by LT were headed to the shelter cellar and followed by Cindy who had stopped to retrieve baby Adam.

Eddie, after making his report, scrambled down from the tower. His combat station was one of the Strykers which covered the area south of the shelter. Three of the big fighting vehicles had been staged behind berms on what had been dubbed windmill hill on the far west border of the farm. Anything coming around the hill south of Buff and Nick's bunker was his. He'd also be protecting the south side of the shelter and the motorhomes which were being evacuated.

Monica had the middle Stryker with the Gatling gun she'd learned to use. There was a large wooden obstruction made from railroad ties in front of her vehicle to keep her from shooting toward the shelter entrance, or Tony, who was 30 feet in front of her inside the storage building, or the motorhomes. She'd be looking far left and far right for targets.

Randy was in the northern-most Stryker on the base of windmill hill, beside his friends Eddie and Monica, even though 150 yards separated the three Strykers. His primary mission was defending the shelter and Jerry, who would be in his sniper position atop the shelter directing the defenses. Jerry had provided a walkie-talkie to everyone, and a command set Tony had rigged in case the attacker's frequency was found.

The elderly deJesus's opened the hatch of middle Stryker of the reserve force and climbed inside. They might be old, but they were ready to fight. They would be protecting the windmill Stryker force from their concealed position between the motorhomes and the parapet in front of the shelter doors.

Sade and Jamal were in the second reserve Stryker. They were responsible for defending the north side of the three Strykers arrayed along the base of the hill where the windmills were located south and west of the shelter. Tia and Tim manned a Stryker which guarded south side of the shelter and protected Buff and Nick's bunker.

Josh and Natalie were manning a pair of bunkers that protected the escape route of the children and the north side of the farm. If they were evacuated, Josh and Natalie would drive the first two SUVs and Cindy the third which were hidden there. The north side of the farm needed the least amount of watching because the heavily wooded area had been booby trapped with noisemakers and flares. Anyone attempting to come at the farm from that direction would give their positions away and have to fight through the tangle of briars and trees. They'd be picked off easily.

Tony was in his office in the storage building and was being protected by Katie and Karen, neither of who could safely shoot the .50 caliber rifles. They'd been armed with AR-15s and would only shoot at enemies that were within 100 feet of their position. They'd also be watching for anyone moving toward the shelter door.

Tony would be alternating between trying to contact the Indiana camp on the frequencies he's been given by Keith, and watching the cameras, giving Kellie as much help as he could.

Kellie was the voice of calm across the radio. She'd be relaying what she saw on the monitors in the shelter. She'd be letting everyone know where the attackers were and where they were trying to get to. Her voice would be the anchor for the people defending their home. She would also keep Jerry appraised of injuries to the people on the farm.

Kellie, protected by the Padre, was also responsible for the kids. If the farm was going to be overrun she was to send the kids and Cindy to evacuate via the SUVs. She would be relaying information to Jerry so he could direct everyone's fire where it was most needed. The Padre was with her to help her watch the cameras and for her defense.

Cleve made it clear in the morning discussion, the most valuable commodity the farm had was the people. The barn and the garage were expendable. The cattle, chickens and pigs were not worth a human's life. They were betting that the invaders wouldn't be using mortars to "soften up" the farm because they wanted to take over the place.

Cleve manned a bunker in the tree line 150 yards to Jerry's left and down the hill. Danny was with him. Buff and Nick were in a mirrored position to the right, protected from any rounds coming from the Strykers by 30 feet of earth. Both were armed with the high-powered .50 caliber rifles and each had clips filled with armor piercing rounds.

Jerry's choice of weapons was an M60 machine gun and a .50 caliber L96 sniper rifle they'd picked up at the Anniston Depot. He had four 10-round clips for the long gun. He'd shot it a few times to make sure the action worked and was impressed with the way it destroyed reinforced concrete walls from 500 yards away. Cleve and Buff told him he wasn't to shoot the weapon unless it was an absolute last resort. The gun was loud and would draw fire and Jerry had to direct the defense, not become an active part. They also said the sandbags would not be protection if a .50 caliber machine gun zeroed in on him.

From where Cleve would be positioned in the bunker, it would be up to Jerry to direct the battle this time. Cleve would be focusing defending the east and south of the farm. Jerry had argued this, but Cleve's military training would be better served with him behind a gun while Jerry had already proven he could direct fire accurately. Jerry also had lived on this property all his life and knew every hill, valley, path and rock.

~ ~ ~

AMANDA SPENT THE MORNING MOVING HER CLOTHES INTO THE

house. She and Chopper walked back to the apartment and got their RV. They saw Audrey and her kids. They were on their way to the clinic to see Dan. Amanda made them promise to stop by in the afternoon and gave Audrey her address and showed her where it was.

As good as her word, the general had the power on and the refrigerator and shelves were stocked full. There was a large freezer filled with frozen meats and vegetables. Amanda didn't want to think about who lived here before her, but whoever it was, was a wonderful house cleaner.

Amanda resisted the urge to turn on every light to banish any shadows, knowing power must still be at a premium and she didn't want to waste it.

Out the back door, through the kitchen, were a patio and a large fenced in yard. Chopper checked it out and Amanda had to find a trash bag to clean up his mess. Walking through the house, there was a gas furnace and water heater, but also a good-sized fireplace.

There were three bedrooms, two bathrooms and a library, a dining room, living room and an office with a computer. The garage had a tool wall and large Mac toolbox. It took Amanda about two minutes to pick the lock on it and see it was a complete set. There was also an air compressor and some wood-working tools. In the top of the tool box was a picture of the family to whom this all likely belonged. It was a handsome colonel and wife and their daughter. The daughter was wearing a graduation gown. Amanda left the picture where she found it.

There were no other pictures on the walls of family or friends and Amanda assumed the lieutenant had made sure it was all cleaned out so Amanda didn't think she was moving into a dead person's home.

Amanda was upstairs, putting her clothes in the closet of the huge master bedroom and Chopper was still sniffing through the other rooms when she heard a knock at the front door.

She raced Chopper to the door and she nearly slid into the door on the wood floor in her socks. She'd have to remember to keep Chopper's nails clipped short to keep from ruining the floor. It was the private that had come to meet her earlier. "Sergeant, I have your uniforms and gear."

"Okay, let me get my shoes and coat and I'll be right there," Amanda told him.

"Oh, no sergeant," he looked over his shoulder, put two fingers in his mouth and whistled. Another private got out of the green Army van and opened the slider. "Private Kerry and I will bring it in. General Parker told me that this afternoon, I am your slave."

Amanda smiled at the young man. She tried to remember his name but couldn't. She tried to get a look at his nametag, but he turned around to go help his friend get the gear out of the van.

Amanda couldn't help herself. "Sweet," she said. The soldier who had come to the door stopped and looked at her. "Yes sergeant?" That was when she remembered his name, Pvt. Sweet.

Covering her memory lapse, she asked "Are you sure you don't want some help?"

"Absolutely not, sergeant. If the general caught you out here hauling this stuff in, she'd have me back on sewage duty." Amanda didn't want to think about what sewage duty was, or how Private Sweet had gotten on the detail before.

The two privates brought in five large boxes of gear and an M-4 rifle. They also had magazines for the rifle and the box for ammunition.

Amanda let Chopper out the back door, but left it propped open if the dog wanted to come back in. When she got back to the foyer, Sweet was sending the other private back to their office.

Amanda was looking at him, wondering why the private was still standing in her house. "Uh, sergeant. General Parker told me to be your slave. She don't say a lot, but when she does, I've learned to do what she says. She's the smartest soldier I ever met and it's a shitpile of a world out there and I would be dead now if it weren't for her and what she's done here." She wasn't going to argue and could use the help getting all this gear squared away before Audrey and the kids came over.

She found out that when on duty, everyone carried their rifles. Amanda had noticed the officers had side arms and every other soldier who wasn't doing PT had their rifles slung across their back. "We've had three mutant attacks in the past month here. They come at night, that's why you see the bright lights around the outside. They don't like the light."

The uniforms already had her name tag. She asked how they knew what size to get her when they got the boxes upstairs, and the private shrugged. "The lieutenant used to work in supply and called it in while you were talking with the general this morning. He said you were a little above average tall, slender athletic size and you had a size seven and a half wide foot. I don't know how he does it, but I bet it all fits."

Amanda pulled the uniforms out of the boxes and sure as shit, they would probably fit better than her previous uniforms. She put on a pair of OD socks and tried on the boots. They felt good on her feet. It'd take a day or two to break them in, but they'd do fine.

Between the two of them, they got everything hung up. Amanda found an iron, but she wasn't going to have this private iron her clothes. This slave work he was doing was not something she liked having foisted upon her.

"Private Sweet, if you can find me a military watch, I will set you free," she told him. "You have been a mighty good slave, and I'll hate to lose you, but I do need a watch."

"I'll get you one sergeant," and off the young kid left in a rush. Amanda wondered if he was even 18 years old. He was back in 45 minutes with three watches. She chose one with luminous hands, a stopwatch and a compass. It had a thick canvass band and when she put it on, it fit and felt good.

"Thank you for your help this afternoon, Private Sweet. Since you are my slave, I give you the rest of the day off. If anyone asks, you're still my slave until sundown," she gave him a wink and walked him to the door. "Thanks again, sergeant. And if you ever need someone on your team, I'm in the personnel pool." She closed the door behind him and leaned against it. Chopper came running in and skidded up to her. He looked thirsty and Amanda rubbed his head and went to find his dishes.

Audrey and the kids stopped by later in the afternoon. They had Dan's daughter with them. Dan was doing better, still coming to grips with losing his foot, and the five of them had been given quarters just a few blocks away in a house not much smaller than this one. Audrey had taken a position as a mechanic in the motor pool for starters. The children would be attending school. They were going shopping for clothing at the base exchange for everyone and all of them were going to the park before going back to visit Dan. Amanda told them to give her best to Dan, but she had re-joined the Army and had a meeting already scheduled for tonight.

Audrey and Amanda talked for a little while longer, sharing some things they'd learned about the base while the kids played with Chopper. Amanda soon understood the civilians weren't told everything she'd learned, so she kept the private things the general had told her to herself. She was happy to hear the kids would all be together in the same house.

After they left, Amanda took a long bath and luxuriated in the water for a long hour. She had soft music on in her bedroom and it wafted in from her bedroom. She might have even fallen asleep for a few minutes, but if she did, it had been a brief nap. She felt relaxed and refreshed. She looked at the digital clock on the master bath's wall. She had more than an hour until she had to be at the general's for dinner. She wasn't sure what to wear, but since they were going to be talking about what position Amanda would fill, she figured it wouldn't be improper to wear her uniform.

By five minutes to seven, Amanda was ready. She wasn't sure if bringing Chopper with her would be the best decision, but she knew Army dog handlers kept their dogs with them or in cages, and general or not, Amanda was not putting Chopper in a cage. She thought about leaving him outside, but there was no shelter for him and she didn't want him to feel abandoned. She reasoned herself into taking Chopper with her. It wasn't far and if the general didn't like it, she could always bring him back.

Amanda was knocking on the general's door at precisely 1900 hours. A car was pulling up just as the general opened the door. "Oh good," General Parker said honestly, "I was hoping you'd bring him along." She reached down and patted the dog. "Hello, Chopper. I'm glad you could make it too. Come on in, both of you. That's Sgt. DeBusk and his wife pulling up now and Lt. Nila and his wife Carol are already here. She was happy to see three of the four were wearing uniforms like Amanda and the general. Only Carol was in civvies.

The lieutenant introduced Amanda and Chopper to his wife and they welcomed Sgt. DeBusk and his wife Sara to the evening. "Okay everyone, let's get comfortable. Supper will be out of the oven in 20 minutes. Drinks?" asked the general.

"I'll get them, general," the lieutenant's wife said. "I've got to check on the roast anyhow. A gin and tonic for you, a beer for my husband, rum and Cokes for the DeBusks and what'll you have, Sergeant Saunders?"

"Um, please call me Amanda, Carol. And I'm sorry. I'm not a drinker," she looked a little sheepish as she said it. "I like ice water, ice tea or a sports drinks."

"No need to apologize, Amanda, neither am I. And I always make sure the general has plenty of tea, coffee, soda, beer, or liquor in her house for whoever she plans on entertaining for the night."

"And that, Carol, is why I like you better than your husband," the general said, her smile and the small chuckle from the lieutenant making it clear it was a joke between people who knew each other well.

"Amanda," the general began, "the other person who you'll hopefully meet in a few days is Major JJ Solomon. He's my executive officer. He's out on a mission right now, but should be back by the end of the week.

"How much did you pick up today from young Private Sweet?"

Amanda wasn't sure if Sweet had been sent to find out her loyalty, if there were some office politics going on or something else she was missing. As her dad always told her to tell the truth because it was easier to remember. "He said something about slavery and a sewage plant I don't think he ever wants to work in again." The lieutenant and sergeant laughed. "He told me how to get to different buildings on post, where the motor pool was, the base exchange and things like that. He actually gave a very good orientation and he was very helpful about getting my gear and weapons."

"That's good to hear," Parker said. "When I first met him, he was locked up at the Provosts Marshall's Office. I heard him screaming to be let out when I got to him. He and I came to an agreement and I let him out. He hasn't made me regret it."

Amanda didn't inquire into why he'd been incarcerated. She took the young man at face value until he showed her a different face.

"Well, here's the basics," the older woman continued as Carol brought out drinks. "I'm probably the most senior officer left in the USA. Major Solomon, from the Air Force is my exec and the Nila is my aide. Solomon was admin, not a pilot which is too bad because we could use some pilots.

"There's also a second lieutenant who is our computer specialist. We are the entire officer corps.

"We have 11 NCOs, you among them, and 64 lower enlisted. We're from all branches of the military, including a Seaman Apprentice from the Coast Guard who was home on leave in Pueblo when Armageddon struck and a Norwegian Lance Corporal who was training here.

"We call our unit the 1st Mid-America Defense Force and we might be the only real military unit left as an active unit, although Col. Hammond in Indiana seems to be making some good progress.

"Our mission is to protect the community that is growing around us. The last order given by the president was martial law, which, according to Solomon, my legal expert, allows me to make the law.

"We have 354 civilians living on base now on a post that once housed tens of thousands of soldiers and families.

"We are slowly combing the surrounding area looking for survivors and salvaging as much of civilization as we can and bringing it here. Fortunately, we also have two computer experts in the civilian populace who are doing what they can to get a computer network running.

"Our mission, as I see it, is to keep the ideals of the United

States, the ideals on which it was built and lasted for more than 200 years alive. The laws that were passed are the laws we will live by. We might truncate some of the legal process, but the laws remain in effect. So far, no civilian lawyers have come forward and the crime rate, as far as we can tell here on post, is negligible.

"There are roving bands of thugs and bandits who we've heard about who are attacking whoever they come across. We've not captured any, but some of the survivors told stories. If we come across them, we'll give them a fair trial and mete out punishment.

"Then there are the mutants, and that's where you come in, Sergeant Saunders. They've killed way too many of us already. There is no reasoning with them and they are not even human. They may have been once, but they aren't now.

"I've assigned you and Chopper to Sgt. DeBusk's platoon. They're the platoon that does most of the salvaging from the surrounding areas. Sadly, it is also the unit with the highest casualty rate. I think with you and Chopper however, that'll change for the better.

The general was interrupted by Carol who said the meal was ready. Everyone moved to the table and they enjoyed lighter talk. The general, it seemed, didn't like to talk business while eating. After dinner, Carol asked Amanda if Chopper could have the bone from the roast as they moved outside to the general's patio. It was a cool night and Amanda was thankful she had worn her military uniform.

Lieutenant Nila told her how she could restock her provisions as they got low and reminded her to pick up her HUMVEE in the morning. It was waiting for her. He warned her about the blackouts that would happen during a mutant attack as power was re-allocated to spot lights and told her she'd be assigned an alert position at a later time. He encouraged the use of the chain of command, which for her was in this room with Sgt. DeBusk as her platoon sergeant.

Sgt. DeBusk said he was pleased she had been assigned to his platoon. He was infantry by training. He knew Amanda was a helicopter mechanic by trade and her general mechanical knowledge would be welcomed. Amanda told him about

Audrey's skills and he agreed that the newcomer would be very welcome in the motor pool.

They talked more about the 1st Mid-America Defense Force and different situations they might be in and Amanda decided staying here, under the command of Parker, might be the best thing for her now. She was safe, believed in what Parker stood for, and didn't have to worry about her next meal.

The conversation lightened up and it was a relaxing evening for everyone.

When the lieutenant yawned, Parker looked at her watch. "I think you're right, Stan. We might all want to call it a night. Sergeant Saunders, it was a pleasure having you over. I hope we haven't overwhelmed you."

"No ma'am, not at all. In fact it was a very pleasant evening for me, ma'am," Amanda said, unsure of the proper protocols for leaving a general's home after a party. She didn't want to seem rude, but she also didn't want it to look like she was waiting for another invitation.

It was the DeBusks who saved her. The sergeant's wife, who wore PFC stripes and who had been mostly silent during the evening, took her husband's arm. "Come on, Robert. You've still got to fix our water heater tonight."

"Yes, dear," her new boss said, kissing his wife on the forehead.

"Still didn't get that fixed yet?" asked the lieutenant as he and his wife walked with them to the door. Amanda didn't hear the rest of the story. She had to collect up the bone Chopper had been chewing on all evening. He came when she called, but he left the bone and she was sure it might not be good to leave his bone on the general's patio.

The general held the door for her as she came in with her dog and walked with her to the entryway door. Quietly she said to her, "Let's just you and me get together in a few days, informal and relaxed. You seemed rather unconfortable tonight, dear. Next time you come over, we'll have hamburgers on the grill on paper plates and we'll wear jeans and tennis shoes."

"Yes, ma'am," Amanda said to her, smiling and feeling comfortable with the informal conversation. "I look forward to it." She was the last one out, and the general waved to them all, closed her door, not stretching the good bye out any longer.

The DeBusks lived on the other side of the base and the Nilas lived in the house between the general and Amanda and they made small talk as they walked across the grass. Amanda thanked them again for a good evening and told the lieutenant she'd see him in the morning.

It felt good to be home. The general had been observant about Amanda feeling out of place and stiff. Chopper went immediately to the back door and Amanda let him out. She'd left one small night light on in the house to find her way. Chopper could do his business in the dark so she left the patio light off. She looked up at the stars and they were clear, just like in Alaska and just like the stars she'd seen from the hill on the farm where her dad told her he had built a windmill for his hole in the ground. She smiled thinking of her dad and his crazy ideas.

Maybe her dad's ideas were not so crazy any more.

Amanda got Chopper's bowls out and filled them. Chopper lapped up some water and nibbled at his food without enthusiasm. He'd been snuck scraps from the roast Carol had made for everyone at the party.

When Amanda went inside, he followed. She needed to get some sleep because tomorrow she would become a soldier again. With clean linens on the bed, a short shower and a warm room, Amanda was asleep within minutes of her head hitting the pillow.

Chopper was her alarm clock, which was fortunate because she'd forgotten to set one. She looked at her watch after having her hand licked, shaking her out of an unusual dream. It was just before six.

~ ~ ~

WAR HAD COME TO JERRY'S FARM.

Everyone was in position faster than Jerry could have hoped which was good because the four HUMVEEs coming down the road were in a hurry and tore through Nick's repaired gate and Tony's high-voltage wire without slowing. The fence sparked and the gates swung on their heavy hinges, opening up for the HUMVEEs.

Two of Kellie's cameras went down as the first and second HUMVEE dragged 150 feet of fence off its posts as the drivers came through the main gate nearly side-by-side. Two shots with armor piercing rounds hadn't stopped the HUMVEEs and the soldiers manning the M-2s seemed surprised someone was shooting in their direction already. They'd been led to believe this would be a total surprise. They started raking the hill to Jerry's left and several rounds hit very near the bunker where Cleve and Danny were ensconced.

"Stop shooting. Cease fire," the public address system for the farm roared with Jerry's voice over the noise of the HUMVEEs. The shooting stopped.

"We are peaceful civilians with women and children. We will defend ourselves, but we don't want to hurt anyone."

The second HUMVEE's gunner heard where the speaker was broadcasting from and shot it to bits. The man on the microphone had said there were women here and the gunner hadn't had a woman in more than a year. When he started shooting again, so did the first, looking for the bunker that had been shooting at them.

Buff and Cleve began shooting in earnest and the armor piercing rounds exploded the glass of the first HUMVEE, injuring the driver and causing the vehicle to drive off into the field of sweet corn that had been planted. The guy manning the M-2 was thrown clear and had his legs crushed when he was run over. Jerry could hear the man's screams from his position high on the hill.

Two other soldiers in the back seat of the truck were thrown to the floor when the HUMVEE went nose first into the culvert that went under the driveway.

The third and fourth HUMVEEs raced through the front gate while the second kept Cleve's bunker busy. They began hammering the garage and barn with their big guns just as they had been ordered to do by Cheryl.

Danny used his sniper rifle to pick off the gunners when the drivers stopped. Neither gunner was killed, but one was wounded and bleeding, sliding back inside to the relative safety of his HUMVEE and the other ducked inside to keep from being hit by the deadly fire.

Jerry, from his vantage point, watched as rounds from the two bunkers hit dirt and metal on the three attacking HUMVEES.

The first HUMVEE that had crashed into the culvert near the end of the drive wasn't dead yet he soon realized. With everyone's attention drawn to the other three, one of the soldiers put the first HUMVEE's machine gun back in action. The sound caught Jerry's attention and he snapped his view to where new shooting was coming from. Following the tracers, he saw a line of rounds walking its way up to the front of Cleve's bunker.

"Get down!" he hollered toward Cleve's bunker, not bothering with the walkie-talkie. He couldn't tell if anyone was hurt with the quick look he took over the sandbags. Buff and Nick were still working on trying to disable the third and fourth HUMVEEs.

The driver of the second HUMVEE that'd come through the gate saw that stopping was a bad idea so began a serpentine drive further into the compound. He wanted to get out of view of where he presumed the snipers were getting shots at him.

Buff was unable to get a good shot at the engine block or the driver. He shot out a tire and Nick peppered the side of the truck, but it was coming at them quickly. "Down!" Buff hollered at Nick as he saw the truck's main gun train on their bunker.

Nick died quickly when he was hit in the face by the attacking soldiers' machine gun fire. Buff's voice came over the radio next, his words accompanied by the sound of machine gun fire. "Nick's gone," he said sadly. He was breathing heavily.

Everyone on the farm was listening to the exchange. Jerry was now calling out targets. There was no joy in his voice, just grim determination. They heard his strong voice "Go get 'em Tia! They're after Buff!" Tia's Stryker, already idling, pulled out from behind the camouflaged berm.

All she had to do was drive the big Stryker, looking through the periscope. The first time she'd ever driven one was when they called her to the depot to drive one back to the shelter.

Tia stopped the HUMVEE 30 feet to the right and behind Buff's bunker. Tim, the refugee from Florida, manning the machine gun atop the vehicle, was a former fisherman and not familiar with conservation of ammunition. He fed nearly the entire belt of ammo in and around the HUMVEE. It wasn't professional, but it was loud and the HUMVEE wouldn't be attacking anymore.

Jerry watched Tim empty his machine gun and screamed for him to stop, but the man had seen vigilantes or brigands tear through his previous safe haven. He wasn't going to let it happed again.

HUMVEEs three and four were circling looking for a place to hide from the snipers during the attack on HUMVEE number two. They heard a different M-2 speaking and saw their number two HUMVEE being torn apart, but not from where the shooting was coming.

The drivers of the HUMVEEs ordered someone to man the M-2 on their trucks again and kept moving. They hadn't seen the Stryker, but they knew if they worked together, they could take out the bunkers on either side of the hill behind the barn and garage. Their job of destroying the garage and barn and making sure any vehicles were disabled was complete.

They hadn't expected such resistance and hoped the captain would call a retreat or send in a reserve force, but she was busy elsewhere. The third HUMVEE came around the hill just enough to shoot at Buff's position while the wingman kept steady suppressive fire on Cleve's position.

As long as they kept moving in the swerving circle, they were a target too hard to hit and they would eventually get the people in the bunker.

On the third circling they finally saw the armored vehicle and quickly switched tactics. Instead of circling and weaving an ever larger racetrack, they hugged the buildings, taking pot shots with their heavy guns at the bunkers as they passed between the buildings and skirting the edge of the hill.

If Tim hadn't used up his ammunition he might have been

able to get off a shot at them. As it was, Tim hollered that he was out of bullets. Tia thought for a heartbeat, and then did the most unexpected action anyone could think of. "I learned to drive in Detroit, you bastards, and that's my boyfriend you're shooting at," Tim heard her say as she took off after the HUMVEEs. Tim was forced to duck back inside the armored truck as Tia maneuvered her Stryker to chase the HUMVEEs and exposed the fighting vehicle to the M-2's .50 caliber machine guns.

Something must have jammed on the first HUMVEE's machine gun, the one in the ditch, because the soldier who stuck his head out of the top was pulling the charging handle. Jerry saw the man clear a round and when it started shooting again it was providing harassing fire whenever they saw one of the farm's defenders shooting. He changed targets from the bunker Buff was shooting from when he saw what Tim had just done to the second HUMVEE. When the Stryker didn't fire at the HUMVEEs they knew its .50 cal was out of ammunition and began shooting at it with everything they had.

"Kayla!" Jerry hollered into his radio. "We need you now!" The two HUMVEEs that had come through the front gate last were blistering the bunkers Jerry and his friends had built, and the one Stryker they had protecting the front of the farm with short, controlled bursts.

One of the reasons five of the Strykers were positioned on the back side, the south side of the farm was because the 16-ton trucks needed some room to maneuver. The landscape in front of the farm lent itself to being defended by the bunkers that had been designed by the former Marine, Buff.

Both the bunkers had been dug out by Danny and the forward facing side built up with tree trunks with slots cut in them for the people manning the bunker. The trunks were buried with rocks from the piles Jerry had removed from his fields over the years and covered with Alabama clay before being camouflaged. There was a narrow escape route in the rear of the bunkers and a grenade hole in the floor. If someone tossed a grenade through one of the shooting slots, the person inside the bunker could kick it down the grenade hole, where it would drop down a 4"-inch pipe that was set at an angle.

When the grenade went off, the explosion would be absorbed by the ground and directed out the end of the pipe which was aimed to the rear of the bunker.

Jerry looked over his sandbags. The first HUMVEE, the one leaning nose-first into the ditch and had a screaming man beneath it, had a new gunner shooting at Tia's Stryker. She was fearless and reckless trying maneuver the Stryker to where she could ram the HUMVEEs. The M-2 on top of her truck was in pieces and two of the eight tires shredded. The rounds were deflected by the armor, but eventually, with the amount of fire being thrown at it, the Stryker would become Tia and Tim's coffin.

Jerry was more than 300 yards away from the first HUMVEE and about 200 feet above it. Tia's Stryker wasn't maneuverable enough to get a ramming shot, nor had the turn radius to box the HUMVEEs into a corner. Her vehicle was being shot from beneath her and she wouldn't last another minute unless something was done.

Neither Cleve nor Buff could shoot without exposing themselves to the HUMVEEs withering fire, so they were forced to keep their heads down.

Jerry heard Kellie's plea in his ear. "Someone help her." Kellie was very fond of Tia and her plaintive cry pushed Jerry to do exactly what Cleve and Buff told him not to do. He got up on one knee, lifted the big L96 to his shoulder, glanced briefly through the scope and took a shot at the HUMVEE in the ditch.

The shot knocked Jerry on his ass and he fell through the sandbags that were double stacked around his vantage point. He'd been kneeling and wasn't prepared for the kick, even though he knew the big gun had one.

The bullet missed his intended target, which was the gunner, but the 23-ounce round traveling at more than 3,000 feet per second tore through the mount of the gun that was shooting at Tia, causing it to fall onto the head of the man whose legs had been crushed. Jerry got off the ground and back to his knees to make sure the first HUMVEE stayed out of the fray. His shoulder ached, but he'd shoot again if he had to.

Now, only the HUMVEEs Tia was chasing could shoot at

her and they were not aiming very well. She had a few more minutes, though her Stryker was still being shot up. He hoped Kayla got the helicopter in the air in time.

The action and the voices on the walkie-talkies had everyone riveted. They assumed Cheryl was in one of the main attacking vehicles and they were not willing to allow her to escape again or to chase them from the farm. Kayla was now less than a minute from lift off with the helicopter and, Jerry prayed silently, she would put an end to this ass kicking they were taking.

"Hold out for two more minutes, Tia! Kayla's coming!" Jerry hollered over the walkie-talkie. Everyone knew it was a risk to use the Apache. Kayla had flown helicopters before and was an accomplished pilot, but it had been years, and never in a flying weapon. The Apache was a state of the art gunship designed for one thing: killing. They never found a helmet for her, so the 30 mm in the nose of the helicopter was able to shoot only straight forward of the Apache.

If the Apache failed to intimidate the invaders, or if it failed to shoot, the farm would be at a further disadvantage and against trained soldiers.

A minute could be forever when lives hung in the balance.

~ ~ ~

PRIVATE SWEET HAD DELIVERED PT UNIFORMS THE PREVIOUS day to Amanda's new home and she felt like using one this morning. She let Chopper out before changing. By the time she'd stretched and changed, he was ready for the run too.

It was cooler than previous morning, but the sun was up and bright in her eyes. While running, she made a mental note to replace the sunglasses she'd left in Alaska. There were a few others out running as well. She fell into the back of a squad of six soldiers whose pace matched hers. The soldier who was singing cadence had a good voice and it was comfortingly familiar for her.

The squad ran a varied course and varying speeds. Chopper kept pace easily. After about 45 minutes the leader of the squad ordered them to a quick time march in front of the lower enlisted men's barracks. Amanda stayed with the squad as they did warm downs and when the leader dismissed the squad for showers she caught him before he went inside.

"I'm Sergeant Saunders," she introduced herself as she rubbed Chopper's ears. He was drooling from the run. "Do you do a run every morning?"

"Yes, we do sergeant," the man told her, as he snapped to parade rest.

"At ease soldier, at ease. Relax. I'm not here for all the lock step. We're soldiers, but this isn't basic training."

The young man relaxed a little, but Amanda could see he was still very new to the Army. "Do you have a name?" she asked him.

"Private Pinkston, sergeant."

"Well Private Pinkston Sergeant, this is Chopper. He and I like a good run in the morning before breakfast. I enjoyed it and by the looks of him, he did too."

"Just Private Pinkston," he corrected her, not getting the joke until after he'd said it. When he did, he finally smiled and hung his head. "Sorry. We try to start around six every work day. Sometimes we have more, sometimes fewer, but Lt. Nila knows I was a runner in high school. She encourages the soldiers to take part in PT, but the work they do every day is rather intensive, so no one is going to get out of shape if they don't do PT.

"And I think the L-T doesn't want to piss anyone off. We need all the help we can get from everyone.

"What do you do here, Private Pinkston?"

"Today I will be transferring more fuel to the storage tanks again. I've been doing it for a week now. We've got almost 5,000 gallons this week.

"What about you, sergeant? I saw you come from officer's country…." Amanda knew immediately why the private stopped his questions. He was thinking she was new here and some officer was trying to impress her by "sharing" his house with her while she got "acclimated."

"Oh shit. No, it's nothing like you're thinking. Chopper is the reason I'm in officer's country. He can smell mutants."

"Oh! You're the lady who killed ten mutants and saved 20

people from Canada. We all heard about you yesterday. I really thought you'd be taller."

Amanda chuckled. "No, those stories are really exaggerated. Anyway, I have to get to the general's office. I've been assigned to Sgt. DeBusk's platoon. If you don't mind, I'll try to join your PT sessions when I can."

"Please do sergeant. The men didn't bitch and complain the entire run like they usually do. You're good for morale." Amanda smiled. There had been no women running with them, but she had seen women out running. Maybe they were afraid, but Amanda wasn't and maybe she'd start a trend.

"Thanks, Pinkston, we'll see you around." She started walking back to her house.

"Oh!" he called to her, "If Sgt. DeBusk is looking for anymore in his platoon, I'm available.

"I'll tell him," she told him. Amanda got the impression, despite the casualties Sgt. DeBusk led the platoon every one wanted to be in.

It took an hour for her to shower, iron her uniform, brush her boots and get breakfast for her and Chopper. She didn't want to show up to the motor pool too early and Lt. Nila was expecting her at 0830.

She sat down at her laptop and wrote for 20 minutes, catching up her journal to the point of contacting Sgt. DeBusk on the highway two nights ago. That was when she realized, she had no idea where the motor pool was.

"Come on Chopper! We've got 45 minutes to find a building on this base, get our truck and get to work!"

She was locking her door when she saw Nila leaving for the office. He was already on the sidewalk and Amanda hurried to meet up with him. She saluted and said "Good morning, sir."

He returned her salute and kept walking. "Morning Chopper," he said to the dog who sniffed at his leg, then ran off to find something more interesting. "You're up early, sergeant."

She told him she was on her way to the motor pool, but didn't know where it was. He pointed her in the right direction and they parted ways. She caught up to Audrey who was a block in front of her. The tattoos and cigarette were a give-away.

"Morning, Audrey!"

"Hey, kid. Good to see you. Nice uniform, I wouldn't want to wear anything like it, but it looks good on you." Amanda grinned. Audrey had a leather jacket over her denim vest over a blue tee shirt and was wearing jeans and cowboy boots. No apocalypse was going to change her.

"I thought you would be off Armying or something."

"Yea, I start today. How's Dan and the kids?

"Good and getting better," Audrey said. "They're going to release Dan this morning and I got the kids on the school van this morning. They're still in some shock and Beth cried, but they need other children to play with. They have a teacher here who was a professor of educational development and he is great with the kids. There're about 20 of them, from Beth's age up to 16 years old."

"I'm glad to hear that they'll have friends about their age." They talked while they walked until they got to the motor pool. The bay doors were already open and there was a black senior NCO in Navy uniform sitting in a chair cleaning parts and smoking a fat cigar.

"Hey," he called to them. "Git yer asses in here. We gots lots ta do ta-day." His voice was scratchy from years of smoking and giving orders. "You the swabs?"

Amanda spoke up first. "Sergeant Saunders. I'm here to pick up a truck that was supposed to be assigned to me?"

"Oh, shee-it! You're the doll who killed those 20 dead things that aren't dead and saved a passel of kids from that tidal wave. Damn glad to meet you girl," he said, standing up and reaching out to shake her hand, after wiping his own hand on a shop rag.

Amanda shook it. "Actually, those stories are getting very exaggerated. This is Audrey. She's been assigned to you."

The senior NCO, who looked to be near 70 years old, heavy in the gut, missing a tooth and most of his hair, looked at Audrey. "Well, I guess I gotta take what I git. Can you make coffee girl?"

Audrey looked the Chief Petty Officer. "I can sailor, but if you call me 'girl' again, I'm going to kick you hard enough, you'll be able to scratch your nuts with a Q-tip.

"Not only can I make coffee, I make it so it'll grow hair on your bald head. I can also rebuild gas and diesel engines, repair transmissions, troubleshoot, do body work, and run every piece of electronic equipment you got in this hole you call a shop.

"Now, do you want me making coffee or fixing these trucks old man?" Amanda didn't say a word. Audrey had obviously encountered people like the chief before in her line of work.

The old NCO rubbed his head and muttered to himself. "I came outa retirement for this shit?" then aloud said, "fine, what's yer name agin?"

"Audrey. Call me Audrey and nothing else or I start kicking your ass."

"Fine, Miss Audrey. I'm Master Chief Cecil Cadwallader. Call me Cal or call me Chief, it don't make me no nevermind. Yer now shop form'n.

"I don't got no time for teachin' anymore so yer in charge of makin' sure the guys they sen' over don' break more shit than they fix.

"The las' kid they sen' me wrecked more trucks than he could make work. Five E-nothings will be here in about 20 minutes and they're all yers. Train 'em how you want, I'm just here for the paperwork and porn on the computers.

"Have at it," there was a pause as he was making sure she knew she had earned his grudging respect, "Miss Audrey."

"As for you little missy," he said looking at Amanda. "Yer a damned hero, little lady, and I gave you the best truck we got. It's right over there." He pointed to a HUMVEE that was painted flat black.

It looked like it was new off the showroom floor with new tires and a heavy-duty winch on the front. "Adm'rl Parker said to give you the best one we gots and that's it. It's got ceramic armor in the doors and bullit-proof glass. That mount on the top is fer one of those super-type machine guns that shoots a million rounds a second.

"Key's are in it." The sailor was a man of a different Navy than the one now, and he was far from any ocean, assigned to a motor pool, doing what he could to be a part of the base.

"Thank you, chief. And it was a pleasure meeting you." She walked toward the truck and called Chopper who had been sniffing the area. When she opened the driver's door he hopped into the passenger seat and Amanda rolled the window down for him. "Let's get to work boy."

~ ~ ~

THE TWO REMAINING HUMVEEs WERE DOING EVERYTHING right to keep the forces on the farm contained and focused on them. They were becoming more confident in their abilities after surviving in battle now for more than six minutes.

The Stryker trying to crash into them had been effectively neutralized…tires were being blown out, main gun empty and the armor was being torn away. It was no longer a major threat even though it was chasing after them.

The bunkers too had been neutralized. The men in them couldn't stick their heads up without being shot at by first one, then the other HUMVEE's heavy machine gun.

Their hunger for battle, something to kill, had been whetted by the zombies at the truck stop earlier that morning. Now they saw an opportunity to satiate their hunger by defeating the entrenched farmers and taking down a Stryker. This morning the reward had been beer and canned food. This evening their reward would be women.

Their confidence was as high as it had been since entering the farm. True, they had lost two of their HUMVEEs and some of the soldiers in those were dead, but the two others were still mounting a good offense. They knew they had the upper hand and were going to end the battle with discipline, superior firepower and a better battle plan.

Everything a looking very good for the invading force until Kayla popped up from behind the tree line that backed up to Cleve's bunker and Jerry's position.

"Oh shit," the driver of the fourth HUMVEE shouted when he saw the Apache monster on which Kayla had painted a bright pink smiley face. Instead of swinging his truck's M-2 toward her, the man panicked and started screaming at his driver.

Dr. Kayla, with surgical precision, followed the instructions she'd read in the helicopter's manual. She flicked the master arm switch, chose "gun" and began hitting the area around the HUMVEEs with 30 mm shells. She could have destroyed the trucks, but Jerry had said he wanted a minimum loss of life. She began circling the HUMVEEs and had to tip the nose down to fire, but she'd put nail polish on the windshield which allowed her to aim the chain gun under the nose of the gunship.

The helicopter was just clearing the trees to take on the three remaining HUMVEEs in the front of the farm when Kellie's voice broke through the talk on the radio again. "Back gate! Trucks coming through!" She then lost her cameras to that part of the farm as three HUMVEEs came crashing through the gate. The Gatling gun on the first vehicle, manned by a pro, took out four cameras and the truck in the middle with the smaller machine gun took out another one.

The men in the three trucks were the most savage of Cheryl's platoon. They were here for the women and the guns and the property. She'd filled them with promises of sex, alcohol, power and food aplenty. They were here for all the things Jerry had worked so hard to achieve but they wanted. Cheryl thought they'd fight the hardest and not have any qualms about killing the men on the farm.

So focused was everyone on the battle in the front of the farm, the attack through the back gate surprised the defenders. Cheryl had planned it that way. She had expected the defenders to all be looking at the front of the farm and ignore the rear entrance. She really believed she was a modern day warrior.

Jamal, from the closest Stryker guarding the rear gate, was able to get off just one shot before his main gun jammed. After a tense few seconds of trying, he told Jerry the gun was broken.

The shot surprised the driver of the first HUMVEE who swerved away from the spot he'd been directed to park and defend. There was no way he was going to stop there and let some farmer with a .50 cal pot shot him and his truck.

Randy, whose Stryker's main gun was pointed too far to the right, swung the barrel around in time to get off a stitching shot into the third truck which swerved and crashed into the first motorhome, the one Tia, her four kids and Buff, lived in. Bullet holes appeared and paint chips flew from the impacts.

Sade, driving Jamal's Stryker, said he was moving to block the back gate, but Jerry told him to hold off. "I want them to have a way out and you have no way to defend yourself. Stay where you are and watch for soldiers on foot," he told them.

Randy wanted to make sure no one snuck up and attacked his dad from the blind side of the tree line. They hadn't expected the attack to come in two waves. It wasn't something anyone had thought about. They weren't military people on the farm except the astronauts, and they were more scientists than military strategists.

He started his Stryker and backed out of the revetment. The big engine coughed and stalled. He couldn't get it restarted. He called his dad on the radio and told him his vehicle was out of action and needed someone to watch his flank. He then climbed out of the Stryker to do something his dad told him to never do.

Jerry was angry because things were going from bad to worse. Three of their six Strykers were now unusable, the one in the front of the farm was being shot up, the helicopter was no guarantee of victory, and now, his son was calling again.

"I got an idea, dad," his son told him as he crouched beside the big truck. Jerry looked to where he knew Randy was parked and he could just see the berm Randy was parked behind through the trees. He watched as Randy did something stupid.

In that moment of time, Jerry's mind raced through all the mistakes he'd made raising his son. He remembered the times when he was too harsh with his words, the times he coddled the boy instead of letting him grow in his own direction, the times he forced the boy left when he wanted to go right. In the time it takes for a memory to be retrieved and remembered, he said a quick prayer to God for the safety of his son.

Jerry's focus came back quickly. He hated making the decision, but he hated more the thought of losing his farm, his friends, and most of all, his family. "Eddie, Monica, cover Randy!" he hollered to the kids in the other two Strykers parked near the far hill.

He hated moving them in case either of the two HUMVEEs in the front of the farm decided to make a run for the shelter entrance. The helicopter could cover both of the still moving trucks, but it would be hard pressed to cover those trucks if one of the others started shooting. The men in the bunkers had taken a lot of fire and were probably still trying to get a grasp on the situation.

From where he was hidden above the shelter and behind sandbags, he couldn't see where the deJesus's were exactly because of trees, but he knew his farm's layout. "It's your turn Mrs. deJesus. Please be careful," he said over the walkie-talkie, his voice a little calmer than the orders he'd shouted to Eddie and Monica.

The deJesuses were older people, he a former correction officer, she a school administrator. Both were in their late 60s and Jerry had hoped putting them in a Stryker, between the motorhomes and the shelter, far from either of the gates, they'd be the last to have to be used.

He almost called Kayla and her helicopter to the back of the farm, but if he did, Tia and Tim and probably both bunkers could be lost. He had five Strykers defending the shelter in back and he had to trust the plan Cleve had devised.

"Jamal and Sade's Stryker is out of action and Randy's Stryker just died," Jerry told them. "You guys have got the entire back of the farm to protect and watch out for Randy because he's running across the field like an idiot!"

Time was both going in slow motion and super speed for Jerry.

Eddie heard the three HUMVEEs in the distance. He had no good view to his far left because of the camouflage, bushes and trees. He scrambled back inside his truck, started it and drove over the front of the revetment he'd been hiding behind. "It's time to show these carpetbaggers how us southern boys play rough!" Jerry heard him say over the radio, surprised Eddie had remembered anything from his fifth grade history class.

Mrs. deJesus pulled her Stryker straight out of hiding when told to by Jerry. She hadn't driven a car in 15 years, but she insisted she'd be with her husband in this battle. Her husband Juan let the main gun clear its throat into the engine block of the first HUMVEE in the line of three. Its engine went up in smoke and came to an abrupt halt 40 feet from the Stryker.

The second HUMVEE crashed into the leader as it tried to swerve out of the way of the stopped vehicle, stopping along side the first. Juan put a burst of rounds through its engine block too, one of which exploded the radiator creating a steam screen of the third truck. The correction officer then pinged a few rounds off the top of each truck, keeping the men inside cowering.

The two dead HUMVEEs were at the far left of Monica's sight and she played with the mini gun on her Stryker, throwing rounds into the tires of the second HUMVEE. She loved the sound of the mini-gun when it burped out 20 rounds with each the pull of the trigger. "This is better than sex with Eddie," she said over the radio.

The gunners in the trucks were thrown around and when they tried escaping or shooting back, Juan or Monica would fire off a few rounds to let them know they were outgunned and out maneuvered. They were surrounded and they were just realizing their Capt. Paxton had led them into an ambush.

Monica's shots kept the trucks from moving off because she was deadly accurate at hitting the tires. She'd wanted to put a few rounds into the trucks themselves, but Jerry had asked everyone to show mercy if they could.

Just for fun, and because she liked the way the Gatling gun sounded, she'd let loose a quick burst. "It looked like that tire was trying to re-inflate," she told everyone.

She had to stop shooting when Eddie's Stryker crossed in front of her at top speed. She kept her hands, which were sweating from the excitement, off the trigger. She'd grown rather fond of Eddie and was pretty sure he felt the same toward her in his own immature way and didn't want to accidently shoot his skinny little ass.

Juan, however, wasn't feeling as good covering the trucks. The old man did not enjoy what he was doing. The heavy machine gun was loud and the vehicle shook his arthritic arms painfully, but he stood his ground.

He'd seen enough hate and pain in his life as a correction officer. He'd seen death and anger and too many convicts with a total disregard for human life. He was tired of it and when he and his wife retired, he had hoped for a dozen years of time with grand children and travel with his lovely bride.

Instead, he was here fighting so he and his wife could live in peace.

Eddie, seeing the third vehicle that had entered the rear of the farm crash into the escape trench after being shot Randy, told Jerry what he was seeing. He also saw Randy running toward the crashed HUMVEE. "You're right Jerry. Your son's an idiot, but God love him, look at that fat ass run."

"Natalie, Josh, watch out for intruders in the trench! Don't let them get to the SUVs," Jerry told the two defenders who were probably the weakest team when it came to shooting. They were in a bunker guarding the escape route for the children if they needed it and Randy believed that was what the soldiers in the third HUMVEE would attempt. Randy wanted to make sure no one was able to take the kids' escape vehicles.

~ ~ ~

CHERYL HAD BEEN CERTAIN THE FOUR ATTACKING HUMVEEs in the front of the farm would draw all the attention away from the back entrance. She ordered the three remaining vehicles in what she claimed was a "classic pincer" movement to attack through the rear gate two minutes after the first began attacking in the front. She was just realizing that the military plan she'd laid out for her platoon was falling apart when the crews in the first HUMVEEs started calling for help on the radios. They couldn't be helped. Cheryl's dip into obsession with the destruction of Jerry's farm and everything on it had taken her from obsessed to insane.

The first truck in her element knocked the gate off without slowing down, and gunners on the front two HUMVEEs shot out the cameras just as they had been instructed. She was feeling confident of her plan until she heard the report of a .50 cal from her left. The first truck was supposed to stop at the back gate and guard it so no one could escape, but instead the driver accelerated. She started to say something on the radio but was interrupted when her truck was hammered from the right and the windows shattered throwing glass everywhere.

Cheryl's plan was going awry and she wasn't sure why. She'd planned the attack, chosen the soldiers and knew she would succeed. She hadn't expected resistance of this magnitude. She knew the farm would put up a fight, but she hadn't expected the heavy weapons.

She was about to order her driver to the front of the shelter when another shot blew out their left front tire. The truck's already injured driver lost control, careening hard left, hitting the big blue motorhome that was the last in a line of more than half a dozen. The HUMVEE came to an abrupt halt when it fell into a ditch, landing on its nose with all four tires off the ground.

The shattered glass that had left her slightly bleeding had really made a mess of her driver's face. He hadn't been wearing his seat belt either and the impact had knocked him out cold. She looked behind her to check on the vigilante from whom she'd wrung so much "intelligence" on the farm. There were five holes in the door in a vertical line and hole in the rear passenger window, head high. The hole in the window told the story of where the man's head had gone.

Cheryl clambered out of the wrecked HUMVEE and into the ditch. She recognized it for what it was: a trench for escaping from the shelter. It hadn't been here when she had been a prisoner here. She'd been all over the farm, supposedly helping Randy while he helped install the security system.

Randy thought she was trying to prove she could be trusted. When Cheryl had been first captured on the farm, only Randy had anything to do with her. He brought her food and listened to her story of how she'd been captured and raped and tortured. He believed every word of her lies. She used his inexperience with women to tease him with her body. She flirted with him; let him believe she was attracted to him. As the days passed, Randy began to trust her more and allowed her more freedom.

Eventually, she talked him into coming to her cell for a

"date." He brought a TV and a DVD player for a movie they were to watch together. She'd teased him into believing she was willing to go all the way with him.

When his back was turned, she clubbed him on the head with a piece of pipe she'd stashed. When he was unconscious or dead on the floor, she escaped the farm after shooting Kellie in the gut and Danny in the head. As she was running, she was chased by a big dog and she shot that too.

This entire mission was her way of getting revenge on the simple farmer and his friends. Now she was after Jerry, who she knew they were protecting in the shelter.

Outside the vehicle, she had just her side arm, so she stayed in the trench. She kept her head down as she followed it back toward the shelter.

The farmer had built a fortress, heavily defended with armored vehicles. She'd underestimated the hick. The electric fences had been new too, but they had not slowed the attackers.

She passed behind the Stryker that was keeping the first two HUMVEEs in her element pinned down and heard another one coming fast. "Where in hell would they get Strykers?" she asked herself.

Someone was also shooting a mini-gun farther away and the bullets were impacting above the trench she was in. She knew it wasn't her group. "Where'd they get a mini-gun?" she asked herself as she moved through the trench.

Cheryl saw the Stryker and thought if she had been in that kind of vehicle instead of the HUMVEEs the colonel had allowed her, she could have taken this place by herself. As it was, her entire professional military force was being wiped out by a bunch of old people and farmers. It wasn't fair.

Then she heard the distinctive sound of a helicopter on the far side of the hill. "Where in hell did they get a bloody helicopter?"

~ ~ ~

AMANDA FINALLY MET THE 14 MEN AND WOMEN IN THE SALVAGE Platoon with whom she'd be working when she pulled her

HUMVEE into Sgt. DeBusk's training area. There were three other new people in the platoon. They were replacements for the three men who had died in the attack by mutants the day Amanda met their convoy on the highway.

Sgt. DeBusk, a former infantry squad leader, was an excellent trainer and team builder. He introduced Amanda as his assistant platoon leader and Chopper as the team's supernumerary.

For two days, DeBusk put the platoon through basic scenarios they might encounter while on salvage runs. He dismissed one of the new privates on his team at lunch and replaced him with a Marine lance corporal.

He had them on the rifle range the third day. Everyone had to qualify with a variety of hand guns, shotguns, rifles and automatic weapons. Another one of the solders was dismissed for repeated poor weapon discipline, leaving the platoon with 15 members.

Amanda remembered Pinkston' request and when she was alone with DeBusk, mentioned that she'd met him running PT the previous morning. She made sure to tell DeBusk it was because he had already shown he was in shape, and was a take-charge type of soldier, not because she thought he was cute. DeBusk radioed the private's NCO and asked for Pinkston to report to the range. The private qualified with the weapons like everyone else and was reassigned the next morning.

Amanda, as DeBusk's assistant platoon leader, was put in charge of six of the more experienced soldiers and the new guy Pinkston. Between missions, she was responsible for the preventive maintenance of the vehicles and weapons and training her soldiers on supporting her and Chopper as they inspected building exteriors. Chopper loved it. He got a lot of attention and snacks all day long.

DeBusk drilled his half on setting up perimeters, laying down suppressive fire and supporting Amanda's team. They trained separately in the morning, but together as a platoon in the afternoon. They trained hard and at 1630, everyone was dismissed and Amanda and Sgt. DeBusk would finish their days with a review of their soldiers' performance and adjusting the training schedule.

They entered their information into the computers for Lt. Nila and the general and called it a day.

They drilled every day for three weeks and every member of the platoon started showing up for PT, which was always led by Pinkston. Soon, other soldiers and civilians were joining, in hopes of getting on the elite platoon or just to feel like they were a part of something.

Amanda, after three reschedulings because the general had pressing business, enjoyed her evening with just herself, Chopper, the general and the charcoal grill. The general, firm, confident and decisive when around others, was a different person when alone with Amanda. She talked about her military career and what brought her to Fort Carson and Amanda told her about her upbringing in Alabama. She mentioned her dad's wind-powered generators and the general made sure to note it on her tablet, telling her it would be a good idea to get something like that on the drawing board.

After eating burgers, tossing a ball for Chopper until he was tired, the two women sat on the patio and listened to music as the sun went down over the fence. "I want to confide in you, Amanda. Not with any state secrets or anything, just some thoughts that I can't bounce off anyone else."

"Ma'am, the conversations between you and me, stay between you and me. I've been keeping my brother's secrets all our lives, and he kept mine. Our dad was a strict man, but fair and honest. He raised us to avoid gossip and if we were caught doing it, we'd be cleaning the barn by hand for a month," Amanda told her, giving the woman more insight into the type of man Amanda had for a dad.

"He sounds like a good father."

"He was ma'am. I miss him and my lazy-ass brother everyday." The general smiled.

After that evening, every other week Amanda would have dinner at the general's or vice versa. In the confines of their own homes, it was Amanda and Angela having girl talk. They never talked about other soldiers or missions, but the general often talked about issues with the civilian government and their demands.

"There are only 392 civilians now and already they have nine representatives and elected a mayor. They're making demands on the military."

Amanda listened to the general talk and made a few suggestions, most of which she'd probably already considered, but what the general really needed was someone she could trust to voice her thoughts to. It helped her frame decisions.

During one of their evenings, Amanda made tacos and a ranch salad, the general offered to make Amanda a lieutenant so there wouldn't be any talk about her living in "officer's country." Amanda thanked her but declined. She liked her current job as DeBusk's assistant. "Maybe we could promote Chopper to lieutenant?"

The next day orders came through, signed by the general and Lt. Nila, confirming Chopper's promotion to second lieutenant. It was the paperwork shuffle and excuse enough so if anyone complained, the quarters were in the dog's names, and Amanda lived there as his attendant.

~ ~ ~

RANDY, RUNNING ACROSS THE OPEN FIELD TO THE WRECKED HUMVEE had his walkie-talkie's ear bud giving him an idea of the battle taking place.

He heard his dad tell Juan and Monica to hold their shooting while he ran through their fields of fire.

He had run about 100 feet when he heard a Stryker off to his right. It was Eddie with his big army truck coming up to support him.

Eddie had the 16-ton Stryker coming at full speed. Randy hoped his friend knew what he was doing. Eddie did because he slid to a halt five feet from Randy.

The smiling Eddie popped his head up through the driver's hatch. "Going my way, sailor?" he asked.

Randy jumped on the Stryker and told Eddie to head to where the last HUMVEE in line had gone into the escape trench. Randy had thought he saw someone get out of the truck, someone he recognized. He wasn't sure and he wasn't going to say anything to anyone, but somehow he knew.

Eddie dropped back into his Stryker and headed to where Randy directed. Randy had to hold tightly to the side of the vehicle to keep from being bounced off.

From what Randy heard on the radio, the battle in the front of the property was taking a turn for the worse. They got to the HUMVEE he'd indicated and Randy jumped off Eddie's vehicle.

Eddie, Randy heard in his ear bud, was called by Jerry to support Tia in front of the property and he threw dirt in a wave as he took off at full speed. Monica and her Stryker were being repositioned by Jerry to cover Jamal and the deJesuses.

Randy saw two men inside the wrecked HUMVEE. One was obviously dead because he had no head left. The other was unconscious, bleeding from the face and his right hand was broken in at least two places by the way it hung through the steering wheel. The man's rifle was broken and unusable, so Randy was certain this man would do no more fighting.

What he also noticed was the passenger door was open. Someone had gotten out of the truck.

Randy didn't see anyone while riding on Eddie's Stryker. The only place someone could have gone was into the trench. It was guarded at one end, but not guarded on the other. He jumped down into the trench.

Over the radio Randy could hear Jerry directing Eddie to a position so the two HUMVEEs being covered by the helicopter had no chance of escaping. The two had been able to slip in behind the barn, out of direct visual sight of the Apache and both bunkers, and where Tia's Stryker couldn't ram them. It was a stalemate for a few minutes and would allow the soldiers in the HUMVEEs to pop out and shoot down the chopper if given enough time to pull their machine guns off the their trucks.

Kayla, who had been working to get a shot at the two HUMVEEs, had been vexed with her ability to maneuver the helicopter into a position where she could get the nose down far enough to bring her nail polish target onto them. She wished she had more time and chances to practice with the helicopter, but they'd only found a small amount of AVGAS and didn't want to waste what they did have.

There had been a hope that just the sight of the mean looking bird would give the invaders second thoughts. Kayla suggested that she take the helicopter up and reconnoiter and when she found the convoy, she'd shoot it up miles from the farm. Jerry mulled it over and thought it was a good idea, but Buff, the former Marine, suggested it might escalate the attack to a new level. A level at which the farm could not compete.

"Say our Sky Dragon Kayla shoots up the convoy, wipes them out to the last man. The major from Ft. Knox would send tanks the next time. We wouldn't stand a chance no matter how much time we had to prepare.

"If Kayla just fired warning shots at the convoy, and they turned back, we lose the element of surprise on them. They'll know we have a helicopter and the next time they come, they'll have rocket launchers and know we have improved our defenses.

"No," the former Marine said, "we need to defeat them here, capture as many as we can so the next time we speak with the major, he'll have to listen to us."

Flying above the invaders now, Kayla felt the helicopter was less effective than she'd hoped. It was fast and maneuverable out in the open, but for close quarters it was more of a flying tank than mosquito. She was sure if she had a helmet, it would have been easy aiming the 30mm under the nose.

As it was, she had to aim the entire bird. If she tipped the craft too far forward, she would overshoot the HUMVEEs and they'd have a shot at her tail rotor. She settled for harassing the two with the low fly-bys and hard turns just 20-feet over their heads.

They had finally maneuvered their HUMVEEs behind the barn which limited her from getting at them. It wasn't ideal, but it kept them from shooting at Tia or the bunkers for a few seconds. Tia's Stryker was already beginning to smoke from the damage. She'd have to bail out and right now, there was no safe place to do that.

Kayla heard the call for a second Stryker to the front and was relieved to see it tearing along the path along side Buff's bunker. She could tell it was Eddie by the way he drove with reckless abandon. She didn't care, as long as he joined the fray.

Eddie's Stryker, directed by Jerry from his vantage point, drove around the bunker and through the shrubbery behind the barn. The two HUMVEEs in hiding didn't see him coming until he rammed them both from behind, shoving them into the sights of the Apache.

Kayla put three rounds from the 30mm through the engine block of the first truck. She lost some altitude with the pitching forward, but with deft hands on the cyclic and collective, Kayla was able to circle the trucks and get back into a position where she then made it clear the next three rounds would go into the driver's compartment if their surrender wasn't forthcoming.

Jerry called for a cease fire again over the PA system. The HUMVEEs were clearly out gunned and out maneuvered by the Apache and the Strykers.

The soldiers stopped resisting with the second call for cease fire. Soldiers started holding their arms out the windows once they got the trucks stopped.

Tia, still feeling the fury of battle, drove her 16-ton Stryker through the cattle pen and up to the passenger door of the lead HUMVEE and revved the motor. She inched closer in little jumps until the winch of her Stryker was pressing against the passenger's window. She pushed a little harder and the window shattered as the HUMVEE rocked.

The passenger, a 22-year-old with a loud mouth, who five minutes earlier had showed such bravado by hanging out his door and shooting his M16A4 combat rifle pissed himself and started crying in fear.

The two trucks the deJesuses and Monica had surrounded shut their vehicles off too. The soldiers were scared, but they surrendered.

~ ~ ~

AMANDA'S FIRST MISSION AS PART OF THE SALVAGE PLATOON came the fourth week she was on base. They were going to the Air Force Academy, primarily to retrieve computer servers and books, but also because one of the radio operators said they heard what they thought was an S.O.S. and they were able to trace it in that direction. They'd stayed away from the Air Force Academy because that was where an entire squad had already been lost, including the captain who had been in charge of the Salvage Platoon.

The six-truck convoy had three HUMVEEs in front of Amanda's and two behind. Amanda had Chopper in her passenger seat. They'd practiced the scenario the previous two days on a mock up built by the engineers.

Amanda was proud of the way the plan worked, just as they had practiced. The convoy circled the building they would be entering. The straight truck that would haul the computers remained behind her truck while the other four set up a perimeter.

When she was given the signal, Amanda and the straight truck pulled up in front of the building housing the computers and disembarked. Each HUMVEE at the corner of the building had its machine gun pointed outward, while the second man in the trucks had their rifles scanning the windows and doorways of the building. When Amanda was satisfied, she allowed Chopper out of the truck.

He bounded out and immediately began sniffing around. Amanda, her M-4 locked and loaded, flicked the safety off because Chopper immediately began growling. The dog everyone had come to think of as a kind and gentle companion, changed into a dog that was ready and willing to kill.

He bared his teeth and stalked to the northwest corner of the building, moving slowly and purposefully. Amanda was beside the dog. When he started barking Amanda stopped him. She saw movement in a second story window. Maybe it was a curtain moved by the wind, but she didn't think so.

She backed away from the building, keeping her eyes up and a hand on Chopper's back, reassuring the dog she was fine. She filled Sgt. DeBusk in on what she had seen and how Chopper reacted and let him make the decision.

"Three rounds, H.E, second story, northwest corner on my mark. You under cover Saunders?" he asked.

"Give me 10 more seconds to get us behind this van and

cover his ears. My squad is pulling up and deploying now." Her squad was three privates in a HUMVEE and they were her protection. Pinkston was the driver for her team.

DeBusk waited and made sure everyone was ready. "Mark!" Amanda had knelt down 75 feet from the building, behind a van's front tire. She sat Chopper down and covered his ears from the noise that was about to happen. He was licking her face when the first of three rounds blew out the northwest corner of the building. Amanda stayed under cover.

With her head down, she didn't see the three mutants who survived the explosion or when they were tore apart by the soldiers in her squad, and the machine guns on the HUMVEEs. They came out of the building, leaping from the second floor like it was an easy step, only to die on the grass.

Chopper growled and barked and tried to pull away, but Amanda held him.

It was all over 15 seconds after the first grenade was fired.

They did it three more times, taking out two more upper floors and the back door area. Only when Chopper stopped growling and led Amanda and her squad inside the building, did everyone start relaxing. Seven mutants were killed, but no one was injured from the platoon.

Less than three hours after arriving on the academy grounds, the straight truck was had enough computer equipment to make even the most hard-core geek weep. When the truck was full of the computers the general had asked for, library books were carefully stacked until no more could be put in the 24-foot straight truck that had been painted flat black.

The Academy was 18,000 square acres nestled into the Rocky Mountains. If there was anyone alive, they had to have heard the noise from the attack, but the perimeter scouts hadn't seen anything while the others worked.

DeBusk was a stickler for doing one stage of the mission completely before starting the second stage, and it wasn't until the straight truck's overhead door was closed and locked did he go over to the commo HUMVEE. "Start your gear, Private Hahn."

Amanda and Chopper walked around the area while the communications specialist called out on every channel of the

CB and the Army frequency the SOS had come in on.

Twenty-five minutes after he started, one of the scouts called out. "Movement, one thousand meters south, south-west!

"White flag!" the scout reported looking through binoculars.

"Keep your weapons at the ready," DeBusk reminded them. "Saunders, report."

"Chopper saw them, but he didn't even growl. Now he's licking his nuts, sergeant. I don't think they are a threat." Her team laughed and DeBusk, who was feeling a little higher-strung than usual, couldn't help himself. He had to laugh at the report.

"Okay everyone, be ready anyhow, I'm going to go meet our guests," DeBusk told everyone.

The two men were former cadets who had hid out in the mountains after the plague and when the mutants started killing and then eating the bodies littering the campus. They were the two remaining from the five known to have survived. The others had died either by accident or by trying to work their way back to the campus for supplies. The two survivors repaired a radio from a wrecked HUMVEE, but the battery died. They'd seen trucks on the freeway a few nights before and came out of their hiding place when they heard the shooting. It had taken three hours to walk to the convoy.

~ ~ ~

JERRY'S CALL FOR CEASE FIRE CAME AT A TERRIBLY COINCIDENTAL time. There was a knock at the cellar door where the children and Cindy were still huddled.

Cindy had kept them calm through the gunfire, and though there was some crying, Cindy sang to them to keep them calm.

LT, thinking the fighting was over, opened the door without checking to see who was knocking. She'd been told that Josh and Natalie would be coming through the door in case of evacuation and thought it would be them.

Cheryl grabbed the little girl by the throat before the door was fully open. The other kids were startled. They went from being happy the battle was over to as quiet as they'd ever been.

Cindy started to scream but Cheryl pointed the gun at her. She then noticed the crib. This was something else that was new on the farm since she'd last been here -- they were having babies.

Good, Cheryl thought to herself. Another hostage for her to use. She pointed the gun at the crib in which baby Adam was sleeping quietly with a bottle and put her finger to her own lips. She said very quietly to the terrified teen: "Shhhh. Not a word," she said just above a whisper. "Not a sound."

Keeping Kellie's little friend between her and the others, she pointed for them to leave out the door she'd just come through.

Cindy was the last out and attempted to pick up the baby, but Cheryl wouldn't allow it. As she was leaving, she told the teen, "If I hear any one of those children screaming, the baby gets it first, and then this one." Cindy, face red in fear and hands shaking turned and Cheryl pushed her roughly through the doorway with her foot and kicked the door shut.

She then turned to the little nine-year-old.

"Where are they?" she asked, slowly and quietly and with fury LT could hear in the crazy woman's voice. The little girl backed away. She was so afraid now, more afraid than she'd ever been in her short life.

LT didn't say anything. Cheryl didn't know if she was being brave or was just too afraid. Her lips were trembling and she had her hands crossed in front of her.

"Oh don't worry little girl. Your hands wouldn't stop a bullet from this. It'd rip right through your hands and blow your heart right through your back. You'd scream in pain but no one would hear you because your lungs will fill up with blood and you'll drown and bleed to death. Now tell me where they are."

LT, afraid and unable process anything Cheryl was saying started to turn and run deeper into the cellar. Cheryl caught her by the collar of her shirt before she got two steps. She pulled her around and pushed her in front as a shield. It was time Cheryl got back in control of things and they started up the stairs.

Whispering in the girl's ear she said, "open the door." The child hesitated and Cheryl grabbed her by the back of the neck and began squeezing, her finger tips digging deep into the little girl's neck. She then slowly cocked the gun and pushed it to her ear. "Do it." LT, crying and choking at the same time, opened the door.

The Padre saw LT first and smiled. He was as happy as everyone the battle was coming to a close. He was just realizing the little girl was crying and there was a stranger behind her when the realization of who it was hit him.

He tried bringing his weapon up.

From 12 feet away Cheryl shot the man who had dedicated the last few years of his life to bringing people forgotten by society closer to God. The noise of the gunshot so near her ear made Hannah jump, but she couldn't scream because Cheryl's grip on her neck was making it hard to breathe.

The Padre, who just the night before had performed his first wedding ceremony, that of Jerry and Kellie, felt the sting of the bullet entering his neck. He lost control of his body and fell to the floor as the bullet lodged his spinal cord.

Of ways to die, Journey "Padre" Stone thought to himself as the final darkness closed over him, this wasn't as painful as he thought it was going to be.

Kellie, sitting at her desk with her back to the door, jumped at the shot and saw the Padre fall. A spray of blood splattered her surveillance monitor and desk. She turned to see Cheryl with her little LT held in front of her as a shield.

Hate boiled inside of Kellie as it had never before in her life. The former special education teacher, who had lived through an abusive husband, the end of the world and her family, survived three vigilante and zombie attacks and being shot in the stomach felt more hate than she thought one person could feel.

She felt her gut clench when she saw the face of the intruder who had just killed her friend and protector, the Padre.

The word hate couldn't encompass how much revulsion Kellie had for the woman who was standing there with the smoking gun that had killed the Padre, grinning visciously with perfect white teeth and choking Hannah.

The woman had shot her, had almost killed Randy and Danny and was the cause of the battle that had just ended. She'd caused many deaths and was now choking a little girl Kellie loved as if she were her own.

Hannah whimpered as her hands tried unsuccessfully to free herself. Cheryl tightened her grip on the little girl's throat until she shut up. Kellie's gun was at her feet. She'd never be able to reach it and shoot the crazy woman holding the little girl. She was also too far away from the microphone to let Jerry know she was in trouble.

"Well, well, well," Cheryl said, waving the pistol at Kellie. "I thought I'd killed you already. Now get that farmer boyfriend of yours down here or I swear to God, I'll kill you after I put a bullet through this little girl's head."

Cheryl's newest plan was to use Kellie and the little girl to control Jerry, forcing him to surrender of the farm. Of course she'd kill them, but right now she wanted to control him just as he had controlled her.

That plan fell apart with the next sound Cheryl heard. It was the sound of a gun's hammer being pulled back with a distinctive "schnick." The sound came from the gun being pushed into the back of her head.

"Well, well, well, babycakes. You want a second chance at killing me too?" Randy asked, pushing his dad's Desert Eagle hard into the back of Cheryl's head. "Ain't gonna happen.

"Drop the gun now. You hurt that girl and even God won't recognize what's left of your pretty face."

~ ~ ~

OVER THE NEXT THREE MONTHS, THE SALVAGE PLATOON FROM Fort Carson went on 11 more salvaging excursions and three rescue operations. No one had been hurt on any of the missions except when Pvt. DeNelis tripped over an exposed length of cabling and broke his wrist.

The non-perishable food supply safety net had grown to 90-plus days. Buildings had been cleared for other sundries as well, things like toilet paper and toothpaste, deodorants and soap. The general knew these supplies would eventually run out, but for now, breathing room had been extended.

The platoon's operation orders, training and leadership was so successful, buildings on base were being cleared of non-essential equipment to store the supplies that were coming in. The straight truck was supplemented by two more and a semi with a flatbed.

Chopper was the real success for the platoon and Amanda, DeBusk and Nila all insisted the dog not be overworked. A dozen other dogs had been found and tested, but most were feral now, too wild to be of use. There were a few hopefuls in training, but that was still a work in progress.

The 12th mission was the last mission Amanda would go on for the 1st Mid-America Defense Force. The platoon was headed to Peterson Air Force Base on the east side of Colorado Springs. A weak signal had been picked up by the communications squad at Fort Carson. The signal had been on the short wave upper side band. The commo man could only make out "Peterson" and "base," but it was enough for a mission to be mounted.

Two semis were prepped and readied for the mission. They would bring back about 18,000 gallons of fuel if they could find it. Two straight trucks would also accompany the five HUMVEEs in case they found anything worth salvaging.

Peterson was only about 45 minutes away from Fort Carson, but it was an area that hadn't been explored or cleared yet.

The convoy left early in the morning as always, on a day when clear skies were forecasted. It was a pleasant drive with the summer sun in their face only for the last few miles. Chopper was getting used to the missions and seemed anxious this morning.

DeBusk ordered the convoy to the airstrip but changed his mind when he saw six 5,500-gallon refueling trucks, parked and ready to drive. They'd have to be checked out, but this would be a good find. There was a fence around the trucks and a lot of clear area for visibility. He positioned two HUMVEEs of each end of the area.

Pvt. Evans was detailed to open the front gates and the

soldier took very few minutes to break through the locks and chains. He swung the gates open and DeBusk had his driver drive slowly through the gate. DeBusk was on his Gatling gun but didn't see anything. He called Amanda to dismount to have Chopper check the area.

Chopper jumped out of the truck and loped over to where DeBusk was parked. Amanda ran behind the dog with her weapon at the ready. Four of her squad were jogging up behind her. Chopper cleared the area quickly, even took a minute to mark one of the 30,000-gallon fuel tanks.

Amanda waited beside DeBusk's truck until Chopper came back to her. He'd just sat down and she walked up to him, kneeling down to congratulate him for a job well done when they heard a gun shot in the distance. Amanda felt a stinging beneath her arm and she covered Chopper with her body. She then started feeling weak and a little sick. Something stung in her back, but she had her arms around Chopper to protect him so she couldn't feel for what it was.

Chopper was barking furiously at something as Amanda fell to the ground, unable to hold onto the dog any longer. She heard machine gun fire and orders being screamed as her helmet hit the pavement.

Consciousness slipped away from Amanda. In the seconds before darkness closed over her, she recalled the last words Shep had uttered before he passed.

All Amanda could work up the effort to say was "Daddy."

~ ~ ~

TONY REACHED FT. BENJAMIN HARRISON ON THE SHORT WAVE three days after the battle.

Colonel Russ Hammond, commander of the Ft. Benjamin Harrison military community, became an admirer of Jerry's when he heard the full story.

Hammond had struggled with an especially harsh winter in Indianapolis, a turncoat officer who had nearly succeeded in taking over the base and ruining nearly all the stores the colonel and his men had been collecting, and a cultural dispute.

Jerry told Hammond everything, including what Keith had

done for them. That information gave Hammond reason to relieve Smith of his command.

Hammond had not been a fan of Smith's. The lieutenant colonel was always asking for more female personnel, more food and more trained military people. Hammond had told him many times through his commo specialist that Smith needed to do more work on making his own community survivable or move the entire compound up to Ft. Benjamin Harrison.

When the colonel heard about the "invasion" Smith had authorized and the loss of life that had befallen too many, he was angry. He got his best officer to put together a squad to go to Ft. Knox and remove the lieutenant colonel of his command and offer the people there a choice.

The personnel, both military and civilian at Ft. Knox had been given the choice of moving to the greener pastures of Indiana or continue to try to make a go of it at Ft. Knox, sans the military leadership.

It was nearly unanimous to abandon the military base and head for a community that was flourishing. It took less than a day for the civilians to pack up what they had to drive the 160 miles to Ft. Benjamin Harrison.

Lt. Col. Smith would never have allowed a vote if it hadn't been for the 10 heavily-armed men and women who showed up very early one morning and took over the guard posts without firing a shot.

A young Hispanic lieutenant, backed by a female NCO with a SCAR Mk 17 rifle that had been locked and loaded, relieved Smith of his command at 0517 hours, 17 minutes after the first guard post was taken over.

The only soldier injured in the take over was one of the defenders whose jaw was broken when he didn't shut up when instructed. The NCO had quieted him with the butt of her rifle.

~ ~ ~

AMANDA WOKE UP 15 DAYS LATER. A NURSE WAS STANDING BESIDE her bed, looking at the monitors and writing notes on a clip board when she noticed Amanda's eyes fluttering open. "Hey, you're finally awake," the nurse said to her, then pressed the button for the main desk.

Word spread quickly throughout the military compound that Amanda had awakened. Parker ordered two guards at each end of the corridor and told them no one except the doctors and nurses were allowed near Amanda's room without her or the doctor's permission.

It was another six hours before Amanda could talk and the next day before she could have visitors. The first three were General Parker, Sgt. DeBusk and Chopper.

The dog was in such a hurry, he skidded by the door and had to come back. He crashed into the bed when he got in the room and Amanda had never been so happy to see anyone. His wagging tail slapped into everything and he nearly licked the skin off Amanda's hand.

The general and sergeant were right behind him. Parker was smiling and there was pure joy in her eyes. DeBusk, who seldom smiled, had a warm grin on his face. She greeted them, smiling and glad she would finally get some answers.

After the sergeant hung his head and tried saying it was his fault, it was the general who cleared things up. "It was no one's fault except the bandits. They were the ones who shot you, Amanda," the general explained. "You were ambushed by 24 bandits who were going to try and ransom all of you for some women."

Amanda closed her eyes and shook her head slowly. "That doesn't make any sense," Amanda said. "There are a lot of women on the base. They could have come up peacefully and made a home here."

"Well, we're not real sure what they were all thinking. All we know is they were being led by a maniac. Two of the 24 got away, but from the one wounded man we captured we were able to put together bit and pieces of it.

"The leader of the group was a religious fanatic and when the end of the world came, he thought he was the messiah. Forty followed him out from Kansas City on foot, walking to Utah, but only 24 believers made it this far.

"When they got to the air base, they heard our comm boys on the radio and set up the ambush for some reason. The bandit who shot you saw the dog and thought they would be found out so he shot at Chopper. You got in the way and were hit. The first bullet hit just under your left arm. The second hit in the middle of your back. The vest you were wearing saved you from dying on the pavement.

"Your squad was already shooting back, and Robert saw you hit the second time and then saw blood. He knew at least one shot had gotten by the vest. He put his driver in charge of the counter-offensive and dragged you back to your truck. He held pressure on the bleeding and Pinkston got you back here in less than 25 minutes.

"I had you on the table 29 minutes after you were shot, but it was still touch and go. You lost a lot of blood."

"You operated?" Amanda asked the general.

"Yes I did dear," she answered. "We played hell keeping Chopper calm. Robert said he kept licking your face and barking on the drive back here.

"Robert, could you excuse us a moment? Girl talk."

"No problem, ma'am," DeBusk told her. He squeezed Amanda's big toe. "I am so happy to see you awake, Amanda. We can't wait to have you back." He left the room so the general and Amanda could have some privacy.

She closed the door behind him and pulled up a chair. There was sadness in the old woman's eyes. Taking her hand, the general held it warmly. "I haven't told you much about my family, Amanda.

"Oh you know I was married, but I never told you what happened.

"Curtis divorced me when I made lieutenant colonel and was assigned to a hospital in Wuerzburg Germany. He wanted to settle down and hang up a shingle and be husband and wife doctors, curing the sick in some small town somewhere and live out our lives.

"I wanted to continue with the Army, so we went our separate ways. What hurt the most was I only got to see our daughter a few times a year. I loved her, and when we divorced, she was 17 and understood.

"We talked often, but I missed her wedding because I was in Iraq. I missed the birth of both her sons because I was on assignment in Afghanistan. I missed a lot of her life because of the choices I made.

"I was here, doing a study for the Secretary of the Army when the end came for my daughter and her family and I missed that too.

When you came along, I think I saw a lot of her in you… you are confident, funny, thoughtful, considerate, headstrong, smart and love dogs, just like she was.

"When they brought you in, the only doctor we have here is a pediatrician. I was a surgeon before moving to administration. He didn't feel qualified, but the bullet had to be removed. I wasn't going to let you go without fighting with everything I could. You're a crutch for me. You're a surrogate daughter and a trusted friend. Without you, all of us here are diminished."

Tears were falling down the general's face. There was even some coming from Amanda. She hadn't realized how close she and the general had become.

Impulsively, Amanda reached over and hugged the general.

~ ~ ~

JERRY'S CLAN HAD TAKEN TWO FATALITIES. NICK AND THE PAdre were both killed in the battle against Cheryl's platoon. A funeral pyre was raised for them that afternoon. There was no rejoicing in the victory over the soldiers, but there were many tears for their fallen friends.

There were four dead soldiers in the HUMVEE Tim had shot up. The 147 rounds he used did a lot of damage and Danny hooked a chain to the vehicle and hauled it five miles down the road buried it as it was in 25-foot-deep hole he dug.

He covered the hole with boulders and clay. If zombies came for the bodies, he hoped they'd never be able to get at them.

The soldier who had his legs crushed by the HUMVEE and a .50 caliber machine gun fall on his head died before Kayla or Monica could get to him. His body was burned with a pile of wood from the barn. The driver of the first vehicle in the first element was wounded and treated before being incarcerated.

The driver of Cheryl's HUMVEE would never be able to fully use his right hand again, and he lost his right eye, but Kayla saved his life.

The vigilante in the back seat was the sixth fatality of the attackers and his body was burned with the dead soldier from the first HUMVEE.

Tony and Danny set up a fenced-in area around a pair of tents and electrified it. A single guard watched the prisoners until they were picked up by the military.

Maybe the greatest insult was the "guard" was one of the teenagers, some as young as 13 years old and some of them were girls. While guarding the prisoners they played with remote controlled helicopters and airplanes, jumped rope, played soccer and rode quads around the field in which the prisoners were being held.

The prisoners were jealous of the freedoms the kids had and the simple joys they were allowed.

They wondered why they had stupidly followed Cheryl instead of doing what they knew to have been right. Cheryl became a pariah and the other prisoners had to be reminded to leave her alone or face more charges.

Col. Hammond sent a school bus to Jerry's farm to take the prisoners off their hands. The soldiers would be tried by military court. Hammond hadn't insisted on taking the prisoners.

If Jerry had wanted to summarily execute the soldiers, there was nothing anyone could have done, but Hammond did suggest turning them over for military trial. "Maybe the United States isn't what it used to be," Col. Hammond told Jerry by radio, "but we are still a nation with laws and by God, we'll give them a fair trial."

The barn and garage were heavily damaged and the farm's four newer SUVs had been shot up to where they were useless. Jerry's Ford F-350 had also been shot up. There were bullet holes along the bed and in the doors, the passenger windows were shot out and three of its six tires were flat, but when Jerry turned the key, the old girl started up with a belch of black smoke.

Of the four wounded from the farm, Danny and Cleve were superficially injured. Both suffered shrapnel wounds from

M-2 rounds that tore up the ground in front of and around their bunker. Both required minor surgery to remove shrapnel. Kayla allowed Monica to stitch them up as practice.

Buff had part of his ear shot off and stone fragments had to be removed from his left eye by the doctor.

Hannah's neck was so badly bruised by Cheryl, she had trouble breathing for a few days because of swelling. She would also have bruises for weeks afterward. Kellie sat with her little helper every waking minute she was under Dr. Kayla's care.

While she was recovering, she was invited, along with her mom Tia, Buff, her brother John and the twins, to sleep in the shelter. Even better, the little girl got to sleep in Jerry and Kellie's room until a new home for them could be found. It was their motorhome that had been wrecked by Cheryl's driver.

Cheryl couldn't believe Randy was still alive. She tried to evoke sympathy and said things like "I cried when I thought I hurt you" and "Please, sweetheart, don't do this to me again." Randy didn't believe a word she said and enjoyed binding her hands. He'd found the leg irons and collar she'd worn and laughed in her face when she pleaded for him not to put them on her again.

She was still wearing the leg irons when the Military Policemen from Ft. Benjamin Harrison picked her up with the other soldiers. He conveniently forgot to give the military policemen a key to the leg irons when she was taken away.

As he was getting the prisoners out of their enclosure, Cheryl was begging him to let her free, offering him anything and everything. She did it when Cindy was standing behind Randy and the teen who had been kicked in the back in the cellar while protecting a baby and the younger kids, socked Cheryl hard enough to draw blood on her knuckles and knocking Cheryl to the ground with blood coming from both her pouty lips.

"Get some respect for yourself," Cindy said to her, standing over the woman who had caused so much death and destruction. "Act like a woman, not like a whore." The soldiers loading the prisoners applauded the young lady. Cindy blushed.

Randy waved as the bus carrying Cheryl and the other soldier/prisoners pulled out of the driveway.

He was glad she was now out of his life for good.

~ ~ ~

Jerry started farming again with Kellie's help. Kellie ran the household with Jerry's help. They were able to provide a safe haven for people of peace moving from one area of the country to another. Their farm would grow with real houses that Jerry and others would build. Word spread about how the farm had survived and he became known as a protector of freedom and the ideals on which the United States had been built.

Col. Hammond rotated a platoon of soldiers to care for the military equipment, but placed the platoon leader under Jerry's authority, giving him what he called a battlefield commission to Lieutenant Colonel and called the citizen soldiers on the farm "The 1st Alabama."

The colonel also came to the farm so he could meet Jerry and so they could drive to the gulf coast with Juan and Randy to do some fishing on the catamaran Jerry and his friends had used to rescue the astronauts. It was their vacation from their communities before harvesting season started.

Randy and Cindy made a cute couple and eventually shared a motorhome. They had become friends when Randy found out she loved video games and could regularly defeat him in sports games. He was better at war games and when the day's work was complete, Jerry could hear the sound of their video games coming from their motorhome along with their laughs and taunts and insults.

She was also the impetus for Randy taking part in the work out program of the astronauts, remarking one day about the "gorgeous abs on Buff."

Monica and Eddie shacked up and would become parents.

When telling everyone about the pregnancy Eddie said "I didn't like what she said about her machine gun over the radio, so I machine gunned her until she was pregnant."

Monica punched him and Randy just hung his head at his friend's sense of humor.

About the only one who didn't realize how close Eddie and Monica two had become was Jerry. When he remarked to Kellie that he'd seen Eddie take Monica's hand weeks earlier, Kellie closed her eyes and shook her head, much like Randy. "I've known she's had the hots for him since I got here."

Tia and Buff had a big family and were the first to get a modular home onto the property and on a basement. Tia had her two children and the twins, but they also took in two more young children whose parents had died. The leader of a reservation in west Texas had heard there was a "family farm" near Birmingham and escorted the children there as a better environment than what he could offer.

After one house was placed on the farm, others were always looking for a modular home that could be used until a few contractors came along.

Cleve adopted five children and their two mothers who survived a zombie attack that killed the dads, brothers and husbands. He'd never had children before, but the kids needed him, so he was there. He was able to share with them his adventures as a spaceman, but it was being a parent he found more satisfying than anything in his life.

Josh, Katie, Marissa and baby Adam found out they too would be having another mouth to feed. Katie, being 42 years old, had given up believing she'd ever have a child, but as late summer turned to fall, her morning sickness was apparent to everyone. Secrets were very hard to keep in their community.

Josh had made a bit of a name for himself as a butcher, bringing back a job title that had almost gone out of use. His knowledge couldn't be lost so he taught classes to others who came to their community and to some who came just to visit.

Tony set up a help network with other camps. Maybe the internet was gone, but people had knowledge they could share with others. He, Tim, Natalie and Karen became a thing and the four laughed and cried and played and worked together, setting up antennas and connecting people from different camps.

No one on the property even questioned or judged the arrangement. As long as they were happy, no one cared.

Kayla drained all the fluids from her helicopter and built a shelter for it. She wanted it ready to use, but didn't know how to maintain it any more than what the instruction book told her. If she couldn't fly that Apache no one would. She continued training Monica and Sara to be medical technicians, even after she met a refugee from Arkansas who was a veterinarian.

Word eventually spread that she was an M.D. and others came to the Saunders farm to learn and take the knowledge back to other camps.

Jamal stayed with the Saunders farm, learning to drive from Danny, but Sade left with the Army men.

Three more pieces of slate were erected in the Saunders' "cemetery" -- Nick's, The Padre's and Keith's. No one would forget their sacrifice as long as Jerry and his son owned the farm.

~ ~ ~

THERE WAS A SOFT KNOCK AT THE DOOR TO AMANDA'S HOSPITAL room. She and the general composed themselves and wiped their faces free of tears before the general said "Come in."

It was Maj. Solomon, the general's exec. "Sorry to intrude, ma'am, but the colonel in charge of the Ft. Benjamin Harrison camp just called on the short wave. He was passing on some information about what he called 'renegade soldiers.' It seems these soldiers sent by Maj. Smith in Kentucky attacked a camp in Alabama and were repelled by some farmers using Strykers and helicopters.

"When he told me the name of the farm, I asked him to do some checking and I think Amanda will want to hear this," the major said then pulled out a sheet of notepaper before continuing. "The farm that was attacked was the Saunders Farm."

He then looked up at Amanda whose eyes were as wide as they could grow. "Jerry Saunders, his son Randy, friend Eddie, wife Kellie and a dozen others are alive and well and now under the protection of the United States Army."

Amanda cried tears of happiness.

~ ~ ~

A WARM BREEZE ROLLED ACROSS THEM AS JERRY AND KELLIE lay in a hammock he'd put up near the shelter hatch. They were looking at the new house being built at the base of the furthest hill. It had been another busy day for both of them, but Kellie was still recovering so they took it easy this afternoon.

Jerry asked Kellie if she wanted him to build her a real home in which to live. She kissed him and told him that this shelter would always be her home and she didn't ever want to live anywhere else.

Molly, Kellie's loyal mutt, barked once when Randy came bouncing through the hatch with Cindy in tow. He had a ridiculous grin on his face, but not for the reason Jerry presumed. Monica and Eddie came through the hatch too.

The four of them were grinning and Jerry assumed they had some stupid idea they were going to pitch. He hoped it was better than their idea of bringing in rocket launchers and howitzers.

Randy pulled a piece of paper out of his pocket and held it up so his dad could see it, but not read it. "Tony just gave me this. It was relayed through Col. Hammond in Indiana."

Randy read aloud from the paper as Cindy held his other hand. She was crying and smiling at the same time. Jerry had thought the girl to be a typical cheerleader-type, but had found out over the past few weeks she was an accomplished pianist and singer, and for whatever reason, was thoroughly taken with Randy.

"Maj. Gen. Angela Parker, commanding general, 1st Mid-America Defense Force, sends her respects and salutations to Col. Russ Hammond, commander, 1st Great Lakes Defense Protectorate and to Lt. Col. Jerry Saunders, commander of the 1st Alabama.

"General Parker extends an invitation to Col. Hammond and his officers and to Lt. Col Saunders, his family and officers to visit and consult at Ft. Carson at their earliest convenience to establish a better working relationship between military units of the United States of America." Randy looked up from the paper he was reading and looked at his dad.

Jerry had been only half listening. The military rank he'd been given and the farm's military designation had done nothing for him.

Sure, it was nice having real soldiers who knew how to maintain the Strykers, help in the field and share the struggles of keeping the farm growing, but as a military unit, it was a bit of a stretch. He didn't think of himself as a soldier, rather just a farmer like he'd always been.

Randy thought his dad was probably already thinking that Cleve or Buff might be talked into going to Colorado because they were former military, although both had "retired" from active duty to become full-time dads.

The next sentence in the dispatch changed Jerry's mind about sending anyone else. "She also advises that she has a soldier in her command named Sergeant Amanda Saunders."

Jerry and Kellie were shocked and looked at Randy in stunned silence.

Jerry, remembering his prayer from so many months earlier, slowly looked from his son's smiling face to the clouded sky above him and sent a silent "thanks."

About the Authors

Terry Stenzelbarton is the author of four novels. He spent 16 years in the military as a photojournalist,

newspaper editor, combat engineer and military policeman.

As a civilian, he has been a sports editor, photographer, traveling salesman, carpenter, computer expert, grave digger and Director of Marketing & Advertising, Information Technology and Software.

Jordan Stenzelbarton is the co-author of two novels. He's an avid gamer, tennis player, reader and volunteer for his church.

www.ingramcontent.com/pod-product-compliance
Lightning Source LLC
La Vergne TN
LVHW091041080826
845145LV00002B/585

* 9 7 8 1 6 1 8 0 8 0 6 6 0 *